THE MIDWILLOW MARTYRS

The year is 1830 and Martha Cavanagh, the minister's daughter, is experiencing the first pangs of love. Gabriel Lawless, the object of her affection, has returned home after seven years but not only is he a common labourer, he is also a rebel. When the landlords cut their workers' wages, the labourers form a friendly society. Their oath of allegiance is treated as treason. With the line drawn, the time has come to take sides. Can Gabriel be the hero Martha dreams of? Or the villain her father seeks to destroy?

Books by Janet Mary Tomson
Published by The House of Ulverscroft:

THE LOVE TOKENS
THE JANUS FACE
SUMMER OF SILENCE
BINDING WITH BRIARS

Janet Mary Tomson was born on the Isle of Wight. After joining the Foreign Office and living in Geneva and Brussels, she moved back to the island where she lives with her husband.

JANET MARY TOMSON

THE MIDWILLOW MARTYRS

Complete and Unabridged

ULVERSCROFT
Leicester

First published in Great Britain in 2004 by
Robert Hale Limited
London

First Large Print Edition
published 2005
by arrangement with
Robert Hale Limited
London

British Library CIP Data

Tomson, Janet Mary
    The Midwillow martyrs.—Large print ed.—
Ulverscroft large print series: romance
    1. Great Britain—History—*1800 – 1837*—Fiction
    2. Love stories 3. Large type books
    I. Title
    823.9′14 [F]

    ISBN 1–84617–026–5

Published by
F. A. Thorpe (Publishing)
Anstey, Leicestershire

Set by Words & Graphics Ltd.
Anstey, Leicestershire
Printed and bound in Great Britain by
T. J. International Ltd., Padstow, Cornwall

This book is printed on acid-free paper

1

'I poach — it is better to be hanged
Than to starve to death.'

Martha Cavanagh, making her daily pilgrimage through Cuckoo Copse, felt that there was something magic about October mornings. The path was ankle deep with leaf mould, her shoes slipping on the russet surface of the fallen chestnut leaves. The ground felt like a sponge beneath her feet. High up in the trees a squirrel the same colour as the autumn foliage scampered from branch to branch and a distant gang of young starlings squabbled vociferously.

Martha stopped to rest her shoulders, lowering two buckets full of water attached to a dairymaid's yoke, to the ground. The bundle of hay tied in a sling across her back made her shoulders ache. She knew she looked like a peasant woman but there was no one to see.

For a moment she raised her head to absorb the stillness. The branches dripped moisture. Beechnuts and sweet chestnuts, those that had escaped the wildlife, were

1

already half-buried in the leaf-mould, settling in for the winter, preparing to burst into life the following spring.

Without actually seeing anything she became aware that someone was watching her. These were dangerous times. Her heart began to flutter.

For a moment she waited, listening. She had a growing desire to scurry from the woods but to do so might bring about the very disaster that she feared. Breathing deeply she tried to calm herself and took up the load.

'Let me carry that.'

Suddenly blinded by unnamed fear she turned her head in the direction of the voice. A man detached himself from the shadows and pushed his way through the ferns. He was young and tall and poorly dressed. His hair was a tangle and he looked rough and unkempt. Worst of all, he was a stranger.

In her haste to pick up the buckets, Martha splashed water over her feet. Ignoring her protests, the man unhooked the pails from their yoke and began to carry them.

'Where are you going?'

She indicated the path ahead and he waited for her to move then followed behind. There was nothing for it but to keep going. Her initial fear subsided but she felt hot and uncomfortable, wondering how he came to be in the neighbourhood, for strangers, especially of the poorer sort, were rarely seen and never welcome. His presence could only mean trouble.

In silence they passed out of the copse, along the narrow lane between two hedgerows and to the gate of a field, where Martha stopped and deposited her load of hay. A shaggy New Forest pony called out and trotted across to greet her. For a moment she felt pleasure at the sight of his familiar face as if his very presence would protect her. His coat was already winter-thick and seemed to grow in all directions, the summer chestnut colouring darkened by the early-morning rain.

'This is for him?' The stranger sounded surprised.

'He's mine,' she said. 'He's old.'

'So it would seem.'

The stranger opened the gate, took the buckets inside and emptied them into the trough. He also picked up the hay and spread it out under the hedgerow. His breathing seemed laboured as if the exercise exhausted him. Indeed, he looked painfully thin. All the time Martha watched and wondered what to say, what to do.

When he had finished he came back out

into the lane. 'Do you know where I can find Isaac Lawless?' he asked.

Everybody in the village knew Isaac Lawless. He was only a common labouring man but somehow he had acquired the status of preacher. Worst of all, he was a Methodist. Martha's father, the Reverend Cavanagh branded him a radical, laid all the troubles of the village at his door.

Martha wasn't sure what to say. In the face of her silence the stranger looked stoical.

'He's my uncle,' he said. 'I've come to visit. He isn't expecting me.'

Relieved that he had some valid reason for being here, she decided to be polite.

'Most of the villagers live over yonder. You'll find his cottage at the end of the street.' She indicated that behind the copse, in the valley, was where the poorer sort had their dwellings.

'Ah, he's still there.' He looked relieved. 'I feared he might have moved.'

She waited for him to move away but then to her discomfort he said, 'And where do you live?'

She frowned at the forwardness of his question. It was time to make things clear.

'I live at the vicarage. My father is the minister for this parish.'

She saw his surprise and felt humiliated,

knowing that from her appearance he had taken her to be an ordinary village maid. As a peasant, it shouldn't matter what he thought but in her present garb she knew that she must look ridiculous and as the vicar's daughter she had a position to maintain. In an effort to regain some dignity, she said;

'Do you have permission to be here?'

'Permission?'

'The parish is overrun with the unemployed. Anyone not belonging here is not permitted to stay.'

'I see.' He tilted his head to one side and studied her thoughtfully. 'If I told you I was born here?'

'Then — then I suppose you are allowed to come.'

'That is generous of you.'

She knew that he was making fun of her and wanted to get away from him. He didn't look like a villager. For a start he had curly black hair whereas the local people were nearly all straight-haired, swarthy skinned — and short. His eyes were a startling blue colour, not the familiar local brown and, besides, there was none of the respect she, as the vicar's daughter, was accustomed to receive from the peasantry.

At that moment, as if remembering his manners, he removed his cap and wiped his hand across his jerkin.

'Gabriel Lawless, ma'am.' He held out his hand but she ignored it.

There were Lawlesses in the village, lots of them. It was a local name. Gideon Lawless was the village smith, Reuben Lawless a shepherd, but most of them were common labourers. Betsy Lawless, Isaac's daughter, came daily from the village to clean at the vicarage.

As his hand dropped to his side Martha noticed with shock the stiff ears of a rabbit protruding from the sack across his shoulders. These woods belonged to Sir Jenison Bowler. The stranger had been poaching!

Not wishing to antagonize him, she said: 'I am Miss Martha Cavanagh.'

'Honoured to meet you, Miss Cavanagh.' He smiled but it was with wry amusement as much as greeting and she blinked back her discomfort. It was time to put an end to this embarrassment.

'Thank you for your help.' she said. 'I must go. My father will be expecting me.'

'Of course. Shall I escort you?'

She could hardly believe his audacity. Here, in broad daylight, a poached rabbit on his back, a stranger in the village, he was proposing to walk with her, an unmarried woman of good character, right up to her front door. She frowned to show her displeasure.

'Thank you. That will not be necessary.'

Clumsily she picked up the pails and hurried away. All the time she could feel his eyes on her, sense his mocking amusement.

As soon as she reached a bend in the path she slowed down and drew a deep breath, silently thanking God that he was not following her. At the back of her mind was the thought that tomorrow and the next day she would have to make this journey again, to feed her old pony. The thought of meeting Gabriel Lawless filled her with unease and some other undefined emotion.

She was five minutes late getting back. Her mother was in the hall and from her anxious expression Martha guessed that her father had been looking for her.

'You're late,' Mama whispered. 'Where have you been?'

You know very well where I have been, she thought, but aloud she said:

'I am sorry, Mama. It is such a mild morning I stopped to look for chestnuts.'

Fortunately Mrs Cavanagh did not ask where were the fruits of her search.

At that moment her father came into the parlour. Clearly he had already been out for he still wore his riding-cloak. Martha sensed her mother wince at the sight of his muddy boots on her rugs.

'You're late,' he echoed.

'I'm sorry, Papa.'

For once he seemed lost for a suitable retort. At the back of her mind she wondered if he might have seen her, have even been spying on her, but she reasoned that he would be much angrier if he suspected that she had walked unchaperoned with a stranger in Cuckoo Copse.

She waited. He looked preoccupied, his pale eyes behind his spectacles, which he only ever wore in the house, focused elsewhere. In this respect Martha took after him, for she too was short-sighted and in the privacy of the vicarage was permitted to wear spectacles.

'There has been more trouble in the village,' the minister said to her mother. 'There was some rick burning down at Hampden Farm last night and our own Squire Wetherby has received another letter threatening to burn down his house. Those Lawlesses have been stirring things up again. You mark my words, Lawless by name and lawless by nature. If we don't stamp down hard on them and their like there will be a revolution in this country. I always feared we'd go the way of France.'

At the name of Lawless Martha thought

immediately of her meeting in the woods. At the time she had been more concerned with the proprieties of being alone with a man, but perhaps she had had a lucky escape. Fortunately, Gabriel Lawless was newly arrived. If he had known how things stood, of the rumblings of discontent, perhaps he would have harmed her. The realization threatened to betray her.

The Reverend Cavanagh, following his own train of thought, grunted his disapproval.

'That's the trouble with teaching the poorer sort to read and write.'

Martha felt the familiar sinking feeling that preceded one of his diatribes on the rightful place of the poor.

One of her duties as the daughter of the vicar was to visit the sick. She thought of poor Widow Shepherd, the last survivor of her family, well over eighty winters old, all her children dead before her. The parish allowed her six pence a week and with that she had to buy everything that she needed, for she could no longer grow her own vegetables or work for her keep. Indeed, she was too crippled to leave the hovel that was her home. Fortunately Betsy Lawless, the Cavanaghs' daily maid often called in to see her. Betsy's brothers cut her firewood and had repaired her leaking roof when the recent storms blew the thatch clean away. By their actions Martha reasoned that there must be some good in them. They could not all be the rabble that her father branded them.

She in her turn delivered the occasional basket of eggs and a loaf of bread to the old lady but it was not enough. She felt ashamed remembering her last visit. With her father's instructions fresh in her mind she had insisted that Widow Shepherd should join her in prayer, thanking God for his goodness, giving praise for the station in life in which he had seen fit to place them. It didn't make sense. Martha indeed had cause to be grateful, but Widow Shepherd, cold, lonely, often hungry — surely that couldn't be right?

'Anyway, your mother and I have to go out, but don't forget what I have just told you.'

With a start she realized that her father had been speaking. Her mother had already slipped away and fortunately he retreated without noticing her inattention.

She took off her bonnet and shawl and went to hang them up. There had been days when she would fling them aside for Betsy to retrieve but today she felt ashamed of her thoughtlessness. This seemed to be a day for regretting her failings. It must be remembered that although Betsy might be poor and a servant, she still deserved Martha's respect.

To ensure that she was suitably occupied, Martha took her embroidery into the parlour and began to sew. She was working on an altar cloth for her father's church. It was strange but she always thought of it as her father's church, not hers or even the village church, but his. It was a place that featured large in her life but without any sense of belonging.

In spite of her best intentions, a mental image of Gabriel Lawless kept returning to her mind. He had looked so thin and dirty, but there was something in the way he had regarded her, those sharp blue eyes, the challenging tone of his voice, that was deeply disturbing. He came from away, probably knew about things that were a mystery to her. She could almost imagine that he could see right through her, read her thoughts and dismiss her as utterly foolish.

As she added a few more stitches to the altar cloth, Betsy came in to stoke the fire.

'Do you have many cousins?' Martha found herself asking.

If Betsy found the question curious, she did not show it.

'I hear that a strange man calling himself Gabriel Lawless has arrived in the village,' Martha continued. 'Do you know him?'

'Gabriel?' Betsy's cheeks flushed. 'Yes.' She

bent down to place some sticks on the fire, hiding her face. 'His father died when he was young. Father raised him as part of our family — he is more of a brother than a cousin.'

Betsy was pretty in that dark, doe-eyed way that was so common amongst the local people. She wore a flannel dress that had once been Martha's. They were much the same size but the dress was one that Martha had outgrown and she noticed how Betsy had let out the side seams and added a strip of fabric along the hem to increase its length. It pulled tight across the bodice and Martha was momentarily intrigued by the curve of the servant girl's bosom. Her own figure was discreetly obscured by the cut of her gown. In a strange way this set them apart. Betsy was actually younger but she seemed much older, more grown up.

Martha did not own to having seen Gabriel Lawless but said:

'I hear there has been more trouble in the next parish. It is quite wicked. Have you heard anything about it?'

Betsy now looked truly uncomfortable. As she replaced the fire irons, she said:

'You must realize, Miss Cavanagh, since the old days many of the people have lost their grazing rights. They don't even have a strip of land to grow a turnip and all through no fault of their own. It might seem wrong to you but when you are desperate you will do whatever you have to do to survive. If I didn't work, Father could not support our family although he toils from dawn to dusk. It — it is very unfair.'

Martha felt embarrassed. Betsy shouldn't speak to her like that. She knew that neither of Betsy's brothers could find work but that was not her fault. She didn't know what to say.

'The local men are asking for a meeting with the masters,' Betsy added. 'Some farmers are more generous than others but where Father works they pay only nine shillings a week. It is generally felt that ten shillings is the minimum that any family can manage on.'

Ten shillings was the monthly allowance that Martha received from her maternal grandmother's estate. Much of it she spent on keeping Willow the pony, now too old to be ridden. Her grant would continue until she was twenty-one at which time she would inherit over £2,000 outright. The time was drawing very near.

'I know nothing about that,' she said aloud. She suppressed the guilty feeling that her pocket-money was more than Betsy's family's income and wished that she hadn't started the conversation. Grudgingly she admitted that perhaps there was some justification in what Betsy said and yet what the men were doing couldn't be right.

As she reached for the scissors to cut the silk she was using to embroider the altar cloth, there was a sudden, violent snapping sound followed by the shattering of glass and a heavy object bounced on to the settle. Martha's hand jerked so violently that the scissors dug into the altar cloth, breaking the stitches. Betsy jumped back in alarm.

'What on earth?'

Betsy moved towards the settle and picked up a large pebble around which a note was tied with twine. She held it out to Martha, her eyes wide with fear.

Her own hands trembling, Martha untied it and read the few words scribbled on the paper.

Rember the pore suport ther cawse
or you will die.

In silence she held it out to Betsy, knowing that she could read. This was one of the things that her father disapproved of: Isaac Lawless's educating his children. Labourers had no need of their letters. It only made them rebellious.

Betsy read the note and looked at Martha with troubled eyes.

'I had better sweep up the glass,' she said, then, as an afterthought, 'Do you think whoever threw it is still outside?'

Martha felt her heart lurch at the prospect of rebels surrounding the house, perhaps burning it to the ground. She stood up and instinctively moved back against the wall. She wished that her parents would hurry home.

'I'll go and look.'

Before Martha could stop her, Betsy was already at the back door. She came back a few moments later shaking her head.

'They must have gone. Should we give this note to your father?'

Martha found herself also shaking her head. The minister would be so incensed he would tear the village apart to find the culprit. Whoever it was needed to be punished, but she knew that her father would only make things worse. Better to let him think that some idle boy had thrown a stone and that it was an accident. True, he'd rant and rave but it had to be hoped that in the end he could be persuaded to accept that every boy is capable of mischief. Besides, the note would only frighten her mother.

Her hands still trembling, Martha threw the note on to the fire, watching it smoke and curl before the flames engulfed it. She handed Betsy the pebble to take back outside.

'What do you think the note means?' she asked.

Betsy shrugged. 'Perhaps whoever wrote it feels that your father could help them if he wanted to. He has influence with the landowners. If he said they should increase the wages they might listen.'

Martha felt it more likely that her father would encourage the gentry to deny the men and to use every method in their means to break their spirit. The future did not feel very bright.

Betsy cleared up the glass and secured the hole with a piece of board she had found in the coach-house. It would do until the minister could arrange for the repairs.

Outside it was already growing dark. Martha thought of the rebels hiding out in the woods. Again she wished her parents would hurry home. 'Will you be alright going home alone?' she said to Betsy.

Betsy nodded. 'I have nothing to fear. The local men wouldn't hurt me.'

She was right. She might live in a tiny hovel of a cottage along with her parents and brothers, with barely room to move, but she belonged here. Martha, an only child, with her comfortable house and her allowance and the possibility of a suitable marriage, was a stranger. The thought caused a tightening in her chest.

Betsy had friends, family, was at home in the village. Martha had only her parents for company, plus occasional formal visits to the houses of people of equal status. Her only friend was now married and therefore no longer her own mistress. They rarely met.

As Betsy returned, tightening her shawl about her shoulders, Martha thought of Gabriel Lawless. Had he not said that he was going to stay with Isaac? Tonight he and Betsy would be under the same roof.

'Perhaps you should stay here tonight,' she said. 'You could sleep in the kitchen near to the fire. That way you would not have to make the journey home.'

'Thank you, Miss Martha, but I must go home. Father will be worried. He will only come to find me.'

At her words Martha felt an extreme burst of discontent, although exactly what for she could not say.

As Betsy made her way to the back door Martha heard her father's gig pull up at the front. Pushing all else aside she prepared herself to face him and to explain what had happened. Inside she was churning as if it was she who had done something wrong.

As she heard the door open she knew that she was about to lie to him, to protect whoever it was who had thrown the stone and sent the threatening note. Yet she did not even know who it was. Why was she doing this? What was happening to her?

As the Reverend Cavanagh swept into the room, he brought with him an air of self-satisfaction.

'We have just been to see Squire Wetherby,' he announced. 'We are setting up a committee to protect the parish against the arsonists. Squire Wetherby and Sir Jenison are going to organize their own militia.'

Martha was glad that she had decided not to tell him the truth. At that moment he noticed the window.

'What on earth?'

'I think there was an accident. I didn't see what happened.' She heard the tremor in her voice. Glancing quickly at her mother, she added: 'Probably just some small boys playing.'

The Reverend Cavanagh tutted and shook his head.

'If I find out who it was . . . ' He didn't say what he would do but it would not be pleasant.

Martha went through to the kitchen to see if the housekeeper, Mrs Porter, was preparing the evening meal. A good plate of beef and gravy always improved her father's temper.

For something to do she took the cutlery through to the small parlour where they dined when they were alone. Everything felt wrong, the rick-burnings, the stone-throwing, the threats, the arrival of a stranger in the village. Where was it all going to lead? The only thing she knew for certain was that she did not know.

2

It did not take Gabriel Lawless long to realize that in his absence things had changed. As he made his way to his uncle's cottage he could feel the air of suspicion in the village. It had not been there before. Still, he had been away a long time. Perhaps his memory deceived him.

His mind flitted over the past nine years. For seven of those he had served a so-called apprenticeship although in reality it had been seven years of servitude in return for a roof over his head. Then there had been one hopeful year working as the head stud groom with the prospect of his own cottage and a wage. By nature solitary, for the first time he began to consider the possibility of marriage, of children, of staying permanently in the village of Lower Hampton. That was when disaster struck.

As he descended across the green and made towards the main street, the injustice tumbled in on him like storm clouds. Four months' hard labour and all because Squire Ponsonby said that he had stolen a saddle.

What would I be wanting with a saddle? he

had asked the magistrates. All the horses he looked after belonged to the squire. To whom would he have sold it? Who did he know with enough money to buy a saddle? It must have been worth five pounds — and the grooms earned a mere six shillings a week. It was an argument that had raged in his head a hundred times.

The real crime was that they had found the saddle in the back of the tack room, but only after he had been sentenced. The squire tried to say that Gabriel had hidden it. He didn't want to lose face, to admit that he had been mistaken. Squire Ponsonby knew the magistrates, of course. To get him off the hook, they said that in view of Gabriel's good character they were being lenient with him — this time!

When he thought about it he felt so angry he could kill someone but what was the point of dwelling on it? No one could undo what had happened.

His thoughts turned to the present strife. There had been talk of an uprising while he was in gaol although it hadn't seemed real at the time. In any case, for the most part what happened outside the prison had little meaning. Survival was all that mattered.

Four days he had been out now and already he knew that the nightmare of that experience would never go away. He only had to look at his wrists, to see the marks where the manacles had been, to feel the rasping in his chest. Four days sleeping under hedges, living on a handful of berries had done little to improve his health, or his temper.

Do you have permission to be here? That's what the girl had asked him. Who did she think she was, speaking to him like that — and her so full of her own importance? Lucky for her he was good at hiding his feelings when he had to.

As he started along the street his heartbeat increased. Nine years ago he had left the safety of that small, neat cottage at the end of the row. His uncle hadn't wanted him to go but, young as he was, he knew that there were too many mouths to feed. His mother was dead. His father was dead. It was up to him as the outsider to ease the burden on the rest.

That boy's a natural with horses. You should get him apprenticed somewhere, learn a trade, get him off your hands. He'd heard the words, heard his uncle say no, that he wouldn't send the child away, but Gabriel had made up his own mind. Now, coming back here was his only hope. If his Uncle Isaac turned him away he had nowhere else to go.

The familiar worries played again in his

head. Even if his uncle took him in there was little chance that he would get a job working with horses, not when they knew that he had been convicted of theft. He tried to be positive, to convince himself that something would turn up, for he would willingly turn his hand to anything. Although he was weak now he'd soon be strong again and he'd always given value for money.

The cottage was only yards away now. Unlike most of them it looked well cared for. The thatch was neat although old, the walls of the cob had been washed over with lime. Standing tall as he did now it looked so small. Funny how everything seemed so much bigger when you were a child. It was hard to believe that seven people had been crowded inside, his Aunt Sarah and Uncle Isaac, Joseph, Matthew and James his male cousins, plus little Betsy. Were they all still there? Were there now more cousins who would look at him with suspicion, an outsider coming into their tiny world?

At the gate he hesitated, suddenly shy, ashamed. What would his uncle think? He couldn't go through with it.

As he was about to turn away the door swung open and a young man came out. He was short and broad shouldered, his dark brown hair mussed up as if from sleep.

'Gabriel? Gabriel Lawless? I don't believe it!'

Slowly his features seemed to rearrange themselves and Gabriel recognized an older version of his cousin Joseph. The last time he had seen him he must have been about ten years of age. Now he was a man.

'Joseph?'

'Come along in, man. Father will be overjoyed to see you. He's never quite forgiven you for going away. How did it go? Where have you been?'

There was too much to explain. Gabriel let himself be escorted into the tiny house, ducking his head under the stone lintel, waiting for his eyes to adjust to the gloom, for the single window was small and deep.

'Gabriel!' His aunt was upon him in seconds, holding him close, then away and then close again. 'Oh my son, my dear sister's son. How shamefully you have neglected us!' She held him again at arm's length and looked him up and down.

'Whatever has happened to you? You are a skeleton. Come, I have a pot cooking, I'll soon fetch you a bowl of good vittals.'

He returned her embrace, overwhelmed by this sudden kindness. Not since he had left Midwillow had he known the joy of physical warmth, not even in the casual liaisons with the women who had come his way.

He looked around for his uncle but he was not there. He was disappointed. Most of all he needed Isaac's approval, his understanding, his permission to stay.

'How are James and Matthew?' he asked.

His aunt looked away. 'James is well. Matthew — Matthew died.' She was silent for a moment before saying, 'We have another Matthew now.' She reached out and drew a young child to her side. He was about three years of age and immediately hid his face in his mother's lap.

'This,' she said to him, 'is your cousin Gabriel, returned home at last.'

He looked around, taking everything in, the pallets piled in one corner for the men to sleep on, the ladder leading to the upper area where Isaac and Sarah slept, with young Betsy when last he had been here.

'And Betsy?' He wasn't sure whether to ask. She would be — what, seventeen now, eighteen? It was hard to believe.

'Betsy's at work. She works at the vicarage.'

The vicarage. Gabriel saw again in his mind's eye the small, bossy young woman who had accosted him earlier. He hoped that she didn't make Betsy's life a hell.

He was increasingly aware of the appetizing aroma of food. His mouth felt dry, deprived of sustenance. Seeing him glance in the direction of the fire, his aunt said:

'Isaac will be here any second, Betsy too, then we will celebrate your return.'

Remembering the rabbit, Gabriel pulled it from his sack.

'I came upon this,' he said, placing it on the narrow ledge that acted as a table.

Sarah and Joseph glanced at each other. Isaac would ask where it had come from. If it were stolen he would have none of it for he always condemned theft.

'It was dead when I picked it up,' said Gabriel. 'The crows would only have had it.'

What he said was true in so far as he had killed the rabbit with his sling. One swift, sure shot and the creature had died without even recognizing a danger.

Sarah nodded. 'Then our thanks to you. Tomorrow we'll have a fine feast.'

Only seconds later they heard the sound of Isaac's boots crunching against the stony path. The little door to the cottage was pushed open.

Isaac Lawless was forty-five years of age. Short, dark haired, his face weathered by the seasons, his thoughtful, measured movements and his deep, searching eyes gave the impression of a serious man. For a second he stood just inside the doorway unfastening the leather jerkin, then, sensing the air of expectation around him he looked up and saw for the first time his nephew.

'God bless us!' He threw the garment aside and came to embrace the younger man. 'Gabriel. I can hardly believe it. To what do we owe this pleasure?'

Gabriel immediately became tongue-tied. Shame engulfed him at the prospect of making a public confession of his position. Sensing his confusion, Isaac eased him towards the fire.

'Come, man, come and get warm. It's turning bitter out there.'

Gabriel let himself be led. As a child, Isaac had seemed like a god: big, strong, and omniscient. Now he looked old and tired, his shoulders drooping as if the weight he had so long borne was too great. Gabriel began to curse himself for coming here and adding to his troubles but then he grasped at the thought that he might be able to ease the burden on his uncle.

Joseph excused himself to go and fetch firewood while Sarah busied herself with the food, little Matthew still clinging to her skirt.

'I've been in gaol,' Gabriel blurted out. 'I was accused of stealing a saddle. It was a lie. They found it later but the master wouldna admit he'd made a mistake. I was released on

Friday. I — I didn't know where else to go.'

Isaac waited, before saying: 'I'm glad you had the good sense to come home.'

Gabriel fought to suppress the tears of exhaustion and relief. The two men sank on to the stools near to the blaze while Sarah dodged between them. She affected not to have heard what was said although it would have been impossible not to. For Gabriel, all that mattered was that for the moment he had a refuge.

'Things have been difficult around here,' said Isaac, 'but I've arranged a meeting for tomorrow with the masters. We're going to put our case to them, tell them that we need more wages.'

'What will you do if they refuse?'

Isaac looked troubled. 'There are plenty of hotheads around. There's trouble everywhere. I hope the owners will have the sense to realize that what we ask isn't unreasonable. They won't want trouble, neither do we. I'm confident that it will turn out well.'

Sarah handed them both a beaker of beer and for a moment they drank in silence, then Isaac said:

'I'm going to ask the minister to stand as witness for us.'

Gabriel thought immediately of Miss Cavanagh.

'What's he like, the minister?' he asked.

Isaac considered for a moment.

'He's — not easy to deal with. I sometimes think he feels that we labouring folk deserve to be poor, as if we are being punished by God. There's bad blood between the church and us non-conformists. He suspects me in particular of causing trouble.'

Gabriel still remembered his uncle's sermons, preached on the green on a Sunday morning. In summer they had the old sycamore for shelter. In winter, if the weather was too bad, they met in the old barn. Unlike the minister, the Methodists could not afford a stone church with all the trimmings. Isaac always said that God was everywhere. The Lord didn't need a building for his flock to reach him. Gabriel suspected that God wasn't anywhere, but he didn't say so.

'The way the minister sees it,' said Isaac, 'he has got a job to do, a position to keep up. The way we see it, we have a right to better ourselves and we don't have need of anyone to intercede on our behalf with the Almighty.' He shrugged as if there was no easy solution.

'We do need someone of good standing to intercede with the gentry though,' he added. 'I just hope that the minister will agree and that justice will prevail.'

'I met his daughter, on my way here,' said

Gabriel. 'She — she asked me if I had permission to be here. I was tempted to tell her that I had a sight more right than she did, being born here and all, but I held my tongue.'

Isaac nodded. 'Always best to think first and speak after. Young Miss Cavanagh's not in an easy position. I suspect that while she is loyal to her father, she doesn't always agree with him.'

At that moment the latch of the door lifted and a blast of cold and light whipped into the cottage, accompanied by the small, neat figure of Betsy. Gabriel rose to his feet, expectant, uncertain as to what she would think. For a second she frowned, then she must have recognized him, for her face transformed into one of smiling welcome.

'Cousin Gabriel? I heard that you were in the village but I didn't believe it.'

'Who told you that?' asked Isaac.

'Miss Cavanagh. She asked me if I had a cousin Gabriel.'

Gabriel smiled to himself. Clearly Miss Cavanagh had not dismissed him from her thoughts the moment they parted.

Betsy removed her shawl from her shoulders and hung it on the nail behind the door. She smoothed her dress down over her hips and came over to kiss her cousin on the cheek. Gabriel was shaken by the surge of excitement that engulfed him.

This was his cousin? Was this the little tangle headed girl who had ridden on his shoulders, tormented him into telling her stories, been his tiny shadow during those childhood days?

Once again the door opened and his other cousin, James, arrived. More welcomes, more expressions of surprise, more stories to tell and lives to catch up with.

James and his elder brother Joseph bore a strong resemblance to each other. Eleven months separated them in age and only the thicker bulb of James's nose, the additional curl of his hair told that they were not twins.

Like Joseph he went through expressions of surprise and delight at seeing his cousin. As soon as the greetings were over, he said to his father:

'The best of news. Widow Merriweather has offered Jo and me six weeks' work helping with the winnowing. We'll be getting five shillings a week.'

A communal gasp of pleasure told of the importance of this extra income.

As they shared the turnip and barley stew that Sarah dished up, taking it in turn to use the spoons and platters, Gabriel pieced their histories together. James was courting a girl from the village although as Sarah confessed, she didn't see how they hoped to marry, not unless his prospects improved. She just hoped the arrival of a babby wouldn't push them into greater poverty.

Gabriel deduced that Sarah herself had lost several infants since he left. Little Matthew was the only one to have survived. Looking at her now he could see that she was with child again. She looked haggard. Her fertile time must be drawing to an end. He hoped for all of them that this would be the last one.

'What about you?' he said to Betsy.

He couldn't keep his eyes away from her. Wherever she was in the room he was aware of her presence. Every part of him seemed to have a heightened awareness. It was a crazy feeling, alarming because it had come on as suddenly as a fever. He longed to be alone with her so that they could talk and he could find out everything there was to know about her.

She smiled and he was mesmerized by her lips, her tiny white teeth. Briefly he wondered how such a rose bloomed in this desert.

'I'm well,' she said. 'I work every day at the vicarage. It helps the family.'

'Not wed, then?' Why did the question seem so momentous?

'I'm betrothed to Ephraim.'

'Cousin Ephraim Carter?' His heart lurched, his soul reached out as if for salvation.

'Ephraim's done well for himself,' said Isaac. 'He has a cobbler's shop next to the forge. He's dead set on having our Betsy.'

Gabriel fell silent. He remembered Ephraim. They were about the same age but that was all they had in common. He remembered his cousin as loud-mouthed, wild, careless. He had never liked him.

Suddenly he was lost for words. He looked at Betsy with her large brown eyes, her thick hair modestly framing her pretty face and her neat yet tantalizing body, and like Saul on the road to Damascus, his life changed irreversibly.

3

Martha slept badly. Lying rigidly in the dark she strained her ears for any suspicious sounds outside. Now that it was dark and she was alone in her room, the memory of the afternoon's attack filled her mind. Might not the rebels come back in the night and carry out their threat? Her conscience troubled her. She should have warned her parents that they were in danger. She should not have lied about the broken window.

A strong wind blew and she feared that any unusual noises outside would be drowned out by the swish of branches, the crack crack of the vicarage gate. She opened her curtains but could see nothing. She must be alert.

As her eyelids drooped she tried to tell herself that they would probably be safe at least until her father had had a chance to prove his support for the rebels' cause. When he did not, though . . . ? She pulled the quilt over her head and tried to think of something comforting but nothing would come.

At last she must have dozed. When she awoke it was already broad daylight. Her first feeling was of relief that they had survived the night. She did not feel like getting up. Instead she decided to wait for Betsy to bring her a bowl of chocolate. She did not want to face the coming day, there were too many unresolved troubles that threatened them all. Closing her eyes she allowed her thoughts to range over the neighbourhood, looking for comfort in the familiar.

The village of Midwillow dated back into the mists of antiquity. It sat astride the river Treadwell which meandered its way across Hampshire, fed by the myriad streams that water the New Forest. Two roads intersected nearby, one running east to west and linking Winchester with Ringwood, the second traversing north to south, connecting Lymington also with Ringwood and beyond. Over the centuries, these routes had lost their importance and now the village was largely undisturbed except by those intending to visit.

The land hereabouts was low lying and rich. In winter the water-meadows were flooded to provide early pasture for the cattle in the spring. In summer the vista was a blaze of ripening wheat and on the horizon the remains of the ancient oak forests stood black against the evening sun. The parish consisted of some two hundred souls.

In many ways the village and the parish

were the same. Although there were one or two isolated settlements they were not considered to be a part of the community, except in times of crisis.

The church, twelfth century and mainly of Norman design, had a squat square tower as proudly self-confident as the man who held the living. Here Martha came regularly to church, had been confirmed and helped with the Sunday school, a task she found daunting for many of the local children could barely be understood, so broad was their dialect. Besides, they smelt. Of recent months however there had been a noticeable drop in their numbers and her father complained that the wicked Dissenters were drawing them away from the fold. The chief culprit was Isaac Lawless.

Martha looked out of the bedroom window. The church and the cemetery filled much of the vista. Standing near to the church was the most important dwelling of the parish — Bilton Manor, the seat of the Bowler family. The manor took its name from the French *belle*, meaning beautiful and was once *Bellton*, whereas the Bowlers took their name from the French *beau* or beautiful as in the masculine form. The second syllable of their name was thought to come from a corruption of the French word *lieu*, meaning place. Hence, *Beaulieu* had modified into *Bowler*.

William the Conqueror had given the surrounding countryside to his kinsman Walter Fitzborne whose tomb had pride of place in the church. The Bowlers prided themselves on direct descent from the Norman conquerors.

Martha lay back and felt that familiar *frisson* of unease. The Cavanaghs too had a distant kinship with the Bowlers, for a century ago the third sister of the grandfather of the current incumbent, Sir Jenison Bowler, had married Martha's great-great-grandfather. For this reason — and also the fact that her father and Sir Jenison held views that were compatible when it came to village affairs, Ignatius Cavanagh had been offered the living.

Sir Jenison had one son, Bartholomew, and Martha's father once nursed secret hopes that a match might be arranged between them. Happily that proved to be unrealistic, for Sir Jenison was looking to advance his position by finding a suitable heiress. Lack of fortune aside, Martha knew that nobody with any ambition would consider wedding his son to a sallow, short-sighted, bookish, mouse of a girl like herself. For once she thanked God for her physical failings, for Bartholomew Bowler was a cruel, selfish boy and she would rather have died than be his wife. It was however a blow that her father had never quite managed to disguise.

Lady Bowler had died a year ago and there was speculation as to whether Sir Jenison would remarry. According to gossip a list of young, healthy, suitable girls had been drawn up, for having only one son the continuation of the Bowler line could be at risk. Undeterred, Martha knew that her father nursed the hope that if all else failed, she might be at the bottom of the list as a possible vessel to pass on the Bowler line. The thought only served to increase her headache.

Lying on her back and studying the ceiling she thought about the person next in importance in the village, Squire Wetherby. The squire lived at the other end of the parish in a fine Jacobean house known as Treadwell Grange. He was well into later life and walked with a pronounced limp, the result of a hunting accident. A short man, he gave the appearance of being broad from the front but from the side view he had a noticeably narrow torso. He reminded Martha of the king on a playing-card.

About a sixth of the 500 acres he acquired on marriage was leased to two brothers — Reginald and Digby Amos. According to local folklore, the brothers married twin sisters whose father had left them well provided for. Although they were only lease-holders, as employers of labour they saw themselves as having some standing in the village, a view her father distrusted — *Not born to it*, was one of his favourite expressions whenever somebody's pedigree was under discussion. There had been times of late, however, when the Amos brothers, along with Squire Wetherby and Sir Jenison, had been pleased to band together against the rising discontent across the county.

Betsy still had not appeared so, in a bad humour, Martha got up and began to dress. She felt at the same time cross and yet guilty as she was forced to find her own stockings and shift and to struggle with the laces of her bodice. Uncomfortably, she wondered how Betsy managed with the fastenings of her own gown when she had no maid to help her. Admitting to her own helplessness and the other girl's efficiency brought little comfort.

As she went downstairs there was a knock at the front door. Her father was on the point of going out and it was he who answered it. The door swung open to reveal Isaac Lawless.

A short, dark man, he seemed to Martha to be upright in every way. He had a soft, slow way of speaking that was at the same time polite and respectful and yet challenging. Martha immediately thought of his nephew Gabriel.

'Excuse me for calling unannounced, Reverend, but there is a matter that calls for your attention.' He held out a letter.

'What is this?' The minister regarded it with distaste as if it might contaminate him.

'There is to be a meeting of local men today outside the church. We wish to discuss our wages with the maisters and we feel that as a man of God, your presence would be helpful.'

'*You* have called a meeting? At *my* church?' The vicar's eyebrows disappeared into his hairline.

'Squire Wetherby, Mrs Merriweather, Daniel Bridle, the Amoses have all agreed to come. Sir Jenison is sending along his bailiff.'

Martha's heart contracted as her father blustered and complained that he should have been approached first. Isaac stood very still and his eyes did not leave the vicar's face. In the end, Ignatius Cavanagh's outrage burned itself out.

'And next time, don't come calling at the front door!' he said.

Isaac bowed in reply and left, walking straight and dignified down the driveway. Martha, half hidden in the doorway, felt

40

uncomfortable as if in some way her father had let himself down. Isaac Lawless was of course their inferior, but his dignity made her feel ashamed. In its shadow, the memory of that other Lawless, Gabriel, remained as constant as a rain-cloud.

'That man needs taking down a peg or two,' said the minister. This was another of his favourite expressions, and he continued to fret that a common labourer should presume to take such a liberty.

He came back into the parlour, screwing up the note Isaac had brought. He flung it into the grate but it missed the fire. For a while he simply stood there brooding on what had taken place, then he flew into a fury.

'Did you hear what he said? Did you hear what he has done? He has the audacity to call a meeting — him, a common peasant calling on men like Sir Jenison and Squire Wetherby to do his bidding. It's outrageous!'

Martha said nothing. Experience had taught her that it was best to weather the storm. Her father continued to bluster.

'The men are holding their betters to ransom, threatening not to work if they don't get their way. A good flogging would do them more good than an extra sixpence to spend on ale and fornication.'

Martha was not sure what fornication was

except that it was one of the things one wasn't supposed to do according to the Ten Commandments. Whatever it was, it must cost money and the local men had little enough of that — according to Betsy anyway.

She thought of poor Widow Shepherd. She could do with an extra sixpence although Martha doubted if she would spend it on ale and fornication.

At last her father calmed down sufficiently to begin his journey. He had not said whether he would attend the meeting, although Martha suspected that he would just so that he could find out what was happening.

After he had gone she retrieved the note from the grate. The writing was strong and well-formed and the language could have been that of a man of letters. It said that being a man of God the minister's sense of what was right and proper would stand them all in good stead. He was sure that the Reverend Cavanagh understood what dire straits the local men were in and no matter how hard they worked, no matter how many hours they put in, they could not earn sufficient even to keep their families in the necessaries. He was however confident that an agreement could be reached that would benefit the men without harming the owners. Isaac said that he hoped the vicar would be sympathetic to the plight of the men with families and he was asking all the local employers to raise their wages to a reasonable amount but that it was desirable that all the local gentry should agree. Perhaps the Reverend, with his sense of fair play, would recommend an amount that was mutually acceptable.

For a moment Martha felt like Solomon, called upon to weigh up the rights and wrongs of a dispute. Perhaps what her father said was right and Mr Lawless was going beyond his authority in arranging this meeting. On the other hand, if the men were so poor and desperate, what else could they do? She hoped that some good would come of it.

The thought of chocolate no longer appealed. Instead she decided to go immediately to feed Willow. That little ripple was there in her chest again. What should she do if she met Gabriel Lawless in the woods? Clearly she must tell him that he was trespassing and that he must not come there. Perhaps more disturbing was the feeling of emptiness that he might already have left the village and that she would never see him again.

It was a beautiful day and she gave herself up to the magic of Cuckoo Copse. There was a particular way that the light lanced through the trees which reminded her of the illustrations from the Bible, as if some celestial light was beaming down on the Lamb of God, except that there was no one else present.

The nearer she got to Willow's field, the heavier her load of hay and water felt. She could not dismiss the thought that it would be good if someone were to come along and help her. Her father strongly disapproved of her foolishness in keeping the old horse which, in his opinion, should be shot. Her mother worried that carrying such a heavy load would make her arms muscular. This was one small act of defiance in her otherwise dutiful and obedient life.

As she walked she tried to convince herself that she was relieved that there was no sign of Gabriel. She wondered what Betsy had thought when she found him at the cottage. Had Isaac agreed that he could stay or had he sent him away? There was little chance that he would find work. They were laying people off at all the farms. She wondered where he had been and why he had come back now.

At the field she filled up the water trough and gave Willow his hay. She noticed with misgivings that he was stiff this morning. He really needed to be stabled at his age but her father would not agree. She gave the pony a carrot and as he crunched it with a pleasing enthusiasm, it occurred to her that perhaps the Lawless family would welcome this simple vegetable to add to their larder. The reality of their poverty hit her anew.

On the return journey the thoughts of Gabriel persisted. She tried to dismiss him as being a common labourer like Isaac Lawless, but then there was nothing common about Mr Isaac Lawless.

Walking home from church one Sunday she had seen a group of people, men and women, under the old sycamore tree down on the green. Isaac was addressing them. The scene reminded her of her father in his pulpit, only Mr Lawless was just standing there, calling the gathering his brothers and sisters and urging them to do right in the sight of God. He sounded like a proper preacher, only there was something different in what he was saying, encouraging his flock to love one another and help each other. Her father did not say things like that even though it said so in the New Testament. For his sermons her father preferred texts from the old book. He was a man who believed in an eye for an eye rather than turning the other cheek.

By the time she reached the vicarage she had met no one and the sudden emptiness of her future cast a cloud over the day.

Later that evening, when her father returned, she heard him telling her mother about the meeting that had been held in the church. So he had gone after all! She could not help but creep up to the half open door to listen. The conversation went something like this:

'How did you get on today, dear?'

'Some of those landlords are fools. Widow Merriweather and Daniel Bridle insisted that the men be allowed to state their case as if it was a court of law.' (Both Widow Merriweather and Daniel Bridle were from outside the village proper and had small farms down near to the parish boundary).

'What happened?'

'That fellow Lawless acted as spokesman. The Devil's got his tongue all right. Smooth as a serpent he is, telling how they labour every hour that God sends and still they cannot afford the necessities. One or two of the owners seemed to believe it but I had a word with Squire Wetherby and we both know the truth. No matter how much these men earned they would squander it on drinking and gambling.'

'I don't think Mr Lawless drinks and gambles, dear. He is a God-fearing man.'

'God-fearing? He's a Methodist!'

From the rest of the conversation it seemed that the farmers and the other gentry had agreed to increase the wages to ten shillings a week. Martha felt a sense of relief. Now perhaps things would settle down. There would be no more threatening notes to spoil their lives.

She heard her father say: 'The gentry will probably get round the increase in their wage-bills by laying more people off, then it will be the parish that has to pick up the pieces.' From the tone of his voice he was getting angry all over again. 'Our people are making a big mistake if they give the rabble an inch,' he went on. 'Show the merest weakness and they will be down on us like a pack of wolves. You mark my words.'

Hearing movements in the parlour, Martha moved away from the door. She thought about poor Widow Shepherd. What her father said was true. If too many more men were thrown on the poor relief then the amount might go down.

She could still hear her father, sense the outrage in his voice.

'The only way to keep the rate down is to make sure that the rules are tightened so that it is harder to qualify. If we don't, every lazy Joe will be expecting us to keep him.'

Martha made a noise before opening the

parlour door. Her father ignored her and she crept near to the fireside and tried to repair the damage done to the altar cloth. Throughout the evening, her father's words stayed with her. Perhaps nothing had been resolved after all. Perhaps all those dire predictions would come true. Another sleepless night beckoned.

4

On his first night back in the cottage, Gabriel found it impossible to sleep. Sandwiched between Joseph and James he lay in the dark and wondered for the hundredth time what the future might bring.

'I think you should come with me tomorrow, lad,' Isaac said, before going to bed. 'I'll have a word with the Sir Jenison's bailiff, tell him how good you are with horses. Sir Jenison has a fine stable. He might take you on.'

Gabriel feared that the thought of having to find food for his nephew was the driving force behind his uncle's suggestion. He did not remind him that a reference might be called for. Perhaps Isaac thought that his word would be enough. As he tossed and turned the prospect of failure haunted him.

There was something else too. Just above his head, through the boards, barely six feet away, his cousin Betsy lay. Her proximity was so disturbing that he could not fight down the fierce urgency of his longing. He had never felt like this before. It was crazy, irrational. Besides, she was spoken for. At the thought of

Ephraim, a rage of jealousy sucked at him.

Ephraim had one brother a poor, half-witted lad called Micah. When Gabriel had been about ten the three boys had gone into the woods to look for chestnuts. It had been too early in the season and the soft hedgehogs of nuts still clung to the trees.

'We'll have to go up and get them.' Ephraim tilted his head back to study the tall straight trunk.

Gabriel, following his example, felt himself sway as sky and earth collided in his mind.

'I'm not going up there. 'Tis too high. Someone will fall and break their neck.'

He remembered the predatory, razorlike pleasure in Ephraim's eyes.

'Mikey can go. Don't matter if he falls.'

Micah was already shaking his too large head, his eyes clouded with fear.

'I don't wanna.'

Ephraim pretended brotherly affection. He put his arm round the frightened boy's shoulders.

'Come along, our Mikey,' he said. 'You're the eldest. If we go back without the nuts father will beat you.'

He glanced at Gabriel. 'You know how cross father gets,' he added. 'It won't do no good us saying it was too high. He'll call you a coward. Come on.'

Micah licked his poor cracked lips, rubbed the palms of his large hands across his breeches.

'I can't . . . ' he started, but Ephraim was already pushing him towards the tree.

Shame descended on Gabriel as he remembered how he had stood there, watching his poor simple cousin cringe and beg. Ephraim, the smallest of the three of them had browbeaten him into submission. Struggling and scrambling, skinning his knees, chafing his hands, Micah struggled up the chestnut tree.

'Go on. Higher than that.'

The inevitable happened and Micah got stuck. His pleas and bellows met with his brother's insults.

'If you don't hurry, Gabriel and me'll go home and tell father how you climbed up there when we told you not to.'

Micah's sobs echoed through the branches. Then, with a squawk and a series of scrapes and scratches he tumbled to the ground, twisting his ankle, bruising his elbows, straining his wrist.

'You bully!' Too late, Gabriel turned on his cousin.

Without bothering to speak, Ephraim hit him hard across the mouth. Together they fell to the ground, twisting and hitting until with one lucky blow, Gabriel felled his cousin who sprawled, stunned, on to the leaf-mould.

That evening they all three received a beating from Ephraim's father. Isaac was furious when he heard of it for he had made it his rule never to lay a hand on his children.

From that day on there had been a rift between Isaac and his brother and Gabriel had never forgiven Ephraim for tormenting the simple Micah. The thought that Betsy might fall into his power paralysed him.

In desperation he dragged his mind from the memories, seeking for anything to lull himself to sleep.

For no good reason the vision of Martha Cavanagh came to him. He sneered at the memory of her sharp, schoolmarmish voice, the vision of her with her milkmaid's yoke and burden of hay. *What right had he to be here?* He'd show her, one of these days.

The next thing he knew, he was disturbed by his cousins getting up and realized that it was already morning. Eyes gritty from lack of sleep, he followed their example. Sarah and Betsy set out bowls and spoons, boiled the kettle, dished up a thin grey porridge, handed each man a cloth wrapped around bread and a small portion of cheese. He tried not to look at Betsy for his fevered thoughts of the night embarrassed him.

'Come along, lad. Best not to be late.'

Dutifully, Gabriel followed his uncle outside. It crossed his mind that as Isaac was a Methodist his recommendation might well harm Gabriel's chances. Perhaps though, his skill with horses might save the day.

It was a damp morning and even the noises of the countryside seemed muffled by the mist that hung as if suspended by some invisible hand. Their footfalls sounded subdued as they traversed the country lanes.

As they walked, Isaac pointed out the changes since Gabriel had left all those years ago.

'Widow Merriweather has the land yonder. Her husband died in a storm three years since. She runs the farm herself now.'

Gabriel looked down across the valley where a ribbon of mist veiled the hedgerows. The sight of the hedge reminded him forcefully of how things had changed. Once that whole area had been common land. Now many of the trees had been cut down. The wood had been the mainstay for heating the villagers' cottages during the long winters. Where did they go for their firewood now?

Isaac professed himself optimistic about the chances of finding work.

'You'll be all right, lad, I'll put in a word for you. Sir Jenison's bailiff is a good man.

Even if there is nothing with the horses he'll do what he can.'

They met the bailiff, Seth Hardwick as they approached the home farm. Two men were already at work, loading logs on to a cart.

'Put your backs into it,' Hardwick encouraged. 'There's plenty more loads when you've cleared that.'

Gabriel thought that there was enough wood here for a thousand fires.

'Morning, Mr Hardwick, sir, this is my nephew, Gabriel. He's just returned to the village and is looking for work.' Isaac paused for breath. When Seth Hardwick did not respond, he went on: 'He's a great one with horses, served his time and been a head groom, but he'll turn his hand to anything, won't you, son?'

Isaac spoke with quiet deference. Once or twice he rested his hand on the small of his back as if some stiffness afflicted him.

Seth Hardwick was a grizzled man of about five-and-fifty. He glanced at Gabriel, wiping his forehead with the back of his hand.

'Can't help you,' he said shortly. 'Sir Jenison has all the men he's prepared to take on.' From his words it sounded as if he personally would have welcomed more.

Isaac seemed crestfallen. His look was apologetic as if it was he who had let Gabriel down. For a moment they stood in silence, neither knowing what to say.

'Don't worry, Uncle. I'll do a tour of the farms, I'm sure I'll find something.' Gabriel spoke to reassure his uncle. He had no great hopes of finding employment.

He was about to take his leave when there was a disturbance in the lane nearby. Seconds later a man on a very fine bay hunter, accompanied by several dogs, came through the gap in the hedge.

Seth Hardwick and Uncle Isaac stepped back and immediately removed their caps. Seth bowed his head, touching his brow.

'Good morning, Sir Jenison, sir.'

The mounted man rode by as if he had not seen them. As soon as he was past the two men relaxed.

'That's Sir Jenison,' said Isaac. 'Looks like he's set for a day's hunting.'

Gabriel did not like what he saw. The man looked arrogant, thin and mean. The horse though, he was a beauty. He felt a pang of regret that there would be no chance of working with such an animal, but his owner — no, he had no wish to be on his payroll.

'Come on, you'd better get to work.' Seth signalled to Isaac to begin loading the logs. For a second Gabriel was tempted to stay and help him but Isaac might feel that he was losing face. In any case, he needed to find paid work of his own.

'I suggest you start with Mrs Merriweather,' said Isaac. 'She might have something for you.' He pointed out the way and Gabriel took his leave.

Mrs Merriweather's farm was one that they had passed on the outskirts of the village. Gabriel increased his stride, wanting to instil some warmth into his feet. He was already sure that there would be no work to be had in the parish. In fact he wondered whether he should keep walking, but his uncle would be worried if he did not return — and besides, he needed to see Betsy, even if only one more time.

The Merriweather farm was visible long before he reached it. The farmhouse itself was a large, single-storeyed construction with a tiled roof. It was separated from the farm proper by a low stone wall. The wall in its turn surrounded a neat garden although most of the blooms that filled the beds were now faded.

He had nothing to lose so he went straight to the front door and asked to speak to Mrs Merriweather personally.

After waiting for a few minutes, her maid ushered him in and he padded into her presence in his stockings. His boots leaked and he left a damp trail across the hallway and on to the carpet. This was not a good start.

Mrs Merriweather was seated in an upholstered chair in her parlour, her feet on a tiny stool, a colourful shawl around her shoulders. The room glowed warm with a comforting fire and there was a great cosiness about it. She looked like everybody's idea of a grandma.

Haltingly Gabriel explained his reason for calling. Sometimes he was not good with words, not when he was feeling nervous.

'It was good of you to come, Lawless,' said Mrs Merriweather, 'but I would have thought you would realize that I am in no position to take on extra men.'

There was nothing to say. He bowed his head and left in silence.

Outside, he had no particular direction in mind but started walking as if by so doing he might leave the bad feelings behind. Fine drizzle chilled his face. As he walked he thought that it wasn't like the old days when a man could rely on staying where he was born all his life. Even in the worst times most families had been guaranteed some work, and if this dried up they could always rely on the few vegetables and some firewood from their own strips and the commons. All this was gone now though, behind Sir Jenison's hedgerows, all certainty of work swept away by those new machines.

He kept walking until the next farm came into view. It belonged to Daniel Bridle and herein perhaps lay the greatest hope of work, for by reputation Daniel Bridle was a man not unsympathetic to the plight of the workers. As he walked Gabriel kept rehearsing what he was going to say, thinking of ways to avoid admitting where he had spent the last months. Sooner or later it would come out but perhaps by then he could have proved himself, show that he was not the sort of man to steal a saddle for which he had no use.

It took about twenty minutes to cross the fields, that being the quickest route. Many of the open spaces that he remembered from childhood were now securely blocked off and twice he had to double back to find a way through a new thicket or over a stream where a bridge had mysteriously disappeared.

He found Daniel Bridle working alongside one of his men, digging a new ditch around his pasture. He was a short man, slight of build, although his strength showed in the muscular forearms, exposed where he had rolled his sleeves up to delve into the muddy trench they were excavating. By a combination of good fortune and hard work he had bettered himself, farming about thirty acres which he rented from the squire, but everything about his demeanour confirmed that he was still a working man, secure in his acres but not ashamed of his roots.

For a while Gabriel watched them work, strangely moved by the sound of axe and shovel, the slurp of mud, the tearing of reluctant scrub. For all its shortcomings, his childhood in this neighbourhood had been a happy one and this familiar harmony of work and rhythm drew him back to more innocent times.

Knowing how much depended on it he took a deep breath and prepared to present his case, clearing his mind of anxieties in the hope of presenting a confidence he didn't feel.

'Good morning, maister.' He removed his hat and wiped the back of his hand across his mouth, the better to get the words out. 'I'm Gabriel Lawless, Isaac Lawless's nephew. I have just returned to the village and I am looking for work.'

He knew immediately that Daniel Bridle saw through the sham. His first words reminded him that news travels fast.

'I hear tell you've been in Sainham gaol.'

In spite of himself, his cheeks grew hot, and he couldn't look the older man straight in the eye. He knew that he was betraying a guilt that wasn't his.

'I was falsely accused,' he said.

'Of what?'

'Of stealing a saddle. I had no use for a saddle. It was later found. Nothing was shown to be true.'

Daniel Bridle removed his hat and scratched his pate thoughtfully.

'I wish I could offer you work, son, truly I do, but even if I believe you — which I am inclined to do, times are difficult and I can't afford another wage.'

Gabriel looked at the ground, wanting to hide the shameful disappointment that showed in his eyes.

'I hear you are good with horses,' said Daniel. 'It might be worth approaching Squire Wetherby. He breeds carriage horses and hunters although this is probably a bad time of the year. Keeping horses through the winter is an expensive business without taking on extra hands, and his mares won't foal until the spring.'

Gabriel thanked him for his suggestion and set off back the way he had come. Of all those employers in the parish, from what he had heard Squire Wetherby, along with his superior neighbour, Sir Jenison Bowler, although the richest men in the village, were the least likely to take him on.

He was half-way home when he changed route and began a tour of the other farms and estates, methodically crossing them off a mental list. He viewed the refusals that greeted him as if he was carrying out a survey. The questions that he was asked, the refusals that followed his answers he accepted as if they were merely curious pieces of information and did not affect him personally. In every case he remained polite, although it was on the tip of his tongue to tell them a few home truths, but what would it gain? Anyway, polite or not, as he crossed the last farm off his list, the answer was still No.

Again he wondered whether to leave the parish, although that would bring its own problems, but the thought of inflicting himself on Isaac, adding to his uncle's burden, filled him with a kind of fury. What pride could a man have in himself when he couldn't even put a meal on the table?

It was dark and cold and wet and he reasoned that if he did not return that night Isaac, being the sort of man he was, would perhaps organize a search party to make sure that he had come to no harm. No, the only thing to do was to go home for one more night and then tell him of his plans to leave.

As he walked into the cottage Isaac was

sitting on a stool near to the fire, a bowl of something hot on his lap. Sarah and young Matthew were with him but everyone else seemed to have gone out.

'How did you get on?' asked Aunt Sarah. He thought how old she looked, far to old to be bearing a child, but the years of want had taken their toll on her. Other than the bulge of her belly, she was skeletally thin. Her hair was grey and her skin had the pallid, dusty look of newly milled flour. He had the fanciful impression that the new life growing inside her was sucking her dry.

In answer to her question he shook his head and the treacherous feelings threatened to betray him again.

'I'm sorry, lad,' said Isaac. 'I really hoped Widow Merriweather might take you on. Her lower fields keep flooding and I hoped she would realize that the only way is to get on with some ditching, but I guess she is like the rest, not willing to pay out for any extra help.'

Isaac stopped to get his breath. He had a nasty cough. Gabriel thought he could do with an easier time but he was unlikely to get it.

For a haunting moment he wondered what would become of them all if Isaac could no longer work. They'd lose the cottage for sure. At present, although Joseph and James had temporary work, being unmarried they were condemned to live at home. It was unlikely that any master would offer them accommodation. If Isaac were to be thrown out of the cottage, what would become of them all? The vulnerability of his uncle's situation struck him anew. Once a man was wed, had children, he was enslaved, condemned to his master's mercy for the rest of his life. However hopeless his situation, Gabriel could always leave, sleep under a hedgerow, take advantage of whatever opportunities presented themselves — as long as he didn't get caught. Marriage though, children — he would never put such a halter around his neck.

Isaac put his bowl aside. 'Well lad, not to worry. We at least have had some good news today.'

Gabriel waited.

'The meeting with the masters went well,' Isaac went on. 'Everyone, even Squire Wetherby and Sir Jenison's bailiff agreed that ten shillings a week would not be an unreasonable sum. The minister heard us out. He didn't say much but I think that he could see the justice of what we asked. The understanding is that as from All Hallows the new wage rates will come into effect.' He sat back and expelled his breath as if throwing off some burden. 'What a difference that will make, to all of us.'

Gabriel sat down on the other stool. Aunt Sarah handed him a bowl of potatoes and gravy, thickened with oatmeal and with generous pieces of the rabbit. His contribution to the supper made him feel suddenly hopeful.

'I'm glad,' he said to Isaac. 'I'm really glad about your news.'

His uncle nodded and leaned forward to poke the fire, adding a few more sticks of wood.

'Where's Betsy?' Gabriel asked. Her absence made the house feel empty. It was a miserable evening and he would have expected her to be at home.

'Up at the vicarage. The Reverend Cavanagh has visitors. He wanted Betsy there to fetch and carry.'

'What time will she come home?'

Isaac shrugged his shoulders. 'I doubt it will be before ten. I'll walk up and meet her.'

'I'll go.' Gabriel felt a curious tightness in his chest, a quickening of his blood. In case Isaac objected, he added, 'You have to be up early.'

The older man nodded and they sat in silence except for the sound of Sarah dunking the used bowls in a pail of water.

Although it was cold and his clothes were wet Gabriel felt impatient to be off again. The thought of seeing Betsy filled him with a foolish, boyish expectation to which no man of four-and-twenty should be prey. He stood up and moved near to the fire so that his breeches steamed, adding a clammy dampness to the already smoky air. His eyes began to sting, increasing his impatience to be off. As he rocked from foot to foot he wondered whether the vicar's guests might offer him employment or, on the strength of his relationship to Betsy, perhaps even the vicar himself? If he worked at the vicarage then he would see even more of her. The prospect fuelled his impatience.

The daydream was cut short as Joseph and James came in, stamping their feet and banging their arms to instil some warmth into their limbs. Aunt Sarah busied herself dishing them up bowls of the broth.

'You have Gabriel to thank for the rabbit,' she announced and he felt again the pleasure of being useful.

The talk was desultory. Isaac told them about the outcome of the meeting and although they expressed pleasure, there was no fire in their answers. They were young and thoughts of women, not work were their main preoccupation. They were not the sort of men to be inspired by the passion for justice and fair play that drove their father.

When at last Gabriel gauged the time to be right he prepared to leave.

Cousin Joseph watched him struggle back into his boots.

'Where'n earth you off to at this time of night?'

'To meet your sister. I thought I'd walk her back home safe, save your father.' As he spoke he wondered if he was implying that her brothers, rather than their father, should be taking care of Betsy's welfare.

Joseph merely said: 'Watch out for the ruts along Dead Man's Lane. They don't look too bad but they're deep as your knees if you step into one.'

Thanking him, Gabriel sank into his jerkin and prepared for the biting wind.

5

As Martha's twenty-first birthday drew near she sensed that her father was growing increasingly panic stricken.

Her grandmother — her mother's mother, had left the sum of £2,000 in her will with the instruction that it should be Martha's to do with as she saw fit on reaching her majority. In darker moments Martha reasoned that perhaps her grandmother thought she would never marry — God knows, she was plain enough. By bequeathing her this sum, perhaps the old lady hoped that her future would be secure. On the other hand she might have done it simply to spite her son in law with whom she had never got on. Whichever, the prospect of this strange bequest began to fill her thoughts.

Martha's mother's portion had of course gone to her husband and Martha reasoned that perhaps Grandmama was determined that she should have the independence denied to her daughter. If she married of course, her inheritance would pass naturally into the hands of her husband but to date she remained single, stubbornly so in her father's view. The prospect of her looming independence seemed to alarm him greatly.

The knowledge of the money had been there for the past three years and yet Martha had always denied herself the indulgence of thinking about it. It was as if, by making plans to spend it, the reality would be spoilt and God (or his representative — Papa) would promptly step in and destroy her foolish dreams. Daydreaming, or 'idle speculation' as the minister would brand it, was frowned upon.

With only two weeks to go Martha began to think that as a matter of seriousness she should consider her future. A strange sense of restlessness immediately claimed her. She knew what she would like to do. To begin with she would like to make things fairer. First of all she would give Widow Shepherd five pounds so that she could have as much food and heat as she wanted and not be dependent on the goodwill of others. It was an empty wish though, for independent or not her father would be outraged at such an irresponsible act. *Have you lost your mind girl? You will have every ne'er do well in the parish coming to your door demanding charity!*

She would like to buy more books, too — not the volumes of sermons and homilies

68

that her father set such store by but some of the new novels that had been written for entertainment. Before she left the village, her friend Rachel had lent her a novel, an exciting story of a young woman who had disguised herself as a man and travelled with an army regiment to be with the man she loved. At first he was thought to be a poor man but it turned out that he was the son of a Scottish laird and as such inherited a vast estate. As a result her parents forgave her and the story ended happily. For a moment Martha tried to imagine herself in such a role, then she shrugged off the foolishness. The buying of such books would not be well received. Her father, regardless of who had paid for them, would probably refuse to have them in the house.

She returned to the problem of her inability to find a husband. It was undeniably a great disappointment to the Reverend Cavanagh. He seemed to feel that having an unmarried daughter of one and twenty — especially as his sole heir, was in some way shameful. Martha was left feeling that by remaining single she was wilfully defying him.

Once, when she was about sixteen, he had introduced her to Mortimer Harvester, who was the then vicar of St Jude's in the neighbouring parish of Lower Rising. At the time she was too naïve to realize the implications. Mr Harvester was a tall, lugubrious man with watery, protruding eyes and a deep sepulchral voice that made her want to mentally wind a handle to make him speak faster. He took to visiting on several occasions and she was aware that his presence produced a flurry of excitement. Her father invariably made a point of leaving them alone and on one occasion, in an effort to be polite and obliging, she regaled the visitor with her views on life. After he had gone her father sent for her. He was clearly displeased.

'What have you been saying to the Reverend Harvester?'

She tried to think what they had talked about. He had asked whether she could sing and if she had had much experience with accounts. When she did not answer, her father said:

'What an ungrateful child you are! I have spent many hours cultivating him, preparing the ground to enable him to ask my permission and now you have clearly offended him.'

Asking permission for what? She was confused.

'What did you say?' the minister continued.

She could not answer and her father sent her to her room where she remained for three days with bread and water until her mother, with unusual courage, interceded on her behalf with the promise that she would go to church twice daily and pray for enlightenment. Mortimer Harvester was now a bishop and the Reverend Cavanagh could not bear to have his name mentioned in the house as it reminded him of what might have been.

Martha looked out of the window at the hostile day. That peaceful, still vista of a few days ago had been swept away by an angry north-easterly wind. As she watched the trees bowed submissively and anything not firmly anchored to its place was at the whim of the elements.

She turned back to the problems at hand. One thing could be said for her father: he did not give up easily. Although he had come to terms with the fact that a union with Bartholomew Bowler would never come about, he was still looking ever more desperately for a suitable match. As a result, Doctor and Mrs Geoffrey Gordon and their son Jonathon had been invited to supper that evening. The excuse was that it was All Saints' Day, a cause for celebration although they had never marked it in such a fashion before.

Jonathon Gordon had recently come down from Cambridge where he had been studying law. He was to join the partnership of Rowhampton and Perkiss, who practised in Lower Rising.

Of course there was no doubt as to the real reason for the invitation. Jonathon was twenty-two and had 'prospects'. Her father's first choice would naturally be a member of the landed gentry or, failing that, somebody in the senior ranks of the church, which often came to the same thing. The saving grace however in Jonathon's case was that his godmother was Lady Boldre and having no children of her own, Jonathon stood to inherit. Lady Boldre was also the sister of Sir Jenison. Knowing this, Martha wondered what desperation made her father think that a union with the Gordons would be possible. With a growing sense of despair she prepared herself for another evening of humiliation.

Jonathon was hardly a catch. She had met him only once and wondered how he would ever practise the law, for he hardly seemed capable of stringing two words together, being plagued by a pronounced stammer. Her mood grew increasingly like the weather. Although she was no beauty she could not rid herself of the hope that a potential bride-groom would stir some feelings of romance in her heart, however slight. The thought of Jonathon, a silent, pimply beanpole with a flat

nasal voice evoked only a sense of hopelessness.

She got up from the settle and began to
pace the room. She wanted to marry. Of
course she did. Even with money of her own
she had no wish to be a pitied spinster,
unfulfilled and shrivelled up. Again she went
to look out of the window, feeding her sense
of rebellion from the angry weather. Inside
her head she said, *I won't marry for the sake
of it*. Her father would be shocked to know
that sometimes she prayed that even if she
never married, she would still find someone
to teach her about the mystery called love.

The day crawled by and that evening she
dutifully dressed in her best silk, brushed her
hair a hundred times to make it shine and
resolved to make interesting conversation
— if only she knew how.

The Gordons arrived promptly at seven
and the minister made a business of making
them welcome.

The meal, as Martha feared, was a disaster.
Her mother, in memory of some dinner she
had had years earlier, had decided upon a
complicated menu which included beef soup
and woodcock. Mrs Porter, who came in to
cook for them, was out of her depth. The
soup was greasy and the lumps of beef floated
like cubes of gristle. Martha watched Mrs

Gordon chase a piece around her mouth for an eternity before gulping it down and laying her spoon aside with the comment: 'very nice.' The men were braver, swallowing the lumps whole. Papa's look defied her to leave any but for once she ignored him, draining the liquid and leaving a rockery of grey lumps in her bowl. In contrast the woodcock were burnt to tiny, shiny conker-coloured parodies of their former selves.

The food aside, the conversation was equally painful. The minister asked the doctor if he was being kept busy which resulted in a monologue about the latest outbreak of fever that had swept the village.

'Of course, I'm a firm believer in the benefits of cider and treacle,' Dr Gordon announced. 'It does wonders for the constitution. My family takes it daily. You should try it yourself, my dear Reverend.'

Martha happened to catch Jonathon's eye and saw the momentary smile that greeted the suggestion. She wondered whether he was amused by or was approving of his father's enthusiasm.

Mrs Cavanagh kept up her end of the bargain by discussing curtain material she had espied at the draper's with little roses woven into the fabric.

'It would be just the thing for when Martha

has a home of her own,' she said in conclusion.

Martha had only been paying partial attention and now wondered what she might have missed. Was she getting a home of her own? For a terrible moment she wondered if some secret agreement had already been made and that this was really a last-ditch attempt to get her married before her majority.

She glanced again at Jonathon but his eyes were boring into the tablecloth. Her father seemed to sense the direction of her gaze. He addressed Jonathon directly.

'Well, my boy, how is the practice of the law going?'

Jonathon cleared his throat and his pimples grew pink.

'V-very well, thank you, sir.'

The minister waited for further enlightenment but when nothing was forthcoming he turned the conversation to local matters.

'You must see some hopeless cases,' he began, addressing the doctor. 'The Lord knows I do my best to steer these people along the course of righteousness but sometimes they seem beyond me. The trouble is, they have no self-respect. They're dirty. They breed irresponsibly — excuse me ladies, that was indelicate of me.' He gave a chastened smile in the direction of Mrs Gordon, who lowered her eyes and grimaced inanely.

'They don't respect authority,' Ignatius continued. 'They lie and steal. I often think there isn't a commandment they haven't broken.'

Doctor Gordon was a long time answering.

'I've always been of the opinion that *judge not that ye be not judged* is a good maxim to live your life by,' he said at last.

The minister looked flustered.

'Well, of course. Some of the poorer sort do try to lead decent lives. I've nothing but admiration for the way they cope, but the fact is, if we aren't very careful the more dangerous element will upset the natural balance. Just the other day now, some of the labourers, the labourers mind you, called a meeting at the church to demand a rise in wages. I told Sir Jenison: give them an inch and they'll take over the village, mark my words.'

'They are hungry. What family can live on ten shillings a week?'

Jonathon's words halted them all in their tracks. Ignatius's fork was half-way to his mouth. His wife was in the process of trying to rehydrate the woodcock with gravy.

The minister sat back. His eyes looked

pinpoint sharp as he formulated his response.

'That sounds a very dangerous attitude, young man.'

Jonathon struggled to find words again. His eyes watered with the effort. 'If you leave people with nothing they have nothing to lose,' he said.

Doctor Gordon defused the tension by saying.

'Fresh air is a great medicine,' he said. 'I walk at least two miles a day. Riding isn't the same. It is the action of the legs pumping the blood around the body. You have a riding-horse, do you not, Vicar?'

The crisis was averted. The minister began to explain how he had acquired his showy black cob as payment for a funeral service, the deceased having left no will. There was general relief that the conversation had been steered away from more contentious issues.

Martha looked at Jonathon. He was very still, his gaze still focused on some inner vista. She thought about what he had said. He had put into words, however painfully, the very thoughts that she nursed. She felt a moment of triumph.

Somehow they struggled through the rest of the evening and when at last the Gordons bade goodbye, Papa closed the door with a sigh.

'That boy will not do. He won't do at all.'

★ ★ ★

As Gabriel drew near to the vicarage it occurred to him that he did not know where he was supposed to wait. A carriage stood outside the gate, a dark-coloured horse slumped in the shafts, his head bent low to avoid the wind. Nearby the driver stamped and paced. At that moment the front door of the vicarage opened and a blaze of light encircled two men and a woman emerging into the night.

'Good-night. God speed and thank you again.'

They came down the path. The lady made a business of feeling her way in the dark, for their bodies cast shadows in the light from the open door. She clung to the older man as though she were afraid of falling. The young man strode ahead, his head bent against the assailing wind. He was tall and gangly and something about him suggested that he was glad to escape.

'My pleasure, dear sir. My pleasure.' The man who remained framed in the doorway was presumably the vicar. He too was tall and willowy, his frame bent slightly forward as if

78

he were carrying out some continual act of worship. Gabriel screwed up his eyes the better to see him, but his face was in darkness.

Meanwhile the coachman opened the door, lowered the step and helped his passengers aboard.

As the front door closed and a spiteful rain splashed across his face Gabriel marched round to the back of the house. Perhaps, with any luck, he would be invited to wait inside.

Through the window he saw Betsy in the candlelit kitchen — along with Miss Cavanagh, the vicar's daughter. He had forgotten about Miss Cavanagh. As he watched she donned a pair of spectacles and in turn seemed to be watching Betsy weave a path across from the kitchen table to the sink and back again, carrying an assortment of plates and dishes and cutlery and pans. Gabriel felt a sense of annoyance that she did not offer to help — foolish, of course, for people like the vicar's family did not demean themselves with humble tasks, even though the Bible preached humility.

Miss Cavanagh wore a dark dress in some silky material with a collar of lace. He conceded that she had a very neat waist, although it was probably the cut of the dress that flattered her. At that moment Betsy struggled to the sink with a kettle of hot water and the resultant steam obliterated his view.

That decided him. If he announced his presence it might speed things up. Miss Cavanagh might even agree that the remaining work should be left until morning. He knocked forcefully on the door.

'Who on earth can that be?' Martha felt a tremor of apprehension. Such late visits always augured the worst. Perhaps someone had died or was ill, and wanted the minister's spiritual guidance.

'Perhaps it's my father,' hazarded Betsy.

Betsy had her hands in the water so, being nearer to the door, Martha opened it, to reveal the tall, dripping figure of Gabriel Lawless.

At the sight of him Martha felt herself to be on the edge of a precipice. Below her was a long, long drop. Her pale cheeks became suffused with a pink blush that spread down to her throat. Hastily she went to remove her spectacles but they caught in her hair and pulled a strand loose so that in addition to everything else she must look dishevelled. She could hardly breathe for shame.

'I've come to escort Miss Betsy home,' said Gabriel.

In silence Martha stepped back as he entered the kitchen.

To his joy Betsy gave him a quick smile, then turned an apologetic face to Miss Cavanagh.

'I'll try not to be too long,' she said, and set to scrubbing the pots and bowls vigorously.

Gabriel went across to the sink, picked up the drying-cloth and began wiping the washed plates, placing them on the table one by one. All the while Miss Cavanagh regarded him as though mesmerized. She had never seen a man undertake such tasks before.

'It's turning mighty cold,' Gabriel observed, hoping that Miss Cavanagh would take the hint and dismiss Betsy, but she didn't. Her breath seemed to be coming unnaturally fast and her bosom, what he could see of it, heaved quite prettily for such a plain little thing. 'The more I help the quicker we'll be done.'

At these words Miss Cavanagh seemed to be startled into action and she began to store the clean dishes away.

Amid the clatter of pots and pans no one heard the opening of the door to the main part of the house. The vicar stepped into the kitchen and stopped in surprise, an expression of cold hostility on his face at the sight of Gabriel.

'Who are you?'

'Gabriel Lawless, sir. Betsy's cousin.'

'And what are you doing in my house?'

Gabriel bit back the desire to say that he thought that must be obvious.

'I have come to escort Betsy home and I am helping her, the quicker to finish her tasks,' he contented himself with saying.

Martha held her breath. His voice was soft, warm as if the fruits of the country had conspired to add to its rich burr.

The Reverend Cavanagh was not impressed.

'Well, next time, wait outside,' he said harshly. He turned to his daughter.

'And what are *you* doing? Are you some sort of servant, to be slaving in your own house?'

Miss Cavanagh lowered her gaze. Gabriel could see that she wanted to run from the room, but the power of her father's presence seemed to keep her rooted to the spot. Mortified by shame she hardly heard her father's parting shot, called out as he turned to leave.

'Just make sure that all the doors are locked after they've gone.'

Martha's heart lurched. Her father's words were so hateful, implying that Mr Lawless was a likely thief. They were living in dangerous times: it did no good to antagonize people. She dropped the spoons she was holding on to the table and sped from the room in the slipstream of her father's anger.

Neither Betsy nor Gabriel spoke. Gabriel wanted to tell Betsy to get her shawl, that they would leave straight away, that she would never have to come back to this house again, but such thoughts brushed up against the harsh reality — that Betsy was lucky to have work. Her few pence meant the difference between hunger and starvation. They finished the work in silence.

Martha waited in the hall, her heart thumping painfully, until she heard Gabriel and Betsy leave. Then she crept back to the kitchen to lock the door.

Later, lying in bed, she relived the encounter, endured again the misery, regretted the loss of something undefined but priceless. Whatever the foolish hopes she might have nursed that Gabriel would at least respect her, they were now dashed. She had never felt like this before. Amid the maelstrom of her emotions was one realization. Gabriel Lawless had aroused in her feelings that she would never have believed possible. No matter what the consequences, she had to follow them through to the end.

★   ★   ★

In spite of the cold, when at last Gabriel and Betsy stepped outside it was as if some oppressive yoke had been lifted. Insanely, Gabriel felt as if this was the moment he had been waiting for all his life. What he said now, what he did could change his future.

He insisted that Betsy walked on the leeward side, sheltering her from the wind. To ensure that she did not stumble over some pothole he held her elbow, its fragile warmth burning into his hand.

'Are you really going to marry Ephraim Carter?' The words came out blunt and awkward, like an accusation. What he really wanted to say was: do you love him? When you think of him, when you hear his name, when someone mentions him, does your heart surge?

The force that swept through him shocked him. He had never experienced anything like it before. He knew that he was fiercely, dangerously jealous. As they walked he hoped to God she didn't detect what was going on in his mind.

'Ephraim has his own business. It will be good for the family,' she answered him.

In a strange, bitter-sweet moment he guessed that she was marrying him to ease the burden at home. He tried not to consider that she might also feel affection for him, be grateful, even feel some physical desire, although he was not sure what women felt in that direction. The only ones he had known closely, so to speak, put on the pretence of caring, but in reality it had always been for the price of a jug of ale or for the gift of a sixpence. Pretty actresses, were women.

He wanted to ask more, to warn her, but to do so would be dangerous so he steered the conversation to safer ground.

'I hear your father has had a pretty victory today,' he said.

In the gloom Betsy sighed. He sensed her shoulders rise and fall as if shaking off some irritant.

'My father is too honest, too straight. They'll not do what they have promised.' She sighed again. 'That is when the real trouble will hit us.'

She spoke with such authority that he found himself asking: 'What trouble?'

Her side momentarily brushed against his, sending shivers of pleasure along his body.

'Why, the rick-burnings, the machine-breakings.'

He could not imagine that they would really take root here.

After a long time Betsy said: 'I am afraid. I'm afraid for my father and my brothers. Father would never do anything he thought to be wrong but by his preaching he influences others. The owners will blame him if trouble comes to our village.'

'What about Ephraim?'

He forced himself to ask the question as if he was merely curious about the cobbler's beliefs.

'Ephraim is hot headed,' Betsy said, 'He piles kindling on the bonfire but he is clever. He won't be there when the blaze starts. He won't be there in the front line.'

He wondered what she felt about it all — her father being the unwitting catalyst, her betrothed the one who fanned the flames, but he could not ask. Besides, the little row of cottages was now within view and reluctantly he released Betsy's elbow, swallowed down his thoughts and prepared for another restless night, lying within feet of the most beautiful girl he had ever known.

6

The conversation with Betsy did little to clear Gabriel's mind. During the night he clung to the small comfort that she was marrying Ephraim not because she loved him but because it made economic sense. Doubts about Ephraim's character gnawed at him. Perhaps his cousin had changed. He drew some comfort from knowing that Isaac would never knowingly put his daughter into danger. Again he tossed in the narrow bed. The real agony came from the fact that even if Betsy liked him, and he had no proof that she did, he had no means of providing her with a secure alternative. As the grey morning light filtered into the little cottage he fell back on the only solution that made sense. He must leave.

'I've been thinking of moving on,' he said to Isaac as the older man pulled on his boots in preparation for work.

'No need for that.' Isaac gave him a reassuring smile. The younger man wondered if he guessed the real reason behind his decision.

'We're managing well enough,' Isaac

added. 'Besides, after Sunday Betsy will have moved out.'

'How?'

'She is to be wed. Didn't she tell you?'

'On Sunday?' The blow was almost physical. Talking to her the evening before Gabriel had assumed that her marriage was some distant plan, something hardly settled, that time and circumstance might change. That it was only a few days away was a crushing blow.

Isaac scratched his head thoughtfully and his eyes narrowed.

'The way they are going about it is going to mean trouble, though. I was all for them marrying proper, in the church. I might not agree with the Reverend Cavanagh but it is what is expected. Ephraim won't have it though. He says that marrying in the parish church would be hypocrisy. He wants me to wed them.'

Gabriel didn't know what to say so he remained silent.

Isaac looked increasingly troubled.

'He may be right, but it's Betsy I worry about. If I perform the ceremony she won't be wed in the eyes of the law. There's them around here that could make trouble.'

Gabriel didn't say anything because he was too busy tormenting himself with visions of

Betsy in Ephraim's bed. It hurt. It hurt so much that he knew he had to get away.

Yet again he wondered what Betsy thought about it. It all came down to what she felt about Ephraim. Surely she wouldn't be browbeaten by him into doing something she felt was wrong? Hot headed. That was how she had described him. Did she approve of him? Was there something about cousin Ephraim that inspired her soul?

'Well lad, I must be going. If you want to make yourself useful there is a pile of logs in the lean-to. It would be a help if you were to chop some.'

Gabriel was grateful to have something to do. Chopping was a good way of venting his anger. He drove into those logs as if they were an enemy. He tried not to think of them as cousin Ephraim.

At the vicarage, Martha was on her way to the kitchen to ask Mrs Porter about lunch when she heard voices on the other side of the door.

'It's the way things have always been done,' she heard Betsy Lawless say above the clatter of dishes. 'You call witnesses together and make a public declaration. There's no need for a ceremony in the church.'

Martha's hand was on the doorknob. Carefully she withdrew it, holding her breath in case she missed the rest of the conversation.

'What do the vicar think?' Mrs Porter's voice had an edge of excitement.

'We won't tell him. Ephraim says it's none of his concern. It's our wedding. We'll do it our way.'

'When are you getting wed then?'

'On Sunday, after the church service. Father will marry us on the green.' There was the sound of laughter as if at a private joke.

'That way everyone can go to church first and then come to the ceremony afterwards so the Reverend can't complain that we're stealing his congregation,' Betsy explained.

Martha hurried back to the parlour, her ears pounding with the rush of her own blood. What she had heard upset her greatly. Why was it that she always felt responsible for things that were beyond her control?

She covered her mouth with her hands as if by so doing she could keep the enormity of the discovery that she had heard at bay. By declaring her intention of tying herself to, of all people, her cousin, Ephraim Carter, Betsy would be living in sin! Martha sank back on to the settle as if the impact of the news had taken away the power of her legs.

It would not be a legal marriage. Mr Lawless was certainly not a proper minister, ordained as her father was, with a right to join people before God in holy matrimony.

She tried to tell herself that it was none of her business. If Betsy wanted to live in such a way, then that was up to her. What really troubled her was the knowledge that when her father got to hear of it he would be furious. Without asking she knew that he would dismiss Betsy immediately from their service. Betsy was a good servant, she pondered ruefully, very honest and hard-working. They would be hard put to find anyone else as trustworthy.

After a while she calmed herself. It was a long time since there had been a wedding in the village. In normal circumstances, when a member of the household married, Martha and her mother would go shopping to find a suitable gift. She felt that sense of unrest again as she contemplated the reality of Betsy and her new husband living together. Their bed would be small and they would be forced to sleep close to each other. What would Betsy feel when Ephraim Carter put his hands upon her? She was shocked at her own excitement.

One small glimmer of comfort came to her. The night before, when Gabriel came to fetch his cousin, Martha had wondered — no — feared, that there might be some understanding between them. Betsy had smiled at him in such a way and he . . . Well, she must have been mistaken. If she had to choose between Ephraim Carter and Gabriel Lawless — but whatever was she thinking about!

When her father came in a while later she wondered if she should tell him, but if she did, he might prevent the ceremony from taking place. If her father tried to interfere, who knew what the villagers might do in retaliation? Best to hope that he did not get to hear of it before Sunday. She remained silent.

At Isaac's cottage it was about half-way through the afternoon when Gabriel heard the rumble of a farm cart. He dropped his axe and went outside to investigate. His cousin Joseph and a man he had never seen before were sitting up on the driver's bench.

'What's amiss?' Gabriel went across and immediately saw that there was someone lying in the back of the cart. It was Isaac.

'It's Father. His back's real bad. I guess he's strained something with all that digging.' Joseph himself looked tired and Gabriel guessed that, like his father, he was probably having a hard time at present, except that he had twenty-five years the advantage.

Carefully they carried Isaac indoors, for he could not walk. There they gently lowered him on to one of the pallets. His face looked grey and he shook his head as if to ward off the pain.

After a moment he said, 'This is the only place I can find any respite. Perhaps if I lie still for a few hours, I'll be better by morning.'

He moved his shoulders a fraction and winced visibly with pain. It was clear that he would not.

'You rest.' A thought struck Gabriel. 'I'll take your place tomorrow,' he said. 'Surely Seth Hardwick won't object?'

Isaac gave the slightest movement of his head. He looked too exhausted to think about it.

As Joseph went to take the cart back, Gabriel moved to stoke the fire. His boots leaked and his feet were frozen. He thought ruefully of Ephraim. He could do with his cousin's services just now. Sarah fetched the quilt from their bed and wrapped it around her husband.

'Don't fuss lass, I'll be well enough,' Isaac said but his face was grey with exhaustion.

As Gabriel stoked the fire he wondered where Betsy was. No doubt she was with Ephraim, making plans for when she moved in — or maybe jumping the gun and behaving as though they were married lovers already.

His thoughts tortured him but he could not get the image from his mind. Again he thought of leaving, but now, with Isaac sick, he could not do so.

Betsy returned soon after. Other than a muffled greeting he tried to ignore her, yet all the time he found himself looking for signs of exhilaration, of that expression of sated, happy love-making that would show in her face. She looked as she always did, calm, serious, utterly beautiful.

It was clear that Isaac would not be able to climb the ladder to the sleeping area. Joseph and James were out about their business and when Aunt Sarah and young Matthew retired for the night, Gabriel found himself sitting with Betsy beside the embers. Isaac was silent and he guessed that at last he slept. An hour since they had attempted to help him to the privy but he was in far too much pain to move so an old pot had been produced instead. Now he breathed heavily, in an uneasy, troubled sort of sleep that went with the pain of both body and soul.

'I hear you are getting wed this weekend,' Gabriel said.

She nodded as if it was of no great significance.

'Congratulations. I had no idea it would be so soon.'

Betsy studied the golden glow in the hearth.

'It will make life easier for the rest of the family, although mother will miss my help.'

Gabriel hesitated. 'You — you don't sound as if you are in the first flush of love.'

Betsy looked at him then and a slow smile turned her sweet lips up at the corners. He ached to kiss her.

'I shall fare well enough,' she said. 'Ephraim's . . . ' she appeared to struggle for the right word.

'Hot-headed?' he offered.

'Aye, that. But he's — fun too.' She shrugged, glancing at him with an embarrassed smile and that searing hurt was there again. They were lovers. Of course they were. What's more, Ephraim made Betsy's cheeks glow, he pleasured her, pleased her. Gabriel envied him with a tidal wave of violence.

'You're not wedding in the church, then?' He said it for something to say.

She shook her head. 'What would be the point? We don't believe in the way the church teaches the gospel. We'll make our vows in the old-fashioned way, out in the open, in front of my father — as long as he is well enough.' She glanced in the direction of Isaac's prostrate figure and her normally warm brown eyes looked grey with worry.

95

'I'll take his place at work tomorrow.'

'That's good of you.' She played with a strand of her long brown hair, the end gently curling about her finger. Only the knowledge that it would be madness stopped him from reaching out and pressing his lips against her small, expressive hand.

'You will be here won't you — for the ceremony?' She looked suddenly nervous, seeking an ally, someone she could trust.

What could he say — that he'd rather plunge his arm into a red-hot crucible than witness her marrying another man?

Aloud, he said: 'I'll be there.'

7

The next morning Gabriel rose early and set out to take Isaac's place at Home Farm. During the night it had rained and beneath his feet the tracks were the consistency of melted toffee. Mud oozed into the cracks in his boots chilling his feet, forming hard, cold casts.

When he found Seth Hardwick he explained what had happened to his uncle and offered his services. The older man looked uncertain.

'I dunno about you working here. I dunno what Sir Jenison will say. He don't like me to make changes without consulting him first.'

Gabriel felt his irritation rising. He knew that this was part of the reason for the present troubles. Men like Seth Hardwick, thousands like him, didn't seem to have any faith in themselves. If they only recognized their own value they could take back much of what was lost to them.

'How often does Sir Jenison come here then?' he said, biting back his frustration.

'Oh, he rides past often but he hardly ever comes to see what we're doing.'

'Well, there you are then. You don't need to change anything. You can still pay my uncle but it will be me who does the work.' He guessed that as far as Sir Jenison was concerned, one peasant was much like another. Would he even recognize the difference? Gabriel raised his eyebrows, waiting for a response. 'I'm younger than Isaac, stronger,' he offered. Because Seth couldn't think of anything else to object to he reluctantly agreed.

After Gabriel's recent privations the work seemed doubly hard. His muscles had grown soft, his energy was low, but he pushed himself all day, unwilling to give Seth any excuse to send him away. The other men didn't say much. He detected their suspicion. It was as if by going away he had in some way betrayed his roots, that he was now truly a stranger in the village. Besides, he was a skilled man, had served his time. That too set him apart. He wondered if he would ever feel at home here again.

When he arrived back at the cottage it was already dark and he was cold, exhausted and hungry. Pushing open the cottage door he was moved by the gentle glow from the fire, the tendrils of heat that reached out to him — and by the sight of Betsy helping with their meal. Uncle Isaac was still stretched out on the floor but he declared himself better.

'I'll be up and about in no time,' he said.

'Well, there's no hurry. I'm quite capable of keeping your place for you.'

Gabriel sank on to a stool and eased his aching back. With an exquisite feeling of pleasure he accepted a bowl of hot stew from Betsy. Her fingers touched his as he took the bowl and an undiluted feeling of desire coursed through him. He thought that he could endure anything if it meant coming home to Betsy every night. She smiled at him and he could not believe that so much joy was possible in such a simple act. In three days she would be wed and lost to him for ever.

Those days passed quickly. As planned, on Sunday after the morning service Betsy and Ephraim presented themselves on the village green for the ceremony. In spite of his protestations to the contrary, Isaac was clearly still in great pain and it took a huge effort to get him up and dressed. Somehow he struggled the distance to the green, taking up a position beneath the ancient sycamore that for generations had sheltered Midwillow folk from the elements. Fortunately the weather was kind, more like an early September day than one in late October.

As Betsy's father was to act the minister, it

was her brother Joseph who gave her away. Gabriel kept himself as far back from the ceremony as possible, fearing that his turmoil must show on his face. His cousin looked beautiful. She wore her Sunday gown and had Michaelmas daisies woven into her hair, a lacy shawl, borrowed from some relative, about her shoulders. As he watched, gall burned bitter in his mouth, for even had she chosen otherwise, he knew that he had nothing to offer her.

He forced himself not to stare at Betsy, instead taking in the people gathered around him. There they all were, the Lawlesses, the Carters, the Brooks and the Brewsters, all drawn together by ties of blood. His blood link was as close as any, his father being Isaac's brother and his mother being Sarah's sister. No doubt that was why Sarah had always been so good to him. He forced himself to look at Ephraim. His cousin seemed uncomfortable in his role as bride-groom. His hair was slicked back, the thick brown locks plastered against his head and his face looked scrubbed. Ephraim's mother, now dead, having been Isaac's sister, he could see a family resemblance between the bridegroom, his uncle Isaac and his cousins Joseph and James. There were the same short, sturdy bodies as if carved from local oak, the squarish faces, some pugnacious, others tending towards oblong; eyes varying in shade from charcoal to hazel, hair in all shades from dark brown to russet. Earlier, Gabriel had caught a glimpse of himself in the dull pewter of Sarah's best plate. Even allowing for the natural distortion of the curved metal, what he saw was alien to everyone around him — a long body, hair black and curly, eyes the blue-green colour of the water. Had his mother borne more live children, perhaps he should not have felt such a misfit.

Isaac stepped forward and the gathering fell silent. He still looked grey and in pain but there was something about the gravity of his bearing that brought everyone to attention.

'Dear brothers and sisters, we are gathered here, before God to witness the binding together of Ephraim Carter, shoe-mender and bachelor, to Betsy Lawless, spinster of this parish . . . '

So it went on. Gabriel recognized the words. He had heard them or others like them in the village church. Now here was Isaac calling upon his daughter to make a vow of fidelity to her cousin Ephraim.

An embarrassed smile played about the bridegroom's lips and, as he made his vows, it spread into a grin. Betsy smiled in response, sharing some secret, and in that moment

Gabriel knew how people could kill when jealousy took them.

Once the ceremony was over the guests retired to the old barn which in wintertime acted as the chapel. Sarah and Betsy had prepared a wedding breakfast of fresh bread and cold mutton with tiny honey-cakes. Where the meat had come from no one said but it was probably a gift from members of the congregation. Isaac would not tolerate strong drink although at that moment Gabriel would have embraced it. Still clearly in pain, his uncle was seated on a bench, his back resting against the wall, supported by a bolster. He gave Gabriel an embracing smile and his nephew felt the familiar gratitude towards him.

As he scanned the faces in the barn he remembered having noticed someone else at the service. He looked around but she was nowhere to be seen. Casting his mind back to the scene on the green he mentally placed his relatives in their groups. Yes, there had been someone, half-hidden behind the sycamore tree, mostly screened by the flow of bodies as they paced and leaned this way and that the better to see. Behind them he recalled the small, still figure of Martha Cavanagh, her pale, peaky little face an anxious blur among the throng.

The significance of her presence hit home. What had made her come to Betsy's wedding? Surely she was not an invited guest — as, indeed, her absence now suggested. What would her father think? Therein lay the answer. He would never, ever approve of what was happening and would certainly have forbidden his daughter to be present.

In spite of his sadness and regret the thought of Miss Cavanagh, defying her father, brought a momentary glow of warmth to Gabriel's icy heart.

★   ★   ★

As her mother had taken to her bed with a headache, Martha stole the opportunity to take a walk after church that Sunday morning. Purely by accident it took her in the direction of the village green, where Betsy's marriage ceremony was to take place. As she drew near she told herself that she did not actually intend to witness the event for to do so would be to give it her approval, and that of course she could never do. It just so happened that a stone became lodged in her slipper and she was forced to stop and remove it just behind the trees that fronted the green.

Nearly all the village seemed to be in

attendance. With something like sadness she thought how beautiful Betsy looked. She had such a slender figure with a curve to her breast that must be the envy of many a girl — and quicken the heartbeat of many a man.

Betsy and her cousin Ephraim, soon to be husband and wife, seemed to smile a lot and be happy with what they were about. Martha tried to keep her eyes on the young couple but somehow they kept scanning the crowd until she found who she was looking for.

Gabriel Lawless seemed to be watching his cousin all the time — Betsy that was. His face looked very tense and Martha wondered if it was because he had found no work. For a while she imagined his gratitude if she were to offer him a place. Tomorrow she would reach her majority. Perhaps she could buy her own house, employ him as her groom and gardener.

Thank you, Miss Cavanagh. I will never forget your kindness and I promise that I will stay in your service for the rest of my life.

She looked up to see him watching her and immediately her face felt like an inferno. Surely her thoughts were transparent? Quickly she dodged back behind the tree and as the wedding party moved off she scurried back to the vicarage.

Her mother still being unwell, Martha did

not go to the evening church service. If she was totally honest in admitting it, although that was wicked, she did not enjoy going to church. She did try very hard but sometimes when her father was preaching she found herself arguing with him inside her head. The fault of course had to be hers, for why otherwise would God have chosen her father as his servant?

Later that evening she heard him return from evensong. By the way the door slammed and the yelp from Dash, the spaniel, she guessed that somebody had told him about the wedding ceremony. As he flew into the room she could see that he was even angrier than she feared.

'Have you heard anything of this?' he asked. She shook her head.

At that moment her mother came downstairs but when she heard what had happened she immediately announced that the shock was so great that she would have to retire again. Martha was left to face the brunt of her father's anger.

'That girl is not to set foot in this house again,' he announced. 'By her behaviour she has made herself no better than a harlot.'

Martha had always been hazy about exactly what a harlot was. Clearly she was a bad woman, but the details escaped her.

Worse was to follow.

'You know who is behind all this, don't you?' said the vicar. Fortunately he answered his own question. 'It is Lawless. That man Lawless. He is setting himself up as a minister. He is challenging God's role in our village. I'll speak to Sir Jenison. I'll have words with Squire Wetherby. We can't have the likes of these Lawlesses in the village. They mean nothing but trouble. They must be driven out. The evil must be expelled!'

Martha watched the spittle gather at the corner of his mouth. She dared not say anything for fear of making things worse. Perhaps someone would be able to intercede and make him see that the Lawlesses were an old, hard-working family who had been in the village for generations — far longer than the Cavanaghs. She did not know what would become of them if they were driven from the parish. Surely they would have no choice but to turn to crime? Perhaps if she pointed that out her father might relent.

Gradually the storm blew itself out. The Reverend Cavanagh announced that he was going to retire to his study. When he had gone Martha tried to let the tension slip from her, but that knot of fear in her stomach was hard to dislodge. All her life she had lived in the shadow of her father's disapproval. Tomorrow would be her twenty-first birthday. For the first time ever she would be an independent person and yet she could not see how things would change. Nursing this painful knowledge she retreated to the sanctuary of her chamber and to yet another night of unrest.

8

As Martha suspected, her transition from child to independent woman was to be in name only. At breakfast on the morning of her birthday, her father announced:

'You must not imagine, Martha, that being a day older will change anything. I shall expect you to continue with your service to the Lord. You will also leave any decisions that have to be made, to me.'

Her mother sat quietly at the breakfast table, her hands in her lap, her eyes lowered in quiescence. Martha wished that just for once her mother would stand up to him but she recognized that years of living with her father's views and certainties had worn his wife down. Not least because, if ever she demurred in any way, her husband called upon his secret ally — God. As he was fond of reminding them, as the representative of the Lord in this parish, who were they to challenge him?

When there was a lull in Ignatius's homily, Mrs Cavanagh handed her daughter a package. In spite of her now being an adult, presents still excited Martha and as she undid the ribbon she hoped for some magical gift that would transform her future. Inside the package however were a pearl necklace and a pair of gloves, also embroidered with pearls.

'Those,' said Mama, 'are for you to wear on your wedding day.'

Dutifully Martha expressed her thanks, thinking that they would be lying in her drawer for a very long time.

The question of her marriage was always there. If she failed to marry then, on her father's death, his estate would pass to his cousin Reginald Price. Cousin Reginald was the product of an unfortunate union her Aunt Charity had made with a man from Reading and as such Martha's father claimed that he was hardly a gentleman. In fact he thought so badly of him that so far Martha had been spared the ordeal of being presented to him as a prospective bride.

The minister rose from the table, casting his napkin aside.

'Well now, your mother and I have to go into Lymington this morning.' He did not say why and Martha was left to contemplate an empty day ahead.

When they had gone she remained at the table. Like some damp blanket she felt the sense of anticlimax drape over her. She didn't know quite what she had expected but it had been something. There was no mention of her inheritance. Foolishly she had hoped that it would be handed over to her to do with as she pleased but she should have known that her father would not release his hold that easily. For the moment she did not even know who held the money in trust. It was probably the firm of Rowhampton and Perkiss, her father's solicitors.

While she was pondering this, Mrs Porter came in to clear the dishes.

''Appy birthday, Miss Martha.' Mrs Porter bustled about rattling the delicate china.

When Martha thanked her she said:

'It seems to be a week for celebration in the village, what with young Betsy's wedding and all — not as how you probably don't approve. I'm sure your papa thinks badly on it.'

Martha didn't know what to say. Mrs Porter was very fond of talking about the villagers and in the past had told her many things that she probably should not know.

'I think a church wedding would have been better,' was the best that she could come up with.

'Ah well, Isaac'll have more room in the cottage now that Betsy's moved out. They'll need it with young Gabriel coming back after all this time.' She paused and lowered her voice. 'I did hear that he's been in gaol but I doubt that's true.'

The news was not to Martha's liking.

'You shouldn't listen to gossip,' she said, but at the same time she wondered where she might find out the truth. If Gabriel Lawless was a gaolbird then all the decent young women in the village should be warned to keep away from him. In fact it would probably be best if all the local girls kept their distance anyway.

'I s'pose you can't blame him,' Mrs Porter continued. 'People who lose their parents when they are young often turn out to be wrong 'uns, 'specially in his circumstances.'

'What circumstances?' Martha cursed herself the moment the words were out but her curiosity was hopelessly aroused.

'Well, the rumour is that his mother died of shame, her husband not being the boy's father.'

'Who was his father, then?' Again she realized that she should not have graced this shameful piece of gossip with her curiosity, but it was too late.

'People say,' said Mrs Porter, 'that his mother was a handsome woman, tall and black haired with vivid blue eyes — not unlike Gabriel.' She paused, savouring the moment before continuing: 'Who *her* father was, always remained something of a mystery but rumour had it that he was a member of the gentry.'

When she was sure that she had Martha's attention, she went on:

'Of course her parents raised her the same as their other children but locally she was always regarded as a cut above the other women. That being so it was hardly surprising that she came to the notice of the master — old Sir Archibald Bowler that is, Sir Jenison's father. He was nigh on sixty by then, but a terrible one for the ladies.' Mrs Porter gave her a sly look.

'Anyway, those things happen, Miss Cavanagh. I doubt if she was willing but there isn't much that a poor girl can do about it if one of the gentry makes up his mind. I guess she was already — damaged — when she married William Lawless. Whether he knew or not, no one knows, but that child — Gabriel, looked not the slightest bit like the rest of the family.'

She sniffed and Martha listened spell-bound.

'But in that case, doesn't it make him Mr Jenison's . . . ?' she asked.

'Aye.' Mrs Porter's eyes gleamed with triumph. 'If it's true, then Gabriel Lawless is Sir Jenison's half-brother.'

While she was contemplating the enormity of this there was a knock at the front door. Mrs Porter excused herself and went to answer it. Moments later she returned.

'There's a young man to see you, the one as come to dinner the other night.'

Martha rose from the table, frowning. What could Jonathon Gordon want?

Mrs Porter had shown him into the drawing-room. When she went in he was standing by the window, looking out at the garden.

'M-Miss C-Cavanagh. H-Happy birthday.'

His hair seemed to sprout rather than grow from his head and lay in unruly directions across his scalp, rather like the grass in the meadow when the dogs had been playing chase. His cheeks were damp from the rain and when he walked, his shoes squelched on the carpet.

'Thank you.' Martha indicated that he should sit down. He folded his legs like some grasshopper as he sank on to the low fireside chair.

'Forgive me for c-calling unannounced, Miss Cavanagh, but my partners are currently away and I thought that being your birthday it might be a good opportunity to discuss with you your estate.'

Martha sat up wondering whether, after all,

she was about to receive the control of her inheritance.

Jonathon looked down at his hands, licked his lower lip, then swallowed as if trying to find the words from somewhere deep inside him. At last he started.

'I — I know that your parents take a keen interest in your affairs but — from certain things I have ascertained, I wonder if you are aware of how your money is invested?'

She shook her head and waited.

Jonathon swallowed again, then blurted out: 'I know it is not my place to sit in judgment on your estate and I should give advice only in so far as your interests are protected but I — I . . . ' He stumbled to a halt and she had no idea what he was trying to say.

'I had been hoping to find out more about my inheritance,' she ventured, hoping that it might spur him on.

He nodded and took a deep breath.

'Well, your money is invested on your behalf — and the returns are very healthy.'

She thought he had finished but suddenly he added: 'The fact is though, the ventures in which you are involved are — to put it bluntly, making you a profit at the expense of other people.' He hesitated, his eyes blinking back his discomfort. 'From the little I have seen of you,' he went on, 'you are the sort of person who would not wish to exploit the poor for your own gains.'

Martha frowned. How could her money affairs affect anyone else?

'I don't understand,' she said.

He came forward, clearing his throat in an effort to get the words out.

'Some of your money is tied up in a mining venture. The men working in the mines are worse off even than the poor labourers in this village. Many die because safety is neglected. Others are injured or get sick and they have no resources to protect them.'

Martha knew nothing about mining but before she could question him he continued, 'Yet more of your funds are invested in a sugar plantation in Jamaica. You receive a healthy return on your investment because people are enslaved, working for you for nothing.'

Could this be true? Her first instinct was not to believe him but he looked so earnest, so uncomfortable with what he was about.

'Then what would you advise me to do?' she asked.

He sat back, clearly relieved that she had not berated him for his audacity in approaching her.

He exhaled loudly, expelling the tension.

'It would be possible for me to find other sources of investment for you that did not involve robbing the poor or supporting the slave-trade.'

'Is slavery not illegal?'

'There are no slaves in England but the battle has yet to be won across the Atlantic.'

His words shocked her deeply.

'I would have no wish to harm others in order to make a profit for myself,' she said.

'That is what I thought.' He smiled briefly and she noticed that he had very regular, white teeth.

'Perhaps you would like some refreshment?'

Jonathon shook his head. 'I must be going.' He paused, then added, 'If you are willing to trust me in this I will look at other ways of protecting your income that are not so — damaging to others.'

Martha nodded, wondering what her father would say.

'I — do I have control of my estate now?' she asked him.

'You do, certainly.'

She sat back and reached a decision. There was no need to tell the minister.

Jonathon stood up, in the process knocking a Bible from the table at his side. Awkwardly he retrieved it and set it back down.

Martha found herself smiling at his clumsiness. So tall, taller even than Gabriel Lawless, but also painfully thin, he seemed too large for the room.

'Well,' she said, 'thank you for taking the trouble to explain to me about my investments.'

For a moment he looked worried.

'The fact is, I cannot guarantee that if you move your money the returns will be as profitable. I want you to know that you personally might suffer a loss if you put the welfare of others before profit.'

'I understand that.' Martha hesitated. 'Mr Gordon — am I actually rich?'

He smiled again. 'In most people's eyes, madam, you are very rich indeed.'

Retrieving his hat which had fallen to the ground along with the Bible, he muttered some awkward goodbyes and tiptoed towards the door. His manner again gave the impression of someone who felt that he was too big for his surroundings and must tread with care.

At the door he stopped and bowed his head in her direction.

'Rest assured that I will inform you of any possible changes to your finances.'

'Thank you and have a safe journey.'

He bounced his head awkwardly again,

fumbled for the door handle and retreated.

Martha leaned back to absorb the things that he had said. Never had it occurred to her that her money might have an effect on the lives of unknown people, especially as far away as Jamaica. It was a strange discovery.

A moment later her mother came back into the room.

'What did he want?' she asked.

'Just to get me to sign some papers.'

She frowned. 'I'm not sure you should do so, not without Papa being present.'

It was Martha's turn to frown.

'Mama, I am an adult and these are my affairs.'

Mrs Cavanagh sank into the chair so recently vacated by Jonathon Gordon.

'I appreciate that, my dear but Papa has reservations about young Jonathon Gordon. I believe his father is sound enough, but Jonathon — well, he seems to have strange ideas.'

Thinking about what he had said, Martha did not think that his ideas were strange at all.

9

After Jonathon had gone Martha sat in the parlour and let the knowledge of her independence drift over her like the warmth from a hot bath. If what he said was true then the doors of her cage were about to swing open. Her anticipation was barbed only by the knowledge that her father would do everything in his power to keep them firmly shut. No doubt she would have to fight for her freedom.

While she was day-dreaming she heard the Reverend Cavanagh come back. The click of the front door and the scrape of his boots were closely followed by the sound of footfalls across the hallway and into the sitting room where she knew that her mother was working. She found herself straining her ears to catch their conversation but it was much too low. Most likely Mrs Cavanagh was telling him about the recent visitor and Martha felt all the old anxieties surfacing. At any moment her father would be bursting in to find out what Jonathon had wanted. Perhaps the fight would come sooner than she had thought.

In the event the Reverend Cavanagh went

straight to his study. With relief Martha guessed that her mother had thought it best not to mention the visitor. Cautiously she returned to her day-dreams, ever alert in case they should be interrupted after all.

When the interruption did come it was from someone knocking at the front door. She heard Mrs Porter go to answer it, then report to the minister. Moments later he was in the hallway.

'How dare you come to my front door! What do you want?'

'I've come for my wife's wages.'

'What wife? You aren't wed.'

Martha rose half-out of her chair. Ephraim Carter was in the hall. She felt a strange mixture of anxiety and excitement. When the voices dropped she tiptoed to the door and turned her head in the direction of the conversation so that she could catch the words.

'Don't you tell me she is owed nothing. It was you as dismissed her. She's done no wrong. If anything you owe her compensation.'

'The only compensation she'll get is if I don't have her publicly shamed.'

There was a tense silence.

'You'd better pay up,' Ephraim said then. 'I'm not going until you do.'

'I'll send for the justices.'

'You do that, maister. You're unpopular enough already.'

'What do you mean by that?'

'What I say. There's some out there that would sweep you and your house away as soon as look at you.'

'Are you threatening me?'

'No. Just give me what you owe Betsy.'

Martha tried to interpret the ensuing silence, the battle of wills. Eventually she heard her father say:

'Here, here's half a crown. Take it. It's more than she deserves and don't either of you come back here again. As far as I'm concerned, she's finished. She'll not find work here any more.'

'D'you think I'd allow her back into a depraved household like this?' Ephraim gave a snort of dismissal.

Martha held her breath, wondering how her father would respond to such a slur but he merely said:

'Get out and don't come back.'

The bang of the front door was accompanied by the retreating sound of boots from outside and her father's hurrumphing as he made his way back to his study.

Quietly Martha crept back to her seat. How dare Ephraim Carter call them depraved! She tried to think what he might mean and could only guess that it had something to do with the fact that he was poor and they were not. Surely he couldn't blame them for that? Everyone strove to improve their lot in life and did not the parable of the talents suggest that everyone should make good use of all their chances? Her father would say that God had chosen to give everybody their station in life and that it was wicked to question Him.

No matter how Martha thought about it, that did not seem to be fair. Why should one person have so much and another so little? Did God not love the poor man as much as the rich one? It was beyond her but one thing was for certain — they would not be having their shoes repaired in the village from now on.

Thinking of what Ephraim had said she wondered if Betsy was under his thumb. It didn't seem likely. Betsy had always seemed strong and from various things she had said in the past, she probably shared Ephraim's view of things. Guiltily she thought that perhaps it was right that she should be dismissed from the household after all.

The thought of Betsy stayed in her mind. She always looked . . . fulfilled somehow. She had a way of swinging her hips as she walked, as if she wasn't afraid of anybody. Martha felt an incipient discontent. Betsy smiled a lot and she seemed particularly at home with men. Martha was sure that she was a good woman and never did anything wrong but she displayed an ease with men that was . . . well, enviable. Perhaps it came from having brothers.

These thoughts only served to make Martha feel more restless. If she was honest, she didn't even know if men liked her. She was never very good at saying witty things and sadly she was not pretty. In foolish moments she thought that she would forgo her inheritance in return for being popular, like Betsy.

Ashamed of her thoughts she glanced out of the window and saw to her surprise that it was beginning to snow. Usually such weather did not arrive much before December but above the hiss of the fire she could hear a deeper, more resonant noise as the wind whipped the branches and whirled the snow in corkscrew spirals.

With shame Martha realized that in the excitement of the morning she had forgotten about Willow. She needed to go immediately to feed him. If the snow settled he would be unable to find any grass; his water was probably already frozen.

She hurried to the kitchen, glad to find Mrs Porter elsewhere so that she was free to boil up some oats to make him a hot mash. When it was cooked she wrapped the kettle in a blanket to keep it warm and crept from the house. As she headed for the stable to collect water and hay she knew that she should tell her parents where she was going but some shameful fear warned her that they might forbid her to leave the house in such inclement weather. Although now her own mistress, she had yet to find the courage openly to disobey them. Before she left she scribbled a note and left it in a prominent position: *Gone to visit Mr and Mrs Hatherby. Their groom will escort me home.*

The ground outside already looked treacherous and she congratulated herself on having the good sense to tie some pattens to her shoes to protect her feet. The snow was settling and her coat, although thick and cosy, soon grew waterlogged.

By the time she reached the field she was thoroughly chilled. Willow was sheltering in a corner, his back to the blizzard, his head hung low. When he saw her he whinnied and came across as fast as he dared, his hoofs slipping on the rutted ground. The water in his trough was frozen but she poured some more on top, urging him to drink while he could, and gave him the oat mixture, placing his hay under the shielding hedge. He felt wet and cold and she longed to take him home. In fact, she decided that she would definitely arrange for him to have his own stable. After all, she could afford it.

As the wind assaulted them she debated whether to lead Willow back with her and to put him in the coach house for the night. That, of course, would mean leaving the carriage out in the elements but a carriage was merely a thing whereas Willow was a living creature and as such more in need of shelter. The thought of her father's expostulations, however, made her change her mind. Besides, she had no halter or bridle to lead him with and after all, nature had provided him with a thick winter coat and he had the shelter of trees. The next morning, though, she would certainly move him, although where to, she was not sure.

Her thoughts were elsewhere and she did not notice in the increasing gloom that the snow had obliterated the path. Cuckoo Copse was criss-crossed by tiny tracks made over the years and suddenly she realized that she was heading away from the village and out towards the exposed hills that made a backdrop to the valley. Wherever she looked there was nothing familiar. Fighting down the growing panic she told herself that sooner or later she would come across a dwelling or some sign that would point her back in the right direction.

It was bitterly cold. As she struggled against the wind it stole her hat. Her ears soon burned with pain. Her gloves were too wet to hold on to the buckets and as tears began to take possession of her, she abandoned buckets and gloves along with the yoke. Her only wish was to find somewhere safe.

It was then that it happened. One moment she was walking in the thick, increasingly crisp snow, the next there was a sharp, metallic sound and something bit into her ankle. She fell forward, landing painfully in a hollow excavated by a long-forgotten stream and now used by cattle on their journey to the watering-place. The thin layer of ice cracked and the water beneath gouged into her like needles. For a moment she was so shocked that she could not think straight, but very quickly all her attention was drawn to her left ankle which throbbed like fire in this otherwise icy world. When she tried to move her leg she could not do so and the answering pain was so great that she wailed with fear.

Stifling her sobs she raised her skirts. Her leg was clamped in the jaws of an evil-looking trap. Desperately she tried to wrench the teeth apart but her hands were too weak and the trap was too strong. Every movement, however slight, sent lightning-rods of agony along her body. She began to sob.

She must have lain there for hours. The wind began to drop and its fury was replaced by an eerie silence broken only by the tiny, cracking contractions of the frozen earth. The earlier gloom gave way to the navy blue of night, broken only by a galaxy of stars. Martha forced herself to watch them, concentrating on their beauty.

Little by little snowflakes formed a blanket around her and gradually the cold gave way to numb acceptance. She longed only to close her eyes and escape into oblivion. As she began to drift away some sense of survival warned her that to succumb to sleep would be never to wake again. Perhaps she had already slept, was already dead? Perhaps it was evening — or night? She did not know. Meanwhile, the tiniest movement of the trapped leg brought the pain raging back.

In spite of the hurt, as she gazed up at the myriad stars she was struck by their wonder. Even in her extreme situation their beauty awed her. She started to sing, any tune that she could think of that reflected the glory of the sky. Her voice seemed disembodied as if she was already drifting away from her injured self. Still she carried on, out of tune, her voice croaking, her cold breath scouring her lungs.

'Who's that?'

At the sound of the voice her first instinct was to fall silent, then as her predicament hit home, she called out:

'Help me, please! I am over here.'

Seconds later someone was slithering down into the hollow.

'What in the name of God . . . ?' With a confused mixture of shock and relief, she recognized the tall, slender form of Gabriel Lawless bending over her, taking in her situation.

He sat back and surveyed her.

'Dear me, Miss Cavanagh, what a strait you find yourself in.'

Her unintended movement meant that once more her ankle burst into tormenting pain. Seeing the cause, Gabriel gave a gasp of shock and with strong fingers grasped the jaws of the trap and tried to force them apart. His action added to her hurt a hundredfold and she cried out.

He glanced regretfully at her. 'I am sorry to cause you pain but there is no other way to release you.'

From somewhere she found an inner

reserve of courage and nodded that he should continue. With a formidable effort he at last prised the evil teeth apart and her leg was free.

By this time she was sobbing and in too great a distress to object when he began to examine her injuries.

'You have some nasty puncture wounds but I don't think there is any damage to the bone.' From around his neck he removed the kerchief that he habitually wore and bound it about her ankle.

When he had done so he looked at her and shook his head.

'How in God's name did you come to be here?'

Between sobs she told him how she had been to feed Willow and lost her way. It sounded weak and foolish and she thought that he must despise her but he merely said:

'You must surely love that horse.'

They both found themselves looking at the trap. Gabriel sighed.

Aloud, he voiced her thoughts: 'What sort of a man would deliberately use such an instrument of torture to catch a man or a beast?'

The woods belonged to Sir Jenison Bowler.

She was about to say that no doubt the trap had been set for poachers when she realized that Gabriel was abroad in the woods at an unearthly hour. What could be his reason other than an attempt to steal wildlife that belonged to the manor? The memory of the rabbit in his sack on that first morning of their meeting came back to her. She remained silent.

As she watched he struggled out of his jerkin and wrapped it around her shoulders even though she was already better clothed than he was.

'Right then. I will try not to jolt you any more than can be helped. Put your arms about my neck and I will carry you home.'

Reaching up she put her arms around him. Bewildered feelings about the impropriety of this action conflicted with her desire to be close to him. In spite of the pain a strange surge of emotion engulfed her. Shamefully she felt glad that her situation had brought her to this moment. Perhaps it was meant to be.

Gradually the warmth from his chest began to seep through to her body. She held him tightly, embarrassment stealing her tongue.

At last she found the silence intolerable.

'It was lucky for me that you should pass this way,' she said. 'What brings you abroad so late?'

He did not reply immediately and again

she thought of the poachers who caused such outrage to the local gentry.

'I had some business to conduct.' His words were brief and warned her not to ask further questions.

All the while they were traversing the woods and before long they came out on to the lane leading back to Willow's field. They had been nearly full circle.

'We'll soon have you home,' Gabriel said. At the rise and fall of his chest she could feel the rasping of his lungs and remembered how thin he had seemed at their first meeting.

'Are you employed these days?' she asked, for something to say.

'My uncle has been ill. I have been working in his place.' He did not say more.

At last the vicarage came into sight. Gabriel halted and Martha guessed that he would not want to have to explain his presence in the woods on such a night.

'You have been very kind to me,' she said. 'If you leave me here I am sure I can make my own way to the door.'

'Nonsense.' He shook his head and carried her forward, then up the path to the porch.

'You go,' she pleaded, suddenly afraid of what her father would say. 'I — I have inconvenienced you long enough. I will see that you are rewarded for your kindness.'

Something about the downward twitch of his lips told her that he thought he knew what she was thinking — that to be found in this compromising situation would do no good to her reputation. In fact it was his welfare that most concerned her, for how could she put him at risk when he had been so kind? With a quizzical shrug of his shoulders, he carefully lowered her to the ground.

'You will have some explaining to do.' He raised his hand in farewell and went back down the path, into the blizzard.

Leaning against the wall of the porch Martha waited until he was out of sight before banging on the front door.

It was her father who answered. When he saw her he looked surprised, gazing around for the sight of the Hatherbys' carriage.

'Martha?' He must have seen how pale she was, how pinched and in pain. When she went to take a step forward, her ankle let her down and she stumbled.

'Whatever is amiss?' The minister took her arm and helped her inside.

'It is nothing.' She tried to hide her pain. 'I had a little fall, nothing more.'

'The Hatherbys allowed you to come home unescorted?' She saw her father's mouth tighten, the sharpness in his eyes hone to pinpoints of disapproval.

'I — I'm afraid I did not get as far as their house.'

'But that was hours ago. Where have you been?'

There was nothing for it. She had to tell at least part of the truth. 'It was on the way back from the field,' she started.

Papa snorted his displeasure. 'That horse again! He will be the death of you. Right, this is enough. Tomorrow he must go.'

'No! Tomorrow I will hire a stable for him.' She spoke with as much determination as she could summon. Gulping down her nervousness, she added: 'I can afford it now.'

For the first time her father did not contradict her, instead helping her into the drawing-room where her mother was resting. She gave a startled squawk at the sight of her daughter and another cross-examination began.

'Whatever has happened to your leg?'

Mrs Cavanagh eased Gabriel's kerchief away and gave a gasp when she saw the marks of the trap.

'My dear child, whatever has happened?'

Before Martha could think of a reply, Mrs Cavanagh came up with her own answer.

'A dog has bitten you. Oh dear, oh dear. Where did this happen?'

'It was an accident,' Martha said, sinking

gratefully into a chair near to the fire.

'An accident? The beast must be found and shot!' Her father was all for going out straight away while her mother was insisting that the doctor should be sent for immediately.

'There is no need.' Martha tried to play down her injury as much as possible.

In the meantime Mrs Porter was sent for to fetch hot water and clean bandages.

'Wherever did you get this — rag?' Mrs Cavanagh took Gabriel's scarf distastefully in two fingers and dropped it to the ground. For a moment Martha thought she was going to consign it to the fire. Somehow she resisted the temptation to snatch it away.

By now she was beginning to feel quite ill. The prolonged cold, the shock of the accident and the injury were all taking their toll. At last her leg was bandaged, a few drops of laudanum administered and she was half carried to bed. Before they left the drawing-room she managed to sweep up the kerchief and tuck it into her bodice while her parents were momentarily distracted. At last, safe and warm and very tired, she secreted the scarf beneath her pillow and slept.

10

Martha slept badly. As she lay in bed she could almost feel the pressure of Gabriel's arms around her. Sometimes she wondered if she had dreamt the whole thing but the pain from her ankle was real enough. When her mother came to wake her it was immediately clear that she could not walk. With something like panic she knew that she had to get out of the house. For a start there was Willow to see to but foremost was the need to find Gabriel, to thank him for his help and just to be in his presence. Gingerly she climbed out of bed, determined to go downstairs but she could barely put her foot to the ground.

'For goodness sake, child. Whatever are you doing?' Her mother pushed her back against the pillow and reluctantly she knew that this time her mother's concern was well-founded.

'What shall I do about Willow?' she asked.

She saw her mother's pained expression. Mention of the pony only brought disagreement between her and her parents. Left to herself her mother would be sympathetic to the pony's needs but her husband's antipathy as always, made her timid.

'You had better ask Mr Porter to go and feed him.'

The thought of entrusting the old animal's care to Mr Porter did little to reassure her, for he was a gruff bull of a man, but there seemed to be no alternative. When Mrs Porter brought her breakfast she said:

'Please will you ask your husband to go and feed my horse? He must do so twice daily and I will pay him sixpence a day for his trouble.'

Giving orders never came easily to her and knowing that she sounded shrewish she forced herself to add: 'I shall expect him to report on the pony's welfare every morning after his visit.'

Mrs Porter sniffed but did not comment. Instead, she said:

'There's been such a to-do. The news is everywhere this morning. Last night someone broke into Sir Jenison's threshing-room and destroyed his new machine.'

Martha's thoughts immediately flew to the evening before. Where she had been trapped, where Gabriel had found her, was less than a mile from the home farm. Was it, could that have been why he was abroad in such bad weather?

'They smashed the machine to pieces,' Mrs Porter went on, 'and when it was dismantled they set light to the barn. It was only luck that the blaze didn't spread to the cow-pens and roast all the livestock.'

The news was doubly painful. In other parts of the country rioters had deliberately maimed the cattle to get their own back on their masters. This was something that Martha could never condone for she knew that the beasts already suffered as much as the peasants did. The thought that Gabriel might inflict further pain on them as a form of revenge made her feel sick.

At that moment the doctor arrived and Mrs Porter retired to her domain.

With Mrs Cavanagh present, Doctor Jamieson examined Martha's leg, prodding at the swelling around her wounds.

'Those don't look like dog-bites,' he said. 'Are you sure that is what happened?'

Her cheeks flushed. 'It was all so sudden. I felt the pain, then I must have fainted.' This did not sound convincing but there was nothing else to say.

'Do you really think there could be a wild beast at large?' Her mother's anxiety showed in her wide eyes. 'Perhaps the gentlemen should organize a hunting party.'

Doctor Jamieson did not comment. 'The wounds are clean,' he announced and rummaged in his bag to produce some salve.

'Right, young lady, this must be applied

137

twice daily. Rest that leg and I recommend that you take a light refreshment of brandy with a beaten egg. It will take about a week for the puncture wounds to heal. I will call again if you need me but if all goes well, you may get up tomorrow but restrict yourself to the house.'

When the doctor had gone her mother said:

'I don't know what things are coming to. The hue and cry has been raised. Sir Jenison and the other magistrates had a special meeting this morning and have set up a search-party to catch last night's culprits. Papa has gone to help them.'

Martha shuddered at the memory of the woods. Not only the horror of the trap but the thought of what Gabriel had been doing there filled her with a sick dismay. There seemed to be only one conclusion. If he was not poaching — and he had borne no evidence of a catch, then he was probably the one who had destroyed Sir Jenison's barn.

She shivered at the thought of what danger she might have been in. In order to protect himself, Gabriel could either have left her there, pretending not to have heard her pathetic singing — or he could have 'silenced' her. After all, she was a witness to his presence.

Her mother brought her a glass with egg and brandy and in spite of her normal revulsion to such a mixture, she took a deep draught, hoping that the spirit might soothe her fears. She could not equate the Gabriel of her thoughts with the present rumours. In spite of herself she relived the events from when he had found her — how he had bound her wounds, how tenderly he had encouraged her with kind words and carried her home.

'You look very pale. You must rest.' Her mother puffed cushions up around her and left her to her torments.

★　★　★

By the time Gabriel arrived at work on the farm, news of the previous night's damage had already preceded him. Everyone was full of it, speculating, expressing dismay, but beneath the condemnation he detected the universal air of excitement. He was already cursing himself for his foolishness of the night before. He cursed Miss Cavanagh too, for she was a witness to his presence in the wood. He wondered whether she would give him away and if she did, what he was going to say.

'Any idea who it might have been?' he asked Seth Hardwick but the older man shook his head.

' ''Tweren't none of us. It must have been someone from outside. Mayhap it was Captain Swing himself.'

Captain Swing was the mysterious leader of a rebellious force rampaging across the south. No one had seen him but work such as that of last night bore witness to his power.

Less than an hour later Squire Wetherby, the vicar and Sir Jenison Bowler himself rode into the yard. They were in high dudgeon asking Seth Hardwick whether all the men were present and was there anything suspicious about them.

Seth had removed his bonnet, as had the others. He looked at the ground as he answered:

'No sir, everything seems the same as always.'

Gabriel glanced around him. None of the men looked directly at the visitors, instead keeping their eyes lowered, their feet awkwardly scuffing the ground. Gabriel glanced at the mounted party. The squire looked worried while the vicar wore his familiar spiteful, self-important expression.

Sir Jenison was riding a bay hunter that Gabriel would have sold his soul to possess. It was clear that he had just suffered a setback and his face exuded anger.

The Reverend Cavanagh took it upon

himself to address the men.

'If any of you here knows of anything, no matter how small, it is your duty before God to tell someone in authority. If you fail to do so you will be breaking the law in the same way as the scum who destroyed Sir Jenison's property.' He glanced at Sir Jenison with the habitual expression of sympathy that he used for the bereaved members of his flock, before turning back to the labourers. 'And do not even consider trying to protect your own. Anyone having anything helpful to say will be rewarded — and just remember, if you want to protect your jobs you need to convince your masters that they have your loyalty.' He waited but nobody said anything. 'You, fellow, how long have you been working here?'

At first Gabriel looked around, thinking that he meant somebody else but it was clear that he didn't.

'I'm here in my uncle's place, he's not well,' he answered.

'And your uncle is?'

'Isaac Lawless.'

'Isaac Lawless *sir*. Remember your manners when you address your betters.'

Gabriel remained silent so the vicar asked:

'And what were you doing before?'

'I was away serving my time. I've just returned to the village.'

'So you arrive here and then this happens.' The minister looked round at his companions as if to emphasize the significance of what he was saying.

'I don't know what you mean to suggest but I had no part in such a thing,' said Gabriel.

Ignatius Cavanagh shot him a filthy glance.

'Watch your tone, man, and only speak when you're spoken to.'

The men began to shuffle their feet but the vicar had not finished. Gabriel wondered whether perhaps the minister knew how he had rescued his daughter and had carried her home through the night. He could not imagine what excuse she had given to explain her condition. Perhaps this was the minister's way of warning him not to say anything that might damage her precious reputation. He remained silent.

Then, looking up he found Sir Jenison staring at him. He had a strange expression on his face, the look of distaste that a man has when a dog has shit in the room and he has stepped in it. Gabriel stared back. Sir Jenison was mounted but he could tell that they were about the same height and they shared a similar colouring. He shrugged off his thoughts. He had heard all the rumours. As he saw it, even if the squire's father had raped his mother — and there was no better word for it, at present he had no way of formal redress. He smiled grimly to himself. He had his own way of dealing with things, though. Time was on his side and revenge, when it came, was always sweet.

'Well? And where were you working before? Who was your master? Is it not right that you were imprisoned for theft?' The querulous tone of the vicar cut into his deliberations.

Somehow he bit back his anger and spoke as calmly as he could manage.

'I was accused to taking something for which I had no use, which I could not sell,' he said. 'I served time in Sainham Gaol. I was released. One day I will prove that I was innocent.'

The vicar looked satisfied as if, by his own words, Gabriel was condemning himself.

'Where were you last night?' It was Sir Jenison who spoke.

'At home.' Gabriel thought they could beat him before he would call his supposed half-brother 'sir.'

'Can you prove it?'

'If necessary.'

Gabriel had no wish to implicate his family into lying on his behalf so he waited.

'What were you doing?'

'Having a sociable time.' He began to feel uneasy.

Fortunately the squire was beginning to lose interest.

'This isn't getting us anywhere,' he said.

The others shortened their reins, pressed their heels against their mounts' flanks and began to circle.

'Just remember what I said,' the vicar called out before his horse, a heavy, lumbering beast, surged forward and he had to give all his concentration to staying aboard.

When they had gone the men relaxed.

'What was all that about?' someone asked. 'Why did they pick on you?'

Gabriel shook his head. 'How should I know?'

Along with his companions he returned to work but all day the events of the evening before stayed with him. At the end of the day he took a detour through the woods to check on the old horse. Either he was not eating or someone else had fed him. Anyway, he didn't delay because it was wet and windy.

When he got home, Isaac and his cousins were already there. Sarah was seated near to the fire sewing some sort of garment — for the baby no doubt. Her time was very near. For a while they talked of the day's events.

Isaac was less than pleased. 'This sort of violent action does the poor man's cause no good,' he said. 'It gives the masters an excuse to impose their will on us. I hear that already the magistrates have been told they may act as they think fit — and no redress if their actions cause damage to innocent men. Does anyone have any idea what happened last night?'

No one claimed to know. They ate in near silence and everyone seemed pleased to retire early. As Gabriel slid into the narrow bed he thought back over the day. Sir Jenison, the squire and their company were clearly shaken by what had taken place. Isaac was right, the men needed to be careful. The gentry felt themselves to be injured and a wounded animal is a dangerous one.

As he closed his eyes his feelings ranged between elation at the thought of someone wreaking revenge on the masters and a very deep sense of foreboding that things could so easily go wrong.

11

Martha endured a day in bed but by the next morning she was determined to get up.

'I don't think you should,' her mother remonstrated.

'The doctor said that I might.'

Ignoring her mother's anxieties she hobbled along the landing and was just negotiating the stairs when there was a knock at the front door. She just managed to settle herself in the parlour when Mrs Porter came in to announce the arrival of Mr Jonathon Gordon, who followed her into the room.

As on the last visit Martha was struck by his height, the illusion he gave of being too big for the space.

'I heard about your accident,' he said by way of introduction, twisting the brim of his hat between his fingers, 'I have called to see if there is anything at all that I might do to be of service?'

Martha glanced at her mother and with obvious reluctance she withdrew. Left alone, Jonathon and Martha regarded each other in embarrassed silence. Jonathon stood there so awkwardly that she felt compelled to invite him to take some refreshment. To her discomfiture he accepted. Her father was in his study writing his sermon and she did not want him coming to investigate. She had not seen him that morning and so had no idea as to what sort of a mood he might be in. Having made up his mind that Jonathon was an unsuitable contender for her hand she knew that if he suspected that this might be the solicitor's motive for calling he was capable of being extremely rude. If on the other hand he learned that Jonathon was 'tampering' with her finances then he was equally likely to vent his outrage. Either event would be very embarrassing.

To break the awkwardness Martha rang for Mrs Porter. When she came she ordered bowls of coffee. Her father always prided himself on ordering the best coffee from Lymington; it was what he called one of their little indulgences.

While they waited she tried to make polite conversation but there seemed to be very few subjects that she could safely broach.

'Has anyone been arrested for the attack on Sir Jenison's property?' she eventually asked.

'Thankfully, no.' Jonathon fought to get his words out. 'How can you blame desperate men for trying to protect their very survival?'

His obvious sympathy for the perpetrators

147

made it difficult to know what to say. Martha was only grateful that her father was not present to hear this expression of support for the troublemakers.

She immediately thought of Gabriel Lawless. The image of him bending over her injured ankle, his body crouched, his face clouded with compassion swamped her senses. She conjured up his tense, under-nourished presence, the hunch of his shoulders, the long curve of his back. Something about his deprivation turned her blood to water, drove her heart to pound as if to compensate for what he lacked. Would she blame him if he were guilty? She felt the now familiar shiver but didn't know whether it was because she was afraid of him or afraid for him. Or was the fear for herself, for this unaccountable madness that swept away all her certainties at the mere thought of him?

To escape from the madness, she said:

'Mr Gordon, I wonder if you would do me a service?'

'O-of course.' The coffee had arrived and Jonathon took a noisy slurp, then lowered his bowl, looking at her expectantly.

'Would it be too much trouble to ride across to Blackponds Field on the other side of Cuckoo Copse and check on the welfare of my old horse, Willow? I am unable to do so myself and I am not sure that he is being properly taken care of.'

'It will be my pleasure.'

He drained his coffee, spilling some on his coat front in the process. Martha watched in fascination as he produced a large handkerchief and proceeded to mop up the mess. When he had finished, he said:

'Bearing in mind that we may well have worse weather to come would you be agreeable to the pony's being stabled at Mount Lodge?'

Mount Lodge was the home that Jonathon shared with his parents. It was a large, low house with a courtyard and extensive stables. Martha had not visited but her mother had pointed it out one day when they were driving back from a visit to Ringwood. This was before her father had decided that the Gordons were not the sort of people to cultivate.

Before she could say anything Jonathon added:

'We have plenty of room. My father employs a groom, so he would be well taken care of while you cannot do so yourself.'

Of course she wanted Willow properly stabled and cared for in this severe weather but what she had in mind was somewhere anonymous where she might come and go as she pleased.

Seeing the doubt on her face Jonathon misread it.

'Of course, you would be welcome to visit whenever you wished,' he added.

'That is most kind of you.'

There was no polite way to refuse. She did not actually give him an answer but he appeared to take her words as an acceptance. He stood up, retrieved his hat and squashed it back on to his head.

'Well then, I had better be going.' He put the coffee bowl back on the table, catching the edge against the wood, which caused it to tip up. Martha held her breath but fortunately he did not break it, for her father put great store by his coffee-set.

In view of his thoughtfulness she made a special effort to be genial.

'I wish you farewell then — and thank you very much for your kindness.'

He bowed and there seemed to be an air of expectation in his eyes. For a moment she wondered if she was misreading the situation. He had not actually given a reason for his visit. Had he really come to press his suit? She tried to imagine what sort of attraction she might hold for him other than her money, but then he had plenty of his own. Were they back to the fact of her distant relationship to Sir Jenison?

She went to stand up but was hampered by her injury. He hastened to reassure her.

'Please, Miss Cavanagh. I will see myself out. I — I will also call again, to give you a report on the welfare of your pony.'

'That is very kind of you Mr Gordon but . . . ' She could think of no way of hinting that perhaps it might be better if he did not come to the house, for how could she admit to her father's feelings?

Nodding and bowing his head he backed towards the door, bumping into a chair and then the piano on the way. As he closed the door with excessive care she sank back and wondered what on earth the future might hold.

Her deliberations were interrupted as the parlour door swung open and the Reverend Cavanagh strode in.

'Am I deluding myself or did I just see that fellow Gordon walking down our path?' he asked.

'No, Papa, you are not deluding yourself.' Martha experienced the too familiar surge of anxiety, the tightening of her stomach muscles, the shortness of breath, the constriction in her throat. This is it, she thought, here we go. Now was the time she had awaited but dreaded, the moment to exert her independence.

'Why was I not called? That man is not welcome here.' Behind his spectacles, her father's eyes were pin-points of affront.

'He has been good enough to take care of my pony,' she started.

'And why should he do that?'

'Because he's — kind.' She hadn't thought about it in those terms before but there was no chance to pursue it for already her father was launching into one of his diatribes.

'Then he's as big a fool as you are. That animal should be shot. It's no use to anyone. Anyway, don't you realize he's only coming here so that he can insinuate his way into your affections.'

The venom of her father's words made her feel ashamed, as if by receiving Jonathon she was doing something shameful. Then the thought of his long face, his earnest expression, the uncertain stutter and his thatch of wild hair gave her courage.

'And why would he want to do that?' she countered. 'He's rich by our standards. What interest could he have here other than a kindness of heart?'

For once her father seemed lost for an answer. He gave a sort of sniff, implying a forlorn sense of defeat because his daughter was a hopeless case.

'Well, *I* certainly don't want to see him.' he said. 'What you do is your own affair.'

As he withdrew, Martha sat in the blessed silence and placed her hand on her racing heart. She felt a surge of triumph. This small act of rebellion had worked. Her father had not forbidden him to call. He had not forbidden her to receive him. Her victory made those other thoughts of Gabriel seem less shameful. Inhaling slowly and deliberately she thought, no matter what people say, no matter what Gabriel Lawless might have done, he saved my life and for as long as I live I will always be grateful to him. What else she might feel about him she chose to ignore.

12

Slowly the calendar inched its way towards the quarter-day, on which the village men were due to collect their wages. For the past month Gabriel had continued to work in his uncle's stead but as Isaac was now back on his feet it was agreed that on this occasion they should both go to Home Farm and that Isaac would make his signature to collect his dues. That way, as the named worker, there would be no discrepancies with the accounts. Ironically Isaac and Gabriel were the only labourers at the farm to know their letters. Had it been otherwise the younger man could simply have made a mark, one cross being much the same as another.

As was the custom, all of the men reported to collect their quarter's pay. For many the money was already spent but for a few brief moments at least they could hold some small wealth in their hands, nurse for a second the illusion of having wealth and power before succumbing once more to the reality of debt and poverty.

It being an inclement day a table was set beneath a canopy especially erected for the occasion. Along with everyone else Isaac lined up to collect his quarter's earnings. According to his calculations he was due ten weeks wages at nine shillings and the past three weeks at ten shillings, the rise having been agreed at the meeting with the employers. This should have given him the princely sum of six pounds. When he received his pay however, it was only five pounds and seventeen shillings, the same as the quarter before.

'I think there has been a mistake,' he said.

The ledger was consulted briefly.

'No mistake. Thirteen weeks at nine shillings makes five pounds and seventeen shillings.'

'But we had an agreement,' Isaac said. 'You were there.' He looked at Seth Hardwick. 'So was the vicar.'

The coins lay on the table before him but he did not pick them up.

'It was agreed,' Isaac repeated.

Seth looked uncomfortable. Then he took a deep inhalation of breath, as if someone was goading him from behind.

'You are on dangerous ground Isaac Lawless,' he said. 'You have been off sick. You aren't the man you used to be. If you want my advice you'll take the money and be grateful.' He paused and his eyes flickered uneasily over the gathering. 'Sir Jenison has instructed me to inform you that as from tomorrow your wages will be adjusted,' he concluded.

The men appeared to relax, ready to accept what they perceived as a compromise, when Seth added, 'As from tomorrow you will all be on eight shillings a week.'

'But that's impossible! No family can live on that!' Isaac voiced their disbelief. Around him the men gasped, looking from one to the other in dismay but even as they protested, the ledgers were packed away, the table removed and the men were left with their shortfall — and their anger.

'I'm not having this, lads.' As one they turned towards Isaac, their natural leader. 'We had a pact,' he said. 'You were all there. You all witnessed it.'

As a group they set off, first in the direction of Squire Wetherby's to see how the labourers there had fared. As at Bilton Manor, the men were bemoaning the fact that the last three weeks had produced no increase in their wages. No mention had been made, however, of a cut in their earnings. Only Sir Jenison, it seemed, had conceived this plan.

'Squire Wetherby agreed to ten shillings but he's only given us nine.'

'He's broken his promise.'

Several more of the squire's men joined the party.

A visit to Mrs Merriweather and then to Daniel Bridle revealed that they had both stuck to the bargain. The Amos brothers however had also paid only the original wages.

At each farm more men joined the original group. When they had made their last call, Isaac turned to them.

'The vicar was there as our witness,' he announced. 'Come along, we'll go and see him, ask him to intercede on our behalf.'

They nodded their assent and made their way, wet, tired and dispirited to the vicarage. It was already growing dark, As they drew near the men slowed their pace. When they stepped into the drive there was a universal sense of going into a foreign territory. Uncertainly they drew to a halt and looked around, seeing the vicarage at close quarters for the first time. It looked large and imposing, intimidating to men with barely two rooms to their name. A lawn and flower-beds fronted the house. As he surveyed it for the first time in daylight, Gabriel thought that the flower-beds alone would be big enough to grow vegetables for several families. The red-tiled house itself looked impenetrable with its central portal and two rows of barred windows on either side. A wing was attached at the western end, making it into the shape of an L. He thought with disdain that although it housed only the vicar, his wife and his daughter, it was bigger than all the labourers' cottages along their row put together.

Through the downstairs windows the glimmer of firelight and the glow of lamps looked inviting. He thought he glimpsed Miss Cavanagh looking from behind the curtains but if so, she quickly drew back.

The last time he had called here officially it had been to escort Betsy home. A wave of sadness swept over him. Since she had been wed he tried not to think about her but everywhere there was something that reminded him of the brief times they had spent together. He cursed himself for his foolishness, knowing that he meant nothing out of the ordinary to her, but as he had already found to his cost, the mind is not master over the heart.

At the steps to the house the men hesitated, looking from one to the other. It was Isaac who stepped forward, leading the way round to the back door. The rest followed behind.

In answer to his knock Mrs Porter from the village poked her nose out. She looked alarmed when she saw the gathering.

'We'd like a word with his reverence,' Isaac said.

Mrs Porter disappeared inside. She was gone a long time. Meanwhile they stood in the downpour, getting steadily more chilled and damp. When at last she came back she looked flustered.

'Mr Cavanagh says as how you are to come back in the morning. He does not receive visits from working men at this time of the evening.'

The men looked at each other, their resolve weakening.

'I think he should see us,' Isaac said. 'It is a matter of importance. By morning we will all be back at work — or maybe not.'

Mrs Porter's look willed him to go away but when he stood his ground she retreated once more into the vicarage.

At last she returned accompanied by her employer.

The vicar looked enraged. He wore a quilted dressing-gown and a cap with a tassel. Everything about him suggested comfort and plenty.

'What is all this nonsense?'

Gabriel thought that if he had been an actor he would have given a good account of himself as an angry man.

Isaac spoke on their behalf.

'Mr Cavanagh, sir. You will recall when we held our meeting with Sir Jenison, Squire Wetherby and the other employers, that they agreed to increase our wages.'

'I recall nothing of the sort.'

Isaac faltered. 'But you attended the meeting. You were our witness as to what took place.'

The vicar's eyes narrowed. The spite in them could have sliced through flint.

'I did no such thing. Your troublemakers presumed to take over the church for your own purposes. I came to ensure that no damage was done.'

'But — '

'But nothing. If you do not leave my property immediately, I will have you and your rabble arrested and flogged for trespass.'

No one moved, stunned to varying degrees by his betrayal. Isaac sighed. 'I think you should take us seriously, sir,' he advised. 'There has already been trouble in the neighbourhood.'

'Are you threatening me?' The vicar began to bluster.

Behind him Gabriel heard the rumbling discontent among his companions.

Sensing that things could get out of hand

Isaac raised his hands in acquiescence.

'Very well, we will go, but this betrayal marks a sad day for Midwillow.'

Still grumbling, humiliated, they started back down the drive and the door shut forcefully behind them. Anger began to bubble up and some of the men were all for storming the vicarage.

As always it was Isaac, good sensible Isaac who calmed things.

'Hold fire, gentlemen,' he said. 'There are more ways of picking a plum than by hacking off the branch. Go to your homes now. I think we need cool heads and even tempers. Tomorrow we will come up with the answer.'

* * *

By the next day Isaac had a plan.

He was up early. James and Joseph had yet to appear, so, while Gabriel went for wood for the fire, Isaac put out some bread and beakers of ale. Sarah was feeling unwell. Her time was drawing near and Isaac insisted that she remain in bed. Gabriel thought that these were the times that the family missed Betsy most. As for himself, weak and foolish as it was, he missed her every single minute of the day.

'Have you thought about what we should

do?' he asked, trying to put his cousin from his mind.

'Oh yes. I know what our response must be.'

Isaac's look was impossible to interpret. There was something intense about it yet at the same time a calm certainty that made Gabriel catch his breath. At moments like this his uncle was formidable.

Isaac took a bite of bread and chewed slowly.

'I want you to spread the word. Tonight I want representatives of all the men to meet here after their labours. Spread the message parish wide. It is a pity that not every man can come but there won't be room. Those who can must report back to their brothers.'

'What are we going to do?'

Isaac smiled his tolerant smile. 'Patience, lad. You'll find out in good time.' Beyond that he would not be drawn.

At that moment James and Joseph stumbled out of their beds and he repeated his instructions to them.

Gabriel put on his boots and jerkin. He could see that Isaac was stiff after his unaccustomed walk of the preceding day and although his uncle protested that he should be the one to go to work, Gabriel reminded him that he had a more important job to

162

attend to. With that, he set off.

In spite of their anger of the day before, all the village men turned up for work at Home Farm. Later that day they heard that the same applied to Treadwell and the Amos farm. As for Widow Merriweather and Daniel Bridle, their workers had received their promised wage increase so they had no cause to stay away.

Gabriel acknowledged that the reason for going to work was simple — if the men failed to do so they would not be paid. If they lost their positions there would be no money, no food. It was this weakness that the land-owners cultivated and he guessed that Isaac hoped to challenge them, although how, he could not fathom.

As a Methodist and a preacher Isaac had long been in touch with other members of the movement around the country. Their interest lay not only with the spiritual well-being of the people but with their physical needs as well. Although not one of their number, for this reason alone Gabriel respected their integrity. In addition to the soul they gave thought to practical issues like work and health, education and wages. As a result of their influence men were beginning to look beyond their own farm or village and parish and address the problems as they related to them all.

With this in mind Gabriel passed on Isaac's instructions.

'You want to watch yourself,' Seth Hardwick warned. 'Stir up trouble and you'll live to regret it.'

Gabriel turned to face the foreman. 'I'm just passing on a message, gaffer. You can come if you wish, report back to your master.'

For a few seconds Seth simply stared at him, then he turned away and went back to his own work.

As Gabriel laboured he pondered that although it would be dark by the time the men finished their day's labours, there would be a full moon to light the way. These nights were cold but clear and there was little likelihood of ice.

At the end of the day he trudged home. His arms ached and his back was stiff with the chill. James and Joseph were back before him and he was glad to see that his aunt was up and seemed to be better.

At the appointed time the men began to arrive. He could not believe what he saw, for upwards of twenty soon gathered in the gloom — not only men either, for the first person to arrive was Betsy.

As soon as he saw her he experienced that breath-catching, jolting feeling in his chest.

Even his cold hands felt damp at the knowledge that she was so close. He nodded to her but did not speak.

They all crowded into the cottage until there was no room for even one more body. While they waited they talked quietly together but there was an air of expectation as if every man was listening out for some signal.

Ephraim wandered in shortly after his wife and stood with his hands behind his back. He looked relaxed, almost amused. Gabriel wondered what he might be thinking, but when Betsy glanced at her husband and smiled his guts turned to water and everything else went out of his head.

As soon as it was clear that no more were coming, Isaac stepped forward to explain what he had in mind.

'Brothers, at the moment, because we are weak we dare not challenge the masters when they threaten us,' he began. 'We all know that we give of our best and yet our rewards are so small that our children go hungry and our wives are in poor health.' He glanced at Sarah, seated on a stool as he spoke. 'This cannot be how God intended his children to be treated. We know too, we see with our own eyes, that our masters have far more than they need. For the sake of an extra shilling per man they would hardly notice the difference whereas we, the men who till the soil and build the barns, face death and destitution for the lack of it.'

There was absolute silence. Everyone waited for his solution.

'The trick,' Isaac said, 'is to take concerted action. If three men decide not to accept Sir Jenison's offer then he will sack them. By the next morning he will have replaced them with three others, for there are always those with nothing, who will take the place of those who have a little. If Squire Wetherby dismissed his cowmen because they complained about their lot he would find more. Against this what can a poor man do? He has two choices, brothers. Either he can accept his lot and watch his children die, his wife suffer — or he can challenge what is happening.'

He leaned forward and wagged his finger tellingly at the crowd. 'If every man working on the farms stands firm, what are they to do then — Sir Jenison, Squire Wetherby, Digby Amos, the others? What would Sir Jenison do if not one man agreed to labour at Home Farm? What would become of Treadwell if not a single man came to care for the livestock?'

They were all beginning to see where this was leading, until someone asked:

'Isn't it against the law for ordinary men to

band together against their masters?'

Gabriel had heard something about it in the gaol. Swift action had been taken against those rioters in the towns and villages to the north. Some men who had shouted too loud were arrested as troublemakers and locked away. Looking at Isaac with his strong, certain sense of right and wrong he felt a trickle of unease. Behind him someone stated what they all knew, that no one was prepared to risk imprisonment — or worse, for the sake of another shilling. On the black side though, without that other shilling it could mean the difference between survival and disaster.

'What do we have to do?' someone called from the crowd. Isaac raised his hands to ask for quiet.

'Brothers, we do not have to break the law. We do not have to threaten. We simply make it clear to our masters that we will work only if they pay us a living wage. If they do not, then none of us will give of our labour.'

'Well,' George Sellars challenged. 'In that case they will make an example. If they cannot sack us all, they will still sack some of us. Who is going to risk being the one to lose his livelihood?'

Isaac had an answer.

'We make provision against that happening,' he said, his attention focussed on

George. 'If every man here agrees that we combine together, if we all make a regular donation to a central fund, then if one of our number is threatened with unemployment or illness, we draw on that money to see him through the hard times.'

'But we don't have enough money now,' someone else pointed out.

Isaac looked at the man questioningly. 'In spite of all, do we not find a spare copper for tobacco, or for an extra jug of ale? If we sacrifice that in the short term then in the long term you will have that extra penny a week, which is all we ask. All I am suggesting is that we agree to pay a subscription to get us started and then we each donate a penny a week. Multiplied by every man in the village that would give us more than enough to support our brothers should they find themselves without resources.'

What he said made sense. Just as they were all nodding their agreement Ephraim Carter began to speak.

'This all sounds very well, my friends. But what are you going to do when one of you fails to pay up? How strong will your determination remain when some of you begin to weaken? I think you are being naïve. Isaac says there is strength in numbers but there is no strength in merely asking for what

168

you want. What you have to do is to take it. You must take matters into your own hands.'

People began to look uneasy. However unhappy they were with their lot, the prospect of violence did not generally appeal.

Ephraim's next words stopped all reservations.

'Does none of you know that Sir Jenison has a new threshing machine arriving this very week? Did you think that he would keep you employed all winter? Think again. This machine will do the work of six of you at the least. No matter how you protest, no matter how much you ask, he won't heed you. Your threats will be useless. If I were you I would be thinking to strike at the source of the trouble. This machine and others like it, they need to be got rid of.'

As a man they looked to Isaac for his reaction. He gave them all time to digest these words, then he spoke.

'The news of this machine is a shock indeed,' he said. 'But if Sir Jenison brings it in, if Squire Wetherby buys one, it alters nothing. If we agree to combine together to protect our rights it will be binding upon us all. Once we have done so no man will be able to back out. Believe me, my friends, if you damage the masters' property then no one can help you. The law will have its way

— and the law is on the side of the masters.'

He glanced at Ephraim. 'Our brother here makes shoes, some of you work with wood or run a forge, thatch cottages or brew ale. You may not be directly affected by what happens to those labouring men in the parish but the less they have, the less they are able to spend on necessaries — no shoes for their children, no windows, no rails — nothing. All we ask is that the artisans give us their support. It might be that if one of us is thrown out of work, he will not be able to pay his bills. If that should happen you tradesmen, you craftsmen will suffer too. If we combine together then we can advance the unem-ployed man the money. Everyone, but everyone, will benefit.'

There was a collective exhalation of breath, a relief that violence need not be the answer to the problems threatening them.

Ephraim shrugged, washing his hands of the meek and gullible. Gabriel saw how his eyes narrowed. He sensed his frustration. Ephraim was a man to strike first and ask questions afterwards. To Gabriel's surprise he found himself thinking that his cousin was dangerous but then he had to admit that he had other reasons for not liking him.

'I am going to get in touch with some people I know who are already formed into a combination, to find out how they set about it,' said Isaac. 'Once we have a proper constitution, once we establish ourselves, we will be a force to be reckoned with.'

Sensing that some of the wilder ones might still be thinking of ways to exact revenge for past slights, Isaac went on: 'We will all remember that this is our village, our parish, our home. We owe it a duty to keep it safe and peaceful. All we ask is for sufficient for our needs, no more.' He looked around the gathering, meeting the men eye to eye, looking for their commitment, then he glanced again at Ephraim. 'All we need to do is to ask, not to threaten.' Into the ensuing silence, he added: 'Remember, brothers, for every hand raised in anger, there will be a blow in return. Peace and strength, that is what we must rely on. Peace and Strength! Let that be our motto. Now — let us pray for success.'

13

For Martha, the feeling of being in prison continued to increase. Rising late, the desert of each day stretched ahead and she spent many hours wondering how to escape from the house. As soon as she hinted that perhaps she should take a short walk, however, her mother grew agitated and her father announced that it would be sheer madness to venture out now that there was such tension in the village. Besides, the weather was cold and the lanes icy. Her leg might be healed but her common sense was still under question.

When she could bear it no longer she announced that her conscience was bothering her so badly that no matter what the cost, she must attend morning service the following Sunday.

As she stumbled over the lie she saw the surprise on her father's face. His mouth, normally so tight and indignant seemed to relax.

'In the circumstances,' he said, 'perhaps a short ride to the church would not do too much harm.'

Martha felt the frustration begin to

dissipate. It was quickly replaced by a trickling sense of anticipation. Once she was out of the house and away from her parents' watchful eyes, she might be able to return Gabriel's kerchief. The very prospect of seeing him tingled through her, immersing her in the fevered, wicked sense of longing that she both feared and craved.

As it turned out, by Sunday the frost had largely dispersed and a weak but welcome winter sun graced the morning. Together with her mother she drove to church in the carriage. As they alighted at the lich-gate the local gentry took time to express their pleasure at seeing her well again. Their concern filled her with a heady sense of importance.

The Gordons were also present, in their box across the aisle. Doctor Gordon nodded in their direction as Martha and her mother walked to their pew. In turn Martha inclined her head, aware that Jonathon kept glancing across at her. Other than a brief acknowledgement, she ignored him. It wasn't exactly a snub but she felt the guilt of ingratitude weigh upon her. His kindness deserved better but for the moment her thoughts were elsewhere.

The minister had taken as the subject for his sermon the theme of *rich man, poor man* and how they both had a place in God's purpose. It was not a monologue that Martha looked forward to. The church was full but, glancing surreptitiously around, she could not locate any member of the Lawless clan. Some wild optimism had left her wondering whether Gabriel, unlike his relatives, might still follow the more orthodox form of worship. Clearly he did not.

It being winter Papa's homily was liberally accompanied by coughs and sneezes from the congregation. Both Sir Jenison and Squire Wetherby, along with their wives, had chosen to attend. Martha wondered whether her father had forewarned them of the subject and they had come merely to underline the validity of the text. To pass the time she studied Sir Jenison from the rear. Occasionally he would turn his head and she got a clear view of his profile. Perhaps it was her imagination but there was something of Gabriel Lawless about the shape of his face, although Sir Jenison's features were coarser and his mouth had a petulant set that contrasted with the determined curve of Gabriel's lips. Could they really be half-brothers? Several years separated them. For a moment she tried to imagine the meeting between Gabriel's mother and Sir Jenison's father. How had their paths crossed? What would she have thought of him? Could a man so much older than her arouse any feeling of attraction, or had she been afraid of him, driven into his arms under duress? Where might he have taken her? Remembering where she was, she stopped the thoughts. After a while, though, she began to wonder what life in the village would be like if Gabriel and not Sir Jenison lived in the manor house. Before too long she visualized herself calling, being helped from the carriage by Gabriel himself — Sir Gabriel, landowner, magistrate, eligible bachelor . . .

The time passed quickly and as she came out of the church she could feel her cheeks glowing from the foolish scenario she had just painted.

As her mother turned towards the carriage she prepared herself for her mission.

'I think I will take a short walk,' she said.

'Whatever for?' Mrs Cavanagh looked at her as if she had lost her mind.

'I — I need to exercise my leg. It is a lovely morning and I will not be long.'

Because there were other people milling around Mrs Cavanagh did not draw their attention by arguing. Gratefully Martha wandered off in the direction of the village.

Concealed beneath her cape was Gabriel's neckerchief. Although it was light and flat she had a foolish notion that she could actually feel it close to her heart, creating a patch of warmth. She had no clear plan as to what she was going to do. If she did not happen upon Gabriel she doubted if she would have the courage to knock at the cottage door. Besides, to do so would be to draw attention to their meeting and she was sure that neither of them wanted that.

As she reached the green local people were beginning to gather under the generous canopy of the sycamore tree, its branches now laid bare. Isaac Lawless was there and she guessed that he was about to give his own sermon. She was tempted to stay and listen but to do so would be indiscreet, so she moved on through the village and down towards the stream.

By that strange quirk of fortune, just as she was approaching Isaac Lawless's cottage, the door opened and Gabriel himself came out. Amid the chaos of her feelings she immediately noticed that his throat was bare. For herself she had a thick woollen muffler wrapped about her neck and shoulders, keeping out the wind. She wondered what it would feel like to press her lips to that very spot where his collarbones left a small indentation.

'Mr Lawless!' A voice other than her own

called out to him but as he turned towards her she knew that it was she who had spoken.

He stopped to wait, his shoulders hunched against the wind.

'Miss Cavanagh. I am glad to see that you are recovered.'

'Thank you, yes. I — I came to return your neckerchief. It was very kind of you to lend it to me.' As she spoke she withdrew it from inside her cloak, embarrassed by its warmth.

Gabriel took it, unfolded it and immediately tied it about his neck. It gave him a wild, gypsy air and at the thought of her body heat touching his skin her face blazed in the winter chill.

For a moment they both regarded each other in silence, then he spoke.

'Are you walking somewhere? May I escort you?'

Foolishly she indicated the stream and they set out, away from the village. As they did so she remembered how only a few weeks ago she had been outraged when he had suggested escorting her home after that first meeting in the wood. Now this moment of togetherness was the stuff of dreams.

'Your horse is well?' he asked. 'I have made a point of checking on him but it seems that someone else has had the same thought.'

'You have been feeding him?'

He must have seen her surprise for he shrugged as if it was of little importance.

'Don't feel concerned, Miss Cavanagh, the hay he has been eating was not mine. Let's just say that it came from a generous source.'

She immediately felt embarrassed that the question of his ability to feed the pony had arisen. As to where the hay came from she had no idea but it felt wise not to pursue it.

Her thoughts returned to the fateful evening when she had injured her ankle. Did he still wonder what she thought about his reason for being abroad? In spite of the passage of time no one had been apprehended but the machine breaking was still very much on everyone's lips. Security was heightened wherever there was anything worth damaging. The vicarage was as secure as a castle. These very thoughts emphasized the difference in their stations. Martha was raised to protect her property and Gabriel was raised to steal it. The knowledge cast a heavy pall.

'Do you have work?' she asked in desperation, for the silence was unbearable.

He looked at her and that same cynical expression she already recognized turned his lips down at the corners.

'Aye, I have been labouring on my uncle's behalf.' He walked a few further paces. 'You

178

do know, I suppose, that I have been in gaol?'

He must have seen her shock for he gave a humourless laugh. 'They say I stole a saddle, Miss Cavanagh. I assure you that of all the crimes I might have committed, that is one that I most certainly did not.'

Among the myriad thoughts she immediately wondered if this was his way of admitting that he had indeed smashed Sir Jenison's machine. As they continued to walk in silence she knew that she wanted something from this meeting. She wasn't clear as to what it was but the situation was running away from her. Clutched in her hand she had a half crown that she had intended to give him, as payment for his kindness. She knew that he could use the money but she did not know how to hand it to him.

The sight of him walking a little ahead of her, his thumbs hooked into the leather belt at his waist, the vision of his long back, his slim hips moving at a gentle gait, caused an uncontrollable, physical, rush of longing.

'I am sorry,' she said.

'For what?'

He turned and looked at her. His eyes were surprised, questioning. For a moment there was none of the cynical hostility that was usually there.

She didn't know why she was sorry. She

felt so foolish, so stupid that tears began to form in her eyes.

He sighed. 'Perhaps you should go home, Miss Cavanagh. Is your ankle troubling you?'

She guessed that he was giving her an excuse for her stupidity and if anything his sensitivity made her feel worse. Wordlessly she thrust out her hand and pushed the coin into his.

'Please take this — for your help — and for caring for the horse.'

Before he could respond she turned and began to hobble away as fast as she could. She didn't know what she wanted. Did she want him to follow her? Did she want him to — no! This was madness, utter madness. She vowed there and then that she must never, ever place herself in such a situation again.

14

After the confrontation with the masters, Isaac made it his business to find out as quickly as possible about setting up a friendly society. To this end he consulted various people he knew of in London and, armed with all the information, he called a meeting to be held at his cottage on Friday evening.

His contacts warned him to keep the proceedings secret, not that such combinations were any longer illegal but there was naturally hostility towards them from the masters. The trick, as he saw it, was to have a group up and running before the employers knew what was happening.

As he walked to work he pondered on the mystery of fate. In a strange way the shock of the masters' betrayal and the failure of the minister to support them had given him a new lease of life. His back still ached but from somewhere he had found a fount of energy and in spite of Gabriel's protests, he had returned to work. What he was about to undertake, the responsibility for his own family and the other village men, alarmed him but he had God to rely on. *Find me the strength, dear Father*, he prayed, *find me the courage to see this through*.

As Isaac left for work, Gabriel found himself once more among the unemployed. He tried to devise ways of keeping himself busy, of earning his keep but there was little that he could do and time hung heavily. Then, on the morning of the planned meeting, Daniel Bridle sent word that if Gabriel wanted some hours clearing ditches then he would be prepared to take him on. The news filled him with a surge of optimism. Of all the local farms, Oak Farm was the one where he would choose to work. Daniel Bridle seemed a decent man and Gabriel had a feeling that if he worked well he might find regular employment as spring and summer approached. With luck he would be able to help with the ploughing. It would be good to get his hands on a horse again, even a slow, plodding pair like Daniel's team.

As he walked home at the end of his first day's labours such thoughts occupied him. His back ached, his hands were stiff and raw and he was tired but it was the exhaustion of a job well done. He intended to hurry straight home in preparation for the meeting but somehow he found himself taking a detour towards the cobbler's shop. With every step he argued with himself that it was sheer foolishness. What did he hope to achieve? Supposing he was fortunate enough to see Betsy, what good would it do? He had no excuse to be there so he would only look stupid. Then, as he slowed his pace it dawned on him that Miss Cavanagh's pony was nearby and here was indeed a reason to be in the neighbourhood.

He increased his pace, trudging his way to the field, but when he got there he was surprised to see that the gate was open and the pony gone. He wondered whether the animal had escaped or had perhaps been moved to somewhere more suitable. A guilty feeling settled upon him because in spite of his best intentions, he had failed to visit regularly and check on the animal's welfare. Anyway, by now Miss Cavanagh was up and well again so the responsibility was hers.

Retracing his way towards the cobbler's shop he decided that in the circumstances there would be no harm in offering to walk with Ephraim to Isaac's house. That way he at least stood a chance of saying hello to Betsy and being rewarded with a smile. As he approached he rehearsed various sentences but they all sounded stiff and unconvincing.

I was in the neighbourhood. I was just passing. His hunger to see her was such that he didn't care what they thought. *It's because*

I love you, he confessed to himself. *It's because just to see you, even from a distance is more precious than all the money in the world.* Such foolishness shamed him but he was as swallowed up by it as he might be by the plague.

For what seemed like an eternity he stood opposite to the shop, shielded by willows, soaking up the glow of candlelight as if it was the warmth of Betsy herself. He was indecisive, undecided. Should he go in or shouldn't he? Surely at any moment Ephraim would come out and then he would be forced to act.

For some reason he thought of the night he had rescued Miss Cavanagh. Perhaps it was the rush of the wind, the billowing of a few new snowflakes. He smiled to himself. Miss Cavanagh was a light little thing and carrying her was no hardship although she was as stiff as a plank in his arms. His smile widened. It seemed unlikely that a man had come that close to her since she was a small child; he couldn't imagine that she'd welcome a male embrace, no matter who it came from. He visualized her in her marriage bed, rigid, unyielding. God help the man she married. She smelt good though, as if her clothes had been layered with lavender or some such thing.

184

The minutes ticked by and still Ephraim did not appear. With a sigh of impatience at his own timidity he brushed past the dripping willow fronds and approached the shop door.

'Hello there. It's me, Gabriel.' He banged on the wooden panel of the door.

A moment later the latch lifted and Betsy peered out at him.

He felt such a rush of anguish, a pure, undiluted sense of pain and pleasure, inextricably mixed together. It was something to be both embraced and feared.

'Is Ephraim here?' he asked.

'He's gone to Father's house, to the meeting.' Betsy looked at him questioningly.

'I — I had something to see to just along the lane. I thought I'd walk with him.'

'He left a while ago.' She stood for a moment, simply staring at him, then she opened the door a fraction.

'Do you want to come in?'

He knew that he shouldn't. The words were there right on his tongue — *No. Thank you, no. I must be getting along.* He stepped inside.

She looked surprised, but only for a second and indicated that he should go closer to the fire.

As she watched him she rubbed her hands carefully down across her skirts. The gesture sent a ripple of desire through him. In his mind his hands followed her own, feeling the warm vibrant flesh beneath the material.

'What is it that you want?' she asked.

'You know what I want.' He felt the madness of his situation. He could not go on as he was, the jealousy eating away at him. He wanted something from her, anything.

She frowned. 'Why have you come here?'

'You know why.'

She stood with her back half to him, shaking her head.

'This is madness,' she said.

'Do you want me to go?' He remained very still, waiting for her to pronounce sentence.

'Of course I do,' she said, 'I am married.'

'Do you love him?'

She shrugged but did not reply. Then, just as the silence grew intolerable, she said: 'He is sharp, amusing.' Her face clouded and she fell silent. 'Sometimes he frightens me.'

Without thinking he stepped closer. 'He hurts you?'

She shook her head. 'No. It is just that he is so — intense. I am afraid that one day he will do something disastrous.'

'You haven't answered my question.'

She stared long and hard at the ground then slowly she raised her eyes.

'Gabriel. Don't. You . . . '

Her expression was enough. In her eyes he saw a kind of truth, an admission that whatever she got from cousin Ephraim, it was not what she wanted.

'Oh, Betsy!' He couldn't help himself. He kissed her, pulled her bodice open, ran his hands over her beautiful, pliant breasts, kissed them, tasted their sweetness. She threw her head back and her body pressed closer. Almost sobbing with the anguish of it he pulled up her skirts and coaxed his fingers into her, rejoicing in the wetness, loosing himself from his breeches and finding escape inside of her.

His seed came quickly. Too quickly. He held her close, wanting the moment to last for ever, fearing that never would such a chance come again.

'I love you,' he said. 'Betsy, I have loved you since the first moment I returned to the village.'

'I know.' Her fingers caressed the back of his neck sending renewed tendrils of desire along his body.

His breath came fast and he parted her legs again but she began to push him away.

'You must not. The time!'

'I must.' He dispelled her objections with kisses, lifted her against him and drove long and hard into her, flying with the storm of his emotions.

When he had done she stepped away and pulled down her skirts. He could sense that she was angry.

'Betsy, forgive me. I have offended you?'

She shook her head but her words spoke otherwise.

'You have just demonstrated the foolishness of this. You should have gone when I asked you to. Now you will be late for father's meeting. People will ask where you have been.' She turned to face him. 'Don't you see that you are incapable of hiding your feelings? This will not be enough. All the time you will want more and more. Sooner or later someone will realize. If it is my father he will be heartbroken. If it is Ephraim . . . ' The thought of Ephraim's anger caused her to clasp her arms about her shoulders for protection against the imagined conse-quences. 'You must go now,' she said.

'Betsy — '

'Go now!'

He bowed his head and turned towards the door.

'Say that I can come again.'

'This is how it will always be — I told you so.'

She was right. It was madness, but that

evening was the moment that gave his life meaning.

As he retraced his steps he was immune to the biting cold, the insidious chill of the snow. When he eventually got back to Isaac's cottage the meeting was over and the first members of the newly formed Midwillow Agricultural Workers' Society had been duly sworn in and gone home.

'What happened?' Isaac looked worried, or perhaps disappointed.

'I had forgotten something I had promised to do,' said Gabriel, remembering the pony. 'Then I'm afraid I got held up.' At the thought of the reason, his face glowed. He was glad that he had not bumped into Ephraim on the way back. Supposing his cousin had returned for some reason and caught him there? Betsy was right. It was madness, but surely the depth of his feelings, the power of his longing, would not exist if it was not meant to be expressed?

Isaac nodded, accepting his explanation. Apart from Sarah and little Matthew he was alone.

'Well,' he said. 'We have done a good night's work.' He showed Gabriel a paper on which were written the new rules and regulations. His face was flushed with satisfaction.

'It's really going to happen then?' Gabriel said.

'It already has. The men have each agreed to pay a membership fee of one shilling and then a penny a week to go to the funds. Anyone who fails to pay up or behaves in such a way as to let his fellow members down, will be expelled.' Isaac's expression relaxed into one of triumph.

Gabriel glanced at the paper. The rules had been printed out properly in London. It gave them an official appearance and, as most of the men could not read, this alone would make them feel that they were part of something important.

The rules laid down conditions of work and wages. They stated that if someone could not work because he was ill, or he was simply laid off, then he would be supported by the central fund until such time as he was able to work again. This was revolutionary indeed and such support would make an enormous difference to welfare of the men and their families.

'We've elected a committee,' said Isaac. 'They've been sworn in. I'm the correspondence secretary.'

'You look pleased with yourself.' Gabriel handed the papers back.

Isaac thought for a while. 'I'm pleased, yes.

Pleased that we are doing something to protect ourselves. The worry is that the masters will try to destroy us. For that reason we agreed that we should all take an oath of loyalty on the Bible. We have a password too, so that only our members can gain admittance to our meetings. We don't want Sir Jenison or the Squire sending along a spy.'

'What's the password then?' Gabriel asked.

Isaac looked slightly embarrassed. 'You haven't been sworn in yet.'

'Then do it now.'

Isaac shook his head. 'It has to be done proper, when the society next convenes. You have to do it before witnesses. Your turn will come at the next meeting.'

Gabriel laughed but he was surprised. Did his uncle not trust him?

'Who else is a member?' he asked.

'Myself, Joseph and James; there are ten of us at present. Including your cousin, Ephraim.'

'Ephraim's not an agricultural labourer.' As far as Gabriel had been concerned, Ephraim was only intended to be a witness.

'Ephraim's behind us good and proper,' Isaac said. 'Besides, the fact that he is not one of our workforce means that no one is going to suspect him if we need a go between. He can be our eyes and ears. His shop is a good place for leaving and collecting messages as well. No one going into the cobbler's shop will look suspicious whereas if people keep coming to my cottage it will arouse curiosity.'

What he said made sense but Gabriel resented the thought that Ephraim should be so active in their cause — especially as at this moment he himself was still excluded.

He handed the papers back to Isaac, who placed them in the niche in the wall that he used as a store-place for all his papers. There was still a little ale left in the jug and he shared it out before sitting down stiffly on a stool close to the fire. Clearly his back was still troubling him and Gabriel wondered for how long he would be able to carry on working. Aunt Sarah made ready to retire for the night and Joseph and James were still nowhere to be seen. The sudden peace of the cottage, the crackle from the hearth, the moving shadows that enveloped the room as the flames wove and danced added to his sense of wellbeing.

'Where were you then?' asked Isaac.

His question caught Gabriel unawares. He sank on to the other stool and took off his boots and socks. All were soaking wet and they would not be dry by morning.

'I promised Miss Cavanagh to keep an eye

on her pony,' he said. It was only a half-lie.
He *had* promised himself that he would do
so.

'I sometimes feel sorry for that girl,' Isaac
commented. 'That father of hers is as big a
burden as anyone would want. Her mother's
nothing but a silly featherbrain. Left to herself
the girl has a kind heart. Betsy always speaks
well of her.'

He thought about Martha Cavanagh,
entombed in snow, her leg being gnawed at
by the evil contraption. She was a brave girl
where pain was concerned. Not so coura-
geous perhaps when it came to defying
convention. The real centre of his thoughts
however, was Betsy. If Betsy thought the
vicar's daughter was acceptable, then who
was he to disagree?

'Betsy was here this afternoon,' Isaac
added. 'She came to give her mother some
news. She's expecting a child.'

His fingers clenched so tight around the
beaker that it was a wonder it did not crack.

'That's good.'

She hadn't told him. She'd said nothing.
This was the depth of the distance between
them, that Ephraim's child already grew in
her womb, put there through his cousin's
lust.

Isaac nodded as if in reply to a silent

comment in his head. 'It is God who blesses,' he said.

When Gabriel did not respond he drained the rest of his ale and stood up again.

'Well, I shall retire. Today has been a busy day.' He put his beaker on the table. 'You should get to bed too, son. You have an early start in the morning.'

He was right. There was a two-mile walk to Oak Farm and Gabriel needed to be there soon after sunrise.

While the older man busied himself about the room his nephew sat and stared into the embers. The dying fire seemed symbolic somehow. He cursed himself for his weakness but the thought that Betsy was with child nearly unmanned him. She and Ephraim had been wed for so short a time that if she was ready to announce to the world that she was with child then the baby had been made before the wedding day. He in his foolishness had managed to cope with the knowledge that she was marrying Ephraim for economic reasons, to make things easier for her family. Somehow he had convinced himself that although she would of course accept her husband's embraces, his intimacies, she would do so out of duty, untouched by any real feeling. If they had been lovers before their marriage that put a different complexion

194

upon it. No longer could he pretend that she was merely the acquiescent, dutiful bride. Instead, his cousin Betsy was a willing partner in this act of . . . love.

Bitterly he drained his ale and longed for something stronger. His small, pathetic triumph of earlier in the evening now seemed very foolish indeed.

He undressed and curled up on his bed in the corner of the room. After a while he heard the ladder creak as Isaac climbed up to the platform above. For a while he listened to all the little sounds, Isaac dropping his clothes beside their bed, the grunt from Sarah as he climbed in beside her, the sudden restless tossing from the young child Matthew, then all was silent.

He couldn't sleep. He envied Isaac the warmth of Sarah by his side. There was something constant about the way they lived their lives, he fretting about the world outside, she the warm, reliable presence, always there when he returned home, her horizons bounded by this humble cottage and the people who inhabited it. Until a few weeks ago, there had been one other person, sleeping a few feet above his head — Betsy. He forced himself to imagine her lying as Sarah did, her body against that of her husband, exuding warmth. Sarah and Isaac were older though, familiar with each other, sharing comfort, not passion. He tossed his head in an effort to drive out the tormenting thoughts. It was time he found himself a woman. Not a wife — he had no wish to be married.

As these thoughts chased each other around in his head he heard the creak of the door, the sudden blast of cold air and the disturbed space where his cousins Joseph and James entered the room. They were noisy in their stealth, a cough, a whisper, someone knocking against a stool, someone dropping their boots to the floor so that the wooden studs reverberated. They brought with them the cold of outside but there was also a sudden acrid smell of burning wood. For a moment he wondered whether a log might have fallen from the hearth and was smouldering and should he get up to investigate. But if it had, they would surely notice it. Instead he closed his eyes and lay very still, pretending to be asleep. The thought of the ashes in the grate, were as nothing compared to those in his heart.

15

The weather, always variable, had by next morning metamorphosed into a benign if damp day. The earlier rains and snow flurries had left the earth waterlogged and leaves dripped pearls of moisture that still dazzled in the weak sunlight. Viewing the panorama from her chamber window, Martha decided that her foot was now sufficiently healed and that today she would go to see Willow.

When she expressed her intention after breakfast her mother was predictably doubtful.

'You really should not be venturing out. Walking can do you no good and you certainly cannot take the carriage. Papa would not hear of such a thing.'

Martha knew that the real reason for the objection was that she would be going to the home of Jonathon Gordon. No doubt her father feared that such a public visit would be interpreted as meaning that there was some sort of arrangement between the two families, and *that* he would never tolerate. She wondered what her mother would say if she suggested buying her own carriage but of course she said nothing.

'Besides, Papa says that in the present climate, you must not under any circumstances venture out alone.'

It took her a moment to realize that by climate, her mother was not referring to the weather.

'Has something happened about the machine-breakings?' she asked.

'Not to my knowledge, but there are things happening in our neighbourhood that you should not become involved in.'

'What sort of things?'

'Things that need not concern you.'

Martha sighed in frustration. 'Mama, I am a woman. Whatever is happening in our village I should know about it, otherwise how else am I to conduct myself sensibly?'

It was her mother's turn to sigh. She appeared to be having a mental battle with herself.

'It is only a rumour but Papa has heard that the men have set up some sort of secret society,' she said at last. 'They are planning to attack Sir Jenison and Squire Wetherby. I shouldn't wonder if they don't storm the vicarage as well.'

'Why would they want to do that?'

Mrs Cavanagh pursed her lips.

'It is what your father says. We must all be on our guard.'

Once she was left alone Martha decided that no matter what her mother warned, she was not going to remain cooped up in the house. Quietly she went to fetch her cape and bonnet and change into her outdoor shoes. Feeling like a naughty child she tiptoed across the hall and when she was sure that the coast was clear she let herself out and hurried for the gate. She did not slow down until she was out of sight of the vicarage. Thereafter she set off towards the point where the Midwillow road met with the narrow twisting lane that led to Willow Halt. This separate but adjoining hamlet consisted of only four, superior houses occupied by the doctor, a solicitor, a colonel and a wool merchant. The doctor in question was Doctor Gordon, Jonathon's father.

Once she arrived at the house, that old enemy, shyness, began to take control. To whom should she address herself? She would feel foolish presenting herself at the front door but at the same time she wondered what would happen if she was found trespassing at the back, near to the stables. In the end she decided that she would indeed wander round to the back. After all, this was where Willow was likely to be and Jonathon had told her that she could call at any time.

Having made up her mind she walked out as purposefully as her now aching ankle would allow, skirting the house and sticking to the neat driveway which circled around to the back. The courtyard was faced with rather unusual grey-black bricks, any surface water running into a channel along the centre. Carefully she picked her way, looking with increasing anxiety at the row of loose boxes on three sides of the quadrangle.

The first one was empty and she realized that the carriage was also absent. Presumably this was where Dr Gordon kept his driving horse and he was now out on his rounds. A rather showy black hunter occupied the next stall. She had not seen him before and held her hand out to him. He immediately flattened his ears against his head and tried to bite her. Quickly she withdrew her hand and stepped back to be out of his range.

The next box again was empty and then, to her joy, in response to her call, there was an answering rustle from the box and Willow poked his greying muzzle over the door.

She gave him a hug and indulged in the pleasure of rubbing her hands along his neck, up over his mane and then fondling his neat ears. To her relief he looked well and happy.

In that same moment she heard the sound

of a horse being ridden up the drive. Its pace was lively and her heart began to beat faster as she wondered how she should present herself. Seconds later Jonathon came into view, riding a smart, dark-bay, big-boned mare.

'Miss Cavanagh!' His delight at seeing her was obvious and she felt trapped by his enthusiasm.

'I was just visiting,' she started.

'I am delighted to see you out and about. You find your pony in good condition?'

She nodded. He dismounted with a surprisingly easy grace and began to unsaddle the mare, who continued to pace and twist, clearly in fine fettle.

'Stand still, Gracey, you silly creature.' He hung the saddle over the stable door and struggled to get a halter on her as he released the bit from her mouth raising her head high to avoid him.

'She's a bit of a handful,' he said, reaching up to lasso her nose. 'A good mare though, very honest.'

It occurred to Martha that in his own environment Jonathon Gordon could be graceful, like a swan on water. In the vicarage parlour, on two legs, he was anything but.

She started to formulate a sentence announcing her intention to leave but he said:

'I am really glad that you are here for I imagine you will have heard the rumours about the troubles in the village.'

'I haven't. I am afraid I have been confined indoors.'

'Your father has not told you?' He led Gracey into one of the empty boxes and started to rub her damp coat with a handful of straw, following her around the stall as she paced and snorted. The smell of her steaming coat was strangely beautiful.

'Why don't you come into the house and I'll tell you what has been happening.'

Her curiosity now thoroughly aroused she agreed, merely waiting for him to return his saddle and bridle to the tack-room. Before leaving he threw an armful of hay in for Gracey and replenished her water. Any doubts she might have had about Willow's welfare were quickly dispelled.

On entering the house she discovered that Jonathon's mother was also absent and she had contradictory feelings of relief that she would not need to explain her presence and yet disquiet at being alone with him. At his insistence she accepted a glass of wine, wondering whatever Papa would think of her drinking alone with a man.

Jonathon invited her to sit and then did so himself, his long legs stretched out in a

V-shape before him. She watched his Adam's apple rise and fall as he swallowed a gulp of the wine.

'Well,' he started, 'you might have already heard that there have been some arrests.'

'No, I have not.' Her heart jolted. Had Gabriel been found out? Had someone said that he was in the woods on the night of the machine-breaking? Would he think that she had betrayed him? She went to stand up but, seeing Jonathon's surprise, with a terrific effort of will she sat down again.

'It happened this morning,' he said. 'It is already all over the village.'

'What has happened?'

'The Lawless brothers and their father.'

She felt the skin of her face tighten.

'Mr Gabriel Lawless?' The words came out before she could stop them.

Jonathon blinked as if his sensibilities were affronted. Perhaps he guessed the true cause of her concern.

'As far as I know it is only Isaac Lawless and his sons, also the Cooper brothers, James Harrison and one or two others. There are eight in all.'

'What have they been charged with?' The relief that Gabriel was not affected was as difficult to hide as the initial fear.

Jonathon sat back and took another gulp at

his drink. 'There is some confusion. They were originally rounded up for questioning about the machine-breakings — it seems that several of them were abroad that night, but since the men have been questioned at length other matters have come to light.'

'What matters?' Why did she feel so afraid?

'It seems that they have formed a Friendly Society,' said Jonathon, seeing her determination to know more.

'Is that against the law?'

'Not in itself, no.' Jonathon put his glass on the table beside him. He said, 'Since the law was changed such societies are permitted but there are stringent rules. Michael Cooper was one of their number. He is saying that the men were sworn to secrecy, that they were forced to take some sort of an oath, and oath-taking in such circumstances *is* against the law. The perpetrators could find themselves fined and even imprisoned.'

Martha tried to think of the implications other than the almost certain destitution for their families, then it came to her that at last she would be able to help. If Gabriel and his family were charged, then she would pay their fines.

'What about the machine-breakings?' Once again she was back in the woods on that fateful evening and her disquiet bubbled to the surface.

'Do not fret yourself, dear Miss Cavanagh,' said Jonathon, seeing her worried expression. 'To date no one has been charged with that offence although I fear that perhaps the magistrates will find a way to implicate the men they have arrested.' His brow creased. 'The charge of taking an oath will be far less severe than that of machine-breaking but nevertheless they have taken a serious risk.'

Without being told she knew that the crime of machine-breaking would carry a sentence of death.

She fought down her panic.

'What is to happen?'

'I don't know yet. Michael Cooper says that there were others present. The magistrates, of course, want to know their names. Once all the facts have been established they will be charged.'

He filled his own glass — and hers. She was too dazed to object and dutifully drank the contents. This second draught seemed to slip down easily.

'I can sense that the welfare of the Lawless family is important to you,' said Jonathon, coming to stand before her.

'Betsy Lawless was in our employ.' She spoke as if in her defence, hoping that he would not guess the true reason for her distress.

Jonathon nodded and she thought he looked relieved. Holding out his hand he helped her from the chair. Her legs felt a little shaky, whether from the unaccustomed exercise or from the wine she did not know, but she did not push his arm away as he offered it to her.

'You must not fret,' he said. 'I have already offered my legal services to the men.'

She was about to protest that they would have no money to pay a solicitor when he added: 'Free of charge, of course.'

'That is very noble of you.'

Jonathon gave a little laugh. 'Noble? That is not a word I would use. We are all what we are. I do not seem to live in the same world as many of my rank and class. All I can see is injustice and greed and theft. Thankfully I am sufficiently well provided-for to be able to stand up against it.'

Remembering her father's words she knew that those with the power — and the money — were unlikely to employ a legal man who did not uphold their right to hang on to their wealth. Jonathon might soon find himself without a clientele. Luckily he had the prospect of Lady Boldre's estate.

She realized that he was looking down at

her and that she was holding his arm in a very intimate manner. He smiled and she registered with surprise that in his passion for the cause of justice, his stutter had disappeared.

In spite of the warmth and sense of peace that was claiming her some distant voice warned that she should not be standing there alone with this man, holding on to him in an almost shameless manner, giving him the totally wrong impression. Shaking off the hazy sense of calm she released his arm and stood apart.

'I really must be going.'

'I will escort you home.'

'No, really . . . '

He shook his head. 'You do not look fit to walk back unaided. I will fetch the pony and trap. Unfortunately my parents have taken the carriage so it might be a damp drive but it will be better than walking.'

She could not seem to find the words to refuse. 'Do you know who else might be implicated in this Society?' she managed to ask eventually.

Jonathon shook his head. 'I think it is in its infancy. Family members are the most likely. I believe Michael Cooper has suggested that there were nine of them. At the moment there are only eight suspects known to the magistrates.'

One more to be discovered! Her head began to feel strangely detached and once more Jonathon Gordon took her arm.

'Come along, Miss Cavanagh. It seems that the warmth from the fireside has caused you some drowsiness. Let's get you home.'

The journey and her arrival passed in a haze. Fortunately her parents were both absent and it was not until she was safely installed in her chamber and resting upon the bed that she remembered that she had not even thanked Jonathon for looking after Willow.

16

The news of Isaac's arrest reached Gabriel at Oak Farm. Shadrack Brown who came to tell him, was so excited that he could hardly get the words out.

'When did this happen?' Gabriel cut across his convoluted account of the events.

''Smornin, at Home Farm. Constable come for Isaac and Michael Cooper then he left to go elsewhere. There's lots on 'em bin arrested.' He glanced up and Gabriel knew that his messenger was thanking his stars that he had not been one of the ones to take the oath. Gabriel in turn cursed himself for failing to have been there.

'What else?'

Shadrack looked uncomfortable. 'It's something to do with some mumbo-jumbo that went on at Isaac's house. Luther Samson heard that they was practisin' magic. Michael Cooper has told 'em everything.'

Gabriel knew that things must be bad. His first instinct was to seek out Ephraim, but remembering what had taken place the night before, he feared, in view of his cousin's naturally tempestuous spirit, that that would only add to the troubles. Instead he turned to Daniel Bridle for Daniel had known Isaac all his life and he might have some suggestion as to what course they should best follow.

Daniel was sympathetic. But for the good fortune that had supplied him with his acres, he too would have remained a labouring man, like Isaac and his sons; had things been different, he might now have been in gaol along with the rest.

The trouble was, Daniel had little influence. Although he was an employer of men, he had none of the power or privileges falling to Sir Jenison Bowler or Squire Wetherby. Indeed, if Daniel were to side openly with men who were accused of destroying property his own position would come under threat.

'The best I can do, lad, is to give you time off work. Take the next few days and I won't dock your pay. Why don't you go into the village and see if you can speak to young Mr Gordon the solicitor? From what I hear he is a bit of a champion of the poor and he will know what is required by law.'

Gabriel felt a momentary lifting of his spirits. Here was something that he could do, here was someone who would know what it all meant.

Daniel drew in his breath as if he was thinking hard.

210

'You would do well to talk with your cousin Ephraim Carter, too.' he added very tentatively. 'Try to persuade him to tone down his language. For all his beliefs, Isaac is respected around here whereas Ephraim's manner is too harsh. If he starts shouting his opinions aloud he is likely to inflame the magistrates.' So saying, he pushed a shilling piece into Gabriel's hand with the instruction to buy food and necessaries for the men in gaol. Gabriel thanked him and made his way to the cobbler's shop.

He found Ephraim sitting cross-legged on his bench, surrounded by leather and knives, needles, thread and a cobbler's last. He looked up as his cousin came in and put the boot on which he was working aside.

In spite of himself Gabriel's first thought was to wonder where Betsy was but there was no sign of her. Swallowing his relief, or perhaps disappointment, he turned to Ephraim.

'News?' the cobbler asked.

'Have you not heard what's happened?' Gabriel told him of the arrests as calmly and succinctly as he could.

Ephraim listened, chewing his lower lip, thinking of the next course of action.

'Right. We must go and see Lawyer Gordon.'

Gabriel felt a moment of surprise and optimism at his cousin's calm reaction; but there was something that he had not told him. As Ephraim slid easily from the bench he said:

'Shadrack says that Michael Cooper has been giving evidence. He's already told the magistrates that he and the others were forced to swear a secret oath and that there was another man helping Uncle Isaac to administer it.'

Ephraim's eyes narrowed. 'I'll get that coward Cooper, if it is the last thing I do!'

Gabriel said nothing for a moment. Michael Cooper had ten or eleven children. He was little more than a simpleton. How could one condemn him for being afraid and for being open to threats or bribery?

'Perhaps they'll not believe him,' he said then.

Ephraim studied him. The intensity of his gaze made Gabriel feel uncomfortable. He wondered for a moment whether his cousin knew what had passed between him and Betsy the night before.

'Has he said who the other man was?' asked Ephraim.

'I don't know.'

'If they arrest me you'll be the only one working,' observed Ephraim, very pointedly.

'Your job's temporary. You have no security. If I'm taken to prison the only source of income left to Aunt Sarah, to Betsy and young Matthew will be gone, that is unless you think you can support them?'

Gabriel didn't know what he was supposed to say. Was this Ephraim's way of warning him not to give him away?

'By the way,' Ephraim added, 'Aunt Sarah's time has come. Betsy is over with her now.'

Gabriel thought of his poor aunt, well past her youth, coping with the shock of her husband's arrest, writhing as another hungry mouth was dragged from her body. He rebelled against the knowledge that in a few months' time Betsy too would be faced with a child to rear.

'You were the other man, weren't you?' he said. 'How come Michael Cooper did not recognize you?'

Ephraim shrugged. 'We wore robes — hoods. The oath-takers were blindfolded.'

'Why?' He recalled Shadrack's mention of some mumbo-jumbo ceremony. Had it come to his turn he would definitely have refused to go along with it. He cursed himself for not having been there. Here was his first punishment for having been absent. He was just wondering how on earth Isaac had agreed to it when Ephraim said:

'The village men are superstitious. I thought it would be best to give the whole thing a bit of mystery. They swore on the Bible, that's all.'

Gabriel did not comment. Ephraim's actions could have put them all in danger.

'Let's just hope they don't identify you, then,' was all that he could say.

They found Jonathon Gordon at the chambers of Rowhampton & Perkiss where he was employed as a junior partner. It was the first time that Gabriel had seen him and this tall, gangly-looking fellow with a mess of hair and a hesitant way of speaking did not give much cause for optimism. He kept reminding himself that they were lucky to find anyone with some knowledge of the law who was willing to support their case.

'R-right, t-take a seat.'

Gabriel and Ephraim sat down in the little office that bore Jonathon's name on the door. It was cluttered with books and papers but there were two seats before the overflowing desk.

Ephraim moved restlessly. 'If the men aren't released, there'll be trouble, I can assure you of that,' he started by saying.

Jonathon glanced at Gabriel before answering.

'I t-think it would be best if we c-come up

with a legal d-defence. Can you gentlemen tell me something of the background?'

Before Ephraim could speak Gabriel started to explain about the meeting at the church and the promise of extra wages, then the fact that Sir Jenison had, instead, cut the men's weekly rate.

Mr Gordon looked pained. 'So, what did they do?'

'We've formed a Friendly Society. It's all legal. We all agreed. This story about machine-breaking is all lies.' That was Ephraim.

Bit by bit Jonathon pieced the story together, stopping them when they got ahead of themselves, challenging some of the things that Ephraim stated as gospel. Ephraim was getting irritated with him and once more Gabriel tried to take control of the story.

'Tell me honestly now,' said Jonathan, 'if I am to defend these men I must know the truth. To your knowledge did these men take an oath of secrecy?'

'No.' That was Ephraim again.

'That means that you were there?' Mr Gordon looked at both cousins. Neither man replied immediately. Gabriel guessed that Ephraim did not want to condemn himself and — well, he hadn't been there had he?

'Well?' Jonathon waited.

'No, we weren't there. We were both at my shop. My wife will confirm it.' Ephraim spoke calmly, his eyes unblinking. By his words he was condemning Betsy to lie on their behalf. Gabriel felt his anger rise but in the circumstances he could not contradict him.

'I see. So neither of you was present when this illegal oath was taken?'

They both shook their heads.

Mr Gordon asked a few more questions, making careful notes, then he put his papers aside.

'Right, gentlemen. I will go to the prison and see the accused. I need to be absolutely clear about what actually took place and if you were not there then you cannot help me.'

He stood up, knocking a pile of documents on to the ground as he did so. Gabriel bent to retrieve them but the solicitor brushed him aside and he guessed that they were confidential although he probably did not realize that Gabriel could read.

Once outside the cousins agreed to go to Isaac's cottage to see how the birth progressed. As they walked Ephraim talked of the troubles and the steps that the men should take but Gabriel was distracted. His thoughts were for Betsy. For her sake he hoped that his aunt would have an easy birth so that Betsy should not be alarmed by what she would have to face later in the year.

As they drew near to the cottage Gabriel saw that the door was open. Something told him that this was a bad omen. He increased his pace. As they drew near, Goodwife Howard emerged. She had attended most of the births in the village over the last thirty years. Her expression told them that all was not well.

'You must not go in.'

'What's happening?'

Mistress Howard shook her head.

'The child is dead. Your aunt has lost a lot of blood — too much.'

'Is she?'

'She is quiet.'

'Where is . . . ?' Gabriel had been about to ask for Betsy but changed his mind.

The midwife continued to shake her head at the hopelessness of the situation.

'She's with her aunt,' she replied. 'It's just a matter of time.'

Even as she spoke, Betsy herself appeared in the doorway. Her face looked shocked and drawn, her eyes darkened by the pain of what had passed. Looking at Goodwife Howard, she shook her head, then she turned to her husband.

'My mother, she's . . . ' Tears spilled down her cheeks and she began to sob, moving into his arms. In silence he held her, patting her awkwardly on the shoulder. Gabriel looked on, helpless to offer her the comfort he longed to give. Such a jumble of thoughts tormented him. His cousin Ephraim was Betsy's husband, the father of her child. It was clear that she needed him. If he were to be arrested how would she cope? Shamefaced he fought the knowledge that if Ephraim was not there, then Betsy might turn to him for that same protection.

After a while they separated and Betsy wiped her eyes on the back of her hands.

'She suffered,' was all that she could say.

The knowledge of his aunt's death and the hopelessness of his love consumed Gabriel with anguish. Tears scalded his lids and he knew that he had to get away. He did not say goodbye, merely turned and walked from the cottage, away from the village. Amid all the pain and sadness was one terrible thought — who was going to break the news to Uncle Isaac?

★　★　★

As he continued to walk without direction, Gabriel knew that he had to be the one to go to the prison, to tell his uncle what had happened. His lungs heaved as if they could not hold in the air that he would need to spell out the tragedy. The prison was three miles away and it had begun to rain. He felt desperately tired, wanting only to go home and sleep — only there was a dead woman lying in the cottage, a dead baby beside her. His anger raged.

'Mr Lawless!'

With a jolt he realized that his steps were taking him back to the village and he was near to the vicarage gates. By the devil's luck, who should be about to enter but Miss Cavanagh. She was struggling to open it, her arms being full of what looked like sketching materials.

Shaking away his tormented thoughts he stopped to undo the latch for her. She nodded her thanks and clutching her parcels, stepped inside.

'I am so sorry to hear about your uncle,' she said. 'It must be a terrible blow.'

For a moment he thought that she was talking about Sarah's death, then he realized that she meant the imprisonment.

'His wife has just died,' he said.

He saw the shock in her eyes.

'I am so very sorry.'

'You should be.' He wanted to hurt someone, anybody. She was the one who was there.

'I — is there something that I might do?'

His fists clenched so hard that his nails dug into his palms. To his own ears his voice sounded like a snarl.

'Your father, your good Christian father could have intervened on the men's behalf. If they had been given the wages that were promised, none of this would have happened. They would not have been forced to act as they have.' He stopped, suddenly afraid that by his words he was condemning them. 'It seems likely that they will also be accused of the machine breaking,' he added. 'They are not guilty and yet the authorities will probably hang them.'

He stepped closer to the young woman, his nostrils pinched, his breath coming in ragged gasps.

'Do you realize what that means, Miss Cavanagh? Have you seen a hanging? Perhaps it should be called a choking, for sometimes it takes a man five minutes to die.'

'Stop, please!' Martha's packages fell from her hands and she reached out to touch his arm.

'The shock of the arrests has killed my aunt,' he said. 'That and the shortages, the lack of food, the hard work, the constant anxiety. You should be ashamed, Miss Cavanagh, ashamed to belong to a family that

220

could have helped and yet chose to do nothing.' He realized that she was crying.

'I'm so sorry. I'm so sorry,' she kept repeating.

He stopped to draw breath. For a moment it felt as if the anger had gone out of him. He looked at her, a small creature muffled in her cape, like some puffed-up sparrow.

'Forgive me. I should not have said those things. It is not your fault.'

She shook her head.

'I am going to the gaol now to tell my uncle that his wife is dead,' he said. 'It is not an easy thing to do.'

'Let me to come with you. I — I will fetch bread and eggs and milk for the men.'

Her suggestion shocked him into silence.

'What about your father?' he asked at last. 'Have you thought about what he will think?'

The girl seemed to grow about six inches.

'Mr Lawless,' she said. 'I am now an adult. I might live in my father's house but I am no longer a child to be told what I may and may not do. If you would care to wait inside, I will prepare some groceries. You too would surely benefit from something to eat and drink.'

He remembered how she had returned his neckerchief, her strange behaviour in weeping for no apparent reason. This quiet, composed young woman did not seem like the same person.

He was about to refuse her offer but he was hungry and she was offering him food, so for the moment he said nothing, instead following her into the vicarage. He wondered where the minister was, then realized that he was probably at the gaol or with the magistrates, cooking up the charges.

'Please, sit down.'

It was only when he had done so he realized that, like a gentleman, he had come in through the front door.

Once they were in the parlour, Martha rang the bell for Mrs Porter. When she came, she said: 'Please tell your husband to prepare the pony and trap. I have to go out again.'

Mrs Porter stared at Gabriel as if he was something nasty that Martha had brought indoors on her shoe.

'And please fetch some cold meat and ale,' she said. 'And pack up a good supply of food and drink for me to deliver where it is needed.'

For a moment Mrs Porter looked as if she might refuse, but after some huffing and puffing she retreated to do as she was asked.

Gabriel waited in silence. He glanced surreptitiously around the room, taking in the comfort, the rugs on the floor, the heavy curtains at the window, the fine hearth with its firedogs and glinting brass poker. This was another world, one he had never experienced, except from the outside.

Martha stood awkwardly, not meeting his eyes. He wondered what her parents would say if they came back and found him there. In the face of their united opposition, would she have the courage to stand against them?

Catching the direction of his gaze, Martha moved across to the fire and busied herself by poking it and adding some logs, drawing pleasure from the thought that perhaps the warmth and peace of the vicarage offered him some brief respite.

When Mrs Porter returned, she slammed the dishes down on the table to show her disapproval.

There was a haunch of cold lamb and Martha began to slice it, placing the tenderest pieces on to a plate which she placed in front of her guest, then she cut bread and spread it with butter, adding pickles to the side of the plate.

'Please eat.'

He seemed to come back from a very long way, then he picked up the knife and began to cut the food into sizeable pieces, eating hungrily.

Her heart felt constrained, every sense

heightened. She thought that just this once she was waiting on him as a wife might do. In her mind's eye she saw him reach and grasp her hand, heard the rich burr of his voice, *Thank you, my love.* Such notions were foolish, she knew, but if she had nothing else, this moment would stay in her memory.

By the time he had eaten he seemed to have regained some of his composure. As soon as he had emptied the beaker of ale he stood up.

'Thank you for your kindness,' he said, 'but I will go now.'

'I will come with you.'

He shook his head. 'Believe me, Miss Cavanagh, you have done enough. I am going now to tell my uncle that his wife is dead. I go to find out when the men will be tried, to see what can be done.'

'If I come, as the daughter of the minister I might have some small influence.' She blushed, knowing that her words were drawing attention to the difference in their ranks.

'Thank you, but no. Mr Gordon the solicitor is giving his services for free. He is a good man.'

She nodded, thinking of Jonathon's twitchy enthusiasm.

'At least take the food with you for your

friends.' She held out the parcel and to her relief he accepted it.

'I will, and thank you again.'

'Please — will you let me know how things go?'

'I will.'

There was nothing more to be said. As they stepped outside, Mr Porter brought the pony and trap to the door.

'Please take the trap,' she said. 'It will save you both time and energy.'

Mr Porter frowned and she turned to him.

'There is no need for you to go. Mr Lawless can drive himself to where he is going and he will return the trap safely.'

With a shrug, Mr Porter climbed down from the box and Gabriel took the reins.

'Thank you again. I — I'm sorry if I shouted at you earlier. You — you didn't deserve it.'

She nodded, ashamed that Mr Porter should hear those words. As Gabriel drove away, those old enemies, tears, were near to surfacing once more.

He had not been gone five minutes when she heard the sound of her father's carriage drawing up at the door. Her insides jolted at the thought of the scene to come, for even as she looked out of the window she saw Mrs Porter open the door and heard her whispering something to Mistress Cavanagh.

Her father greeted her with the words:

'Where is the pony and trap?'

Her mouth felt dry but she forced the answer out.

'I have lent them to Mr Lawless to go to the prison.'

'You have done what?' She recognized the show of disbelief, the mounting rage that so easily assailed her father.

'Mr Isaac Lawless's wife has died in childbirth,' she said, trying to keep her voice steady. 'He is locked away. Someone needs to go and tell him, to offer him words of comfort.' For a wild moment she wondered whether her father might decide that that person should be him, but he blew out his cheeks and shook his head as if facing something unbelievable.

'I understand that you invited that scoundrel his nephew into my house,' he continued. 'That you even gave him food.'

Martha's heart beat so loud that she could hardly hear her own voice but she struggled on.

'If you mean Mr Gabriel Lawless, he was exhausted, hungry. Surely as a Christian one should offer succour to the poor and suffering?'

'Do not try to be clever with me, young

woman. Do you not know that he has been in prison? He is a layabout and a thief of the lowest order. Worse, he is a radical, a public enemy.'

'I did know about the gaol. He told me himself.' Her voice quavered as she tried to challenge his attempt to shock her.

He continued to shake his head then turned to his wife who stood rigid and silent like a rabbit cornered by a weasel.

'Tomorrow,' he said, 'you will send for Doctor Hughes. I told you there was something wrong with that girl.'

'I don't need a doctor.'

The minister fixed his daughter with his hell-fire stare.

'Madam, kindly be quiet. Your mother and I have been aware for a long time that you have been behaving strangely. I think it is time that we sought professional advice.'

Before she could protest, he added: 'And I hear that young Gordon has been calling here in spite of my instructions to the contrary. I hope that you are not still entertaining foolish ideas of a union with him. I thought I had made it clear that he is totally unsuitable.'

'I am not entertaining any ideas,' she said. From somewhere she found the courage to add, 'You might find him unsuitable as a son-in-law. I find him suitable as a friend.

Now, if you will excuse me, Papa, I shall retire to my room.'

She didn't know what they expected, probably that she would ask for forgiveness for some perceived failing, as she usually did. Instead, as she left the room there was silence.

As she mounted the stairs she felt a strange mixture of exhilaration and pride. She had stood up to her father. She had not resorted to tears. Perhaps at long last he would begin to recognize that she was no longer a child under his jurisdiction. If he found her way of doing things not to his taste, then perhaps she should move out, find a lodging of her own.

The wildness of her thoughts took her breath away and she sank into a chair with a thump. The fire was lit but there were no candles and moisture ran down the inside of the window-panes. Shut in this quiet room she felt strangely isolated. Amid all the other thoughts, one gradually came to the fore. As far as her father was concerned, she was an unmarried daughter of a clergyman who had a position to maintain. As far as she was concerned, she now had wealth of her own and she should be the one to control it. She shivered. Whatever happened next, she would need to be very careful indeed.

17

Gabriel kept the pony going at a trot, the wind whipping around him, the rain stinging his face. All the time he wrestled with the same problem — how to tell his Uncle the unthinkable? Words alone would not change the tragedy of the news but the method of telling might ease that first pain and he did not have the gift with words for offering comfort. He almost turned back, thinking that perhaps Isaac was best left in ignorance, but then he feared that his uncle might hear of it from someone else.

The prison was built about half a mile from Lower Rising and had a long history of human misery. Whereas the village nestled around the church and the manor house, the prison was in isolation, hidden up a winding track behind sentinel oaks. It had always been a place of terror to Gabriel as a boy. In style it was ominously similar to Sainham Gaol and the sight of it brought back bleak memories. At the prospect of going inside he was seized by panic, sucked in by the same nightmare fear he had known at Sainham, when the gate slammed shut, stealing his friends, his hope, his life.

He tried to breathe deeply to calm himself, bringing the trap to a halt near to the entrance. The pony was a docile beast so he hitched his rein to a ring outside the prison gate and banged hard to ask for admission.

'Who are you?' A gaoler peered hard at him through the bars, looking him up and down with suspicion. He was a short man of middle years and his hat was pulled so far forward that it was hard to see his eyes. Gabriel remembered the shilling piece that Daniel Bridle had given him and was glad of it, for there was a good chance that he would need to bribe his way in.

'I'm Gabriel Lawless. My uncle and cousins are being held here. I have to see my uncle — his wife has died in childbirth and he must be told.'

To his surprise the guard unlocked the gate without comment. It swung open with a creak, the sort of sound heard on windy nights when footpads and ne'er-do-wells were abroad. Entering that yard was like being dragged back into the nightmare that was Sainham. His courage threatened to fail him but he knew that he had to go ahead. Clutching the parcel of food he followed the gaoler into the grey monolith that was Chantry gaol.

'A legal man was here this afternoon,' said the gaoler over his shoulder. 'He warned us that someone might be coming with provisions and said that we was to let you in.'

Gabriel felt a moment of warmth towards Jonathon Gordon.

'Do you know what is happening?' he asked, sensing that the man was not unsympathetic to his prisoners.

The gaoler shrugged. 'I reckon the magistrates have got it in for this lot. They're land-owning men you see, the magistrates. That and men of the cloth. They don't like peasants who are uppity and they don't like Dissenters. What your uncle and his kind are doing threatens their way of life.' It was not what Gabriel wanted to hear.

Immediately they entered the building proper he was swallowed up by the damp, cold gloom as if the pain and misery locked inside had invaded the very stone of the walls. In silence they made their way down a long corridor, turning twice to left then right. It was so dark that Gabriel almost had to feel his way along, his feet slithering on the slime of the floor. His chest rasped with the desire to be back in the fresh air.

At last they stopped and the guard unlocked one of several identical doors.

'Five minutes,' he said. 'If you don't come

231

out as soon as I come back you'll have to stay there all night — and no funny business. What you got there?'

For the first time he seemed to notice the parcel.

'Just food.' Gabriel held it out to him. The man reached out and prodded the package, feeling its uneven shape, the softness of the contents. Bending forward he sniffed it and the smell of the cold lamb inside must have convinced him, for with a nod he pushed the door open just wide enough for Gabriel to squeeze past then slammed it shut again.

'Gabriel?' He heard his uncle's voice, the rustling of several men, the clanking of chains as they heaved themselves up from the floor.

'Uncle Isaac.' It took a few moments for his eyes to grow accustomed to the gloom. He was not prepared for what he saw. His uncle and his companions were all dressed in the rough prison garb and their heads had been shaved. For a moment he was lost for words.

The place was dark and fetid. On the floor a few strands of sodden straw provided all they had for bedding. Someone, it seemed, had taken pity on them and given them some sticks with which to light a fire but the wood was so green that the resulting smoke must have threatened to suffocate them. He could dimly make out the pile of charred sticks and ash where they had stamped it out, no doubt finding the cold the lesser of two evils. A plume of choking fumes still hung in the air.

The sight of his uncle's face, the lines of anxiety etched across his brow hit home with naked force. Behind Isaac, cousin Joseph and a man Gabriel knew as George Akers stared at him with troubled eyes.

'Is there any news?' asked Isaac.

By way of reply he held out the parcel. Joseph took it and tore it open, descending on the food like a ravenous wolf. Sheepishly he remembered his father and friends and handed it over to Isaac.

'Where's James?' asked Gabriel.

'In another cell with the others. They've split us up.'

Gabriel tried to form the words, to tell them the terrible news, but they would not come. Instead, he asked:

'Have you been formally charged yet?'

Isaac shook his head. 'Not yet. They keep questioning us.'

'I heard that you were all to be charged for belonging to the society and that you might also be held on suspicion of machine-breaking as well.'

'At first we did hint that we might know something about it to put them off the scent of the new union,' Joseph answered, 'but now they have found out about our meeting we have denied the charges. All the others confirm that we were with them at the cottage that night. We couldn't have been in two places at once, could we?'

'Where did you go that night?' asked Gabriel. 'After the meeting.'

Joseph looked sheepish. 'We — Jem and I, we had an arrangement with a couple of lasses from the village.' He looked apologetically towards his father. 'We found a nice little spot where we could light a fire and keep warm. Nothing bad happened' he added, knowing that Isaac would disapprove.

'How's Sarah?'

Isaac's sudden question hit Gabriel as hard as if he had been punched in the chest. For a few moments Joseph's story had driven from his mind the reason why he had come. Suddenly unprepared, he lost all the words he had been planning to say along the way. Instead he blurted out:

'Uncle, I'm so sorry, I'm afraid she..'

Isaac remained very still, almost as if he too had died. Behind him, Joseph gave a sob of disbelief.

'No!'

Anything Gabriel had thought of before deserted him.

'I'm sorry,' was all he could manage again.

Isaac bent his head forward and let out a long, anguished sigh.

'The baby?'

Gabriel shook his head.

'Then God has seen fit to release them from their suffering.'

Gabriel could almost feel his uncle reaching out to an external presence to make sense of what had happened. Part of him wanted to argue with the older man, to say that no god worth bothering with would treat one of his own so badly, but he said nothing.

After a very long silence Isaac spoke.

'I blame myself,' he said. 'If I had not started along this road then perhaps none of this would have happened.'

'No, you are wrong. If you had not started this, many more of the villagers would die of starvation. Things seem bleak now but I know that in the long run you will win through,' said Gabriel. Aware of the defeated men around him he added: 'It just seems wrong that you should have to suffer for what you believe.'

Isaac began to sob, a quiet, controlled expression of his grief and in that same moment the guard banged on the door.

'Out you come now.'

'I'll stay,' Gabriel said to Isaac but his uncle

shook his head, his voice suddenly sounded strong.

'You go now. You look after everything out there. Look after young Matthew, and my daughter.'

Gabriel nodded and patted Isaac helplessly on the arm.

'I'll come back tomorrow,' he said and because the guard was threatening to lock him in, he slipped back outside.

Once in the open he gave vent to his rage, shouting at the empty sky, cursing the god that Isaac believed in so implicitly. Not least, he felt guilty because he was able to walk away whereas the others had no choice but to stay in that hell-hole. He had walked a good hundred yards before he remembered the pony and trap and had to retrace his steps to fetch them.

The pony was dark brown, the sky and the ground were black. Everything about him seemed to be shrouded in darkness and despair. As he listened to the clip clop of the animal's hoofs, he thought of Isaac's last words — *take care of my daughter*. What did he mean by that? Surely Ephraim, as her husband, would look after Betsy? Then he began to wonder. Did Uncle Isaac too have doubts about Ephraim? Was he sending a clear message? Was this perhaps a sacred trust his uncle was imposing, and if so, how should he go about it?

Taking heart he shook the reins and clicked to the pony who, realizing that he was going home, increased his pace. The thought of Betsy being placed into his care by her father was the first glimmer of hope that he had felt since before the arrests.

The prospect of returning the pony and trap and perhaps confronting the Reverend Cavanagh in the process did little to cheer him but fortunately it was Will Porter who heard his arrival and came to take charge.

He remembered Will Porter from childhood. He had always been a dour man, not popular with the boys. Once he had been in trouble with Isaac because he had taken a stick to Cousin Joseph — for cheeking him, so he claimed.

'If my boys offend you then you come to me. I will be the one to punish them,' Isaac had said. 'Lay one more finger on them and I'll have the constable on to you.'

That phrase had stayed with Gabriel all these years, that and the feeling that Uncle Isaac was always strong, reliable, always there to take care of them. Will Porter had threatened and blustered but in the end he had gone away and, to his knowledge, he never touched one of Isaac's boys again.

He accepted the pony without comment.

'Please thank Miss Cavanagh for me,' Gabriel said.

Will did not reply but just as Gabriel was leaving his curiosity got the better of him.

'How are things at the gaol then?' he asked. 'Have they charged them or are they going to let them go?'

'I don't know. We've got a solicitor helping us — a Mr Gordon.'

Will gave a cynical grunt. 'Huh. He's always here, hanging around Miss Cavanagh.'

The news surprised Gabriel.

As he took his leave the immediate future seemed to clasp him like some grey wilderness. Where should he go? Back at the cottage, Aunt Sarah and her baby lay unburied. Would he, could he spend the night there? What were the alternatives? He knew the answer of course — to go to Ephraim. They would squeeze him in. Already they had young Matthew. That great emptiness beneath his ribs began to open up again. He needed to go to Ephraim's to tell them what had happened but the prospect of sleeping under their roof while, a few feet away they shared the same bed was like hell-fire.

Struggling with these torments he set out for the cobbler's shop. When he arrived, what he both hoped for and feared came about.

Ephraim had gone out on some business of his own, Matthew was tucked up in a narrow truckle bed against the wall — and Betsy was alone.

'What news?' Her face was sick with worry and he reached out to squeeze her arm — that gesture again, that useless gesture that implies bad news whilst attempting to offer comfort.

With an effort of will he spoke calmly.

'There is some change with regard to the charge. Joseph and James were suspected of the machine-breaking but they couldn't have done it because they were with the others at the cottage so there is some hope that that charge will be dropped.' In an effort to comfort her he added: 'I'm sure that when all the facts emerge all the charges will be dropped.'

'And father?'

He shook his head. 'I have told him the news. He is upset of course but he has company to help him through the night. I promised I would go back tomorrow. I'll go and see Mr Gordon, perhaps he will know something more.'

She bowed her head and sighed.

'What about the funerals?' he asked, wondering whether Ephraim might have gone to see the minister. As far as he knew, although there was a strong following for the Methodists, they had no burial place of their own. Every man in the parish had still been baptized in the parish church and should therefore have a place in the graveyard.

Betsy did not know.

'Don't fret yourself. I will go at first light and see to things.' They were standing close and quite naturally Betsy moved into his arms, resting her head against his chest. He cuddled her, stroked her hair, feeling that his heart would burst. Isaac's words came back to him, *take care of my daughter*. He hoped this moment would never end but too soon she pulled back.

'We've prepared the bodies,' she said, smoothing down her skirts in a familiar gesture. 'Ephraim has fetched a coffin from Richard Wood. We owe him two shillings. The baby can go in with her.' She hesitated. 'By rights we should return to the cottage tonight and be with them but I can't take little Matthew there.'

He thought that this was her way of asking him if he would hold a solitary wake.

He found himself wondering what Sarah's baby looked like. Where was the sense in all that growth, only to be snuffed out even before it drew breath? He realized that he did not even know if it was a boy or a girl — it made a difference, gave the child some sort of identity.

'What was the baby?'

Betsy gave a sad smile. 'A girl. Father would have liked that.'

He nodded. 'Shouldn't she have a name?'

'I think perhaps we should call her Sarah, after Mam.'

It was his turn to nod. The living-room behind the cobbler's shop was quite small and a good fire blazed. The warmth reminded him how tired he was. He was still debating whether he should stay here, suffer all the cruel temptations, or return to Isaac's cold, morgue of a cottage when he heard footsteps outside, the quick, restless steps of his cousin Ephraim.

Ephraim looked surprised and Gabriel couldn't deduce what he was thinking. Perhaps it was his imagination but he thought that his cousin looked sheepish. He wondered where he had been and what he had been up to.

'Cousin.' Ephraim began to take off his boots, making for the fire to warm his hands. 'Make us a brew, there's a good lass,' he said to Betsy.

'We are nearly out of everything.' There was an edge to her voice. In theory, Ephraim was doing better than the rest of them. Was he careless with his money? Did he keep Betsy short? Was that his way of controlling her?

Such thoughts tumbled in Gabriel's mind. He remembered their wedding day, the way they had shared a private joke during the service, two people happy in themselves. Had things changed since she had committed her life to him?

When he did not answer her, she did as he bid and boiled water on the fire, adding a few precious tea-leaves to the old pot. While the kettle was boiling Gabriel told his cousin what had been happening. 'I will go to the vicarage in the morning to arrange the burial,' he said in conclusion.

As he talked, Ephraim looked thoughtful. When he had finished, Ephraim said:

'I have spoken to every labouring man in the parish. If the men aren't released we will rise up and set them free.'

Gabriel wanted to shout out that to do so would be to bring disaster on everyone, but the hope that they would indeed soon be free, together with the exhaustion that claimed him, meant that he merely said:

'Let's wait and see what happens.'

Betsy filled two beakers with tea and added some honey, then brought it across. Ephraim took his without a word and Gabriel cursed himself for resenting his cousin's lack of feelings. He thought, if she were mine, to be waiting on me, whatever she did she would always get my thanks.

'You'd better stay here,' said Ephraim. 'Perhaps you can squeeze in with the young lad.'

Gabriel looked at Matthew, his limbs flung wide, his young head tilted back as he gently snored. In the shadowy gloom of the room it looked as if his cheeks were stained with tears. Apart from the fact that he had no wish to wake him, there was really no room for two bodies, however tightly packed, in the little bed. Besides, he wondered what he should say if the child awoke crying for his mother in the night. That decided him. He would return to Isaac's.

Quickly he finished his tea and stood up. Betsy saw him to the door.

'Thank you,' she said. 'Will you — will you say a prayer for Mam and for baby Sarah?'

'I'm not much of a one for praying,' he confessed. 'I'll send them your . . . love though, to help them on their way.'

She gave him a hug, the brief, affectionate embrace of a relative. He touched her cheek and for a second it felt as if his fingertips were pouring into her all the love that he felt. Regretfully he pulled away.

243

'See you in the morning then.'

'Until tomorrow.'

He walked back to the cottage filled with the sort of feeling that comes only when extreme events have taken place. His aunt and her child had died. His uncle and cousins were in gaol. There was a possibility, perhaps even a probability that they would be imprisoned for a long while. Foremost though, always there, was the sense of bereavement he felt because he had lost Betsy. True, she had never been his, but the possibility, the *what might have been*, burned into his soul.

To his shame he called in at the alehouse and with the shilling that Daniel Bridle had given him, he bought some gin. Isaac would have been disappointed. He never allowed strong liquor in his house but if Gabriel was to get through the night he needed this Dutch courage.

As he approached the cottage he found it difficult to go inside. He did so only because he told himself that this was what Betsy wanted. In doing this, he was doing it for her, and for Uncle Isaac. As he stepped inside the door he was immediately aware of the rough oblong of the coffin, dominating the room, laid along the table. He walked around it warily as if, should he go too close, it might attack him.

The place was cold but he did not feel that he could light a fire in case it affected the bodies. Instead he found a piece of tallow candle and set it on a stool, crowding close to be drawn into its fragile light, then he opened the jar and took a swig.

The liquid was raw, making him gag, but as it spread through his body it brought warmth, a blessed numbness. He drank some more.

After a while he forced himself to look at the bodies. Sarah was laid out flat on her back, her hands folded across her breast. Her face looked waxy, unreal but there was an eternal stillness about her that gave him courage. The babe was shrouded in a cloth, lying against her mother's side, her face hidden by the cover. He did not have the courage to expose her tiny features.

His head was beginning to feel woolly. He took a deep breath and sat on another stool, taking another long draught from the jar. Well God, he thought, I've got a message for you from my cousin Betsy. She wants you to take care of her mother. A pity you didn't do a better job while she was still alive.

Feeling the need to relieve himself he went outside. His legs felt as if they belonged to someone else and twice he had to steady himself against the cottage wall. The stream of piss wavered, just missing his boots.

When he had done he looked around him. By now it must be well after midnight and everything was still. Perhaps it was his imagination but there was a tension in the air as if something was about to happen. The rain had stopped and the wind had fallen. Trees stood out black against the black of the night. Above him, more stars than he could imagine were possible flickered and flirted. Somewhere close to hand an owl screeched. He thought to himself, this world is a beautiful place. Beautiful. Where on earth was the link between the beauty out here and the ugliness and suffering that happened alongside it?

Having no answers he stumbled back inside. Leaving the candle to burn itself out he fell into his bed in the corner and slept.

18

Martha came down to breakfast the next morning as if nothing had happened. Her father breezed into the room moments later with an air of businesslike preoccupation. He appeared too absorbed to speak to either Martha or her mother. Then, just as they were about to eat, Mrs Porter poked her head around the parlour door.

'It's that Lawless man, he wants a word with you,' she announced. 'It's the one who took the pony and trap.' Her words seemed to imply that they had been stolen.

Martha felt all the familiar sensations, tightness in her chest, a suspension of breathing, a dry mouth, heat in her cheeks. Somewhere in the cacophony that filled her head she heard her father say:

'Tell him if he wants to see me, he can go to the church.'

There was a movement by the door and she realized with shock that Gabriel had followed Mrs Porter into the room.

'Forgive me for this rudeness, Reverend, but I have much to do today and I need to arrange my aunt's funeral.'

The sound of his rich country dialect did strange things to Martha's heart. She longed to look at him but to do so would be to reveal her soul so she kept her eyes lowered to the whiteness of the tablecloth.

'Is your aunt a member of my congregation?'

'My aunt was born and bred and baptized here. I believe your predecessor married her and my uncle in the church.'

'When did she last attend a service? When did she last take Holy Communion?'

'I don't know.'

Martha held her breath. She was reminded of two cock pheasants, sparring, each one waiting for the advantage to strike his foe.

'Then there's the babe,' Gabriel said.

'What babe?'

'My aunt died in childbirth.'

'Was the child baptized?'

At the thought of Mistress Lawless's poor, dead baby and Gabriel's pain Martha had to blink back treacherous tears.

'No, she was not.'

'Then it cannot be buried in consecrated ground.'

'But — '

Her father pounced. 'Your family brings nothing but trouble. Your uncle preaches treason. There is no room for the likes of them in the cemetery, or in this village.'

'In *our* village, I think you mean.' There was venom in Gabriel's tone. After a terrible silence he asked 'You are refusing to bury them?'

'I most certainly am.'

Holding her breath against some catastrophe Martha endured the silence then Gabriel turned and strode from the room. Seconds later she heard the angry banging of the front door. In its wake, his anger circled like a swarm of bees.

Martha and her mother sat in frozen silence. Any spark, any twitch might set off the inferno of her father's wrath. For a wild moment Martha was tempted to run after the young man, to ask his forgiveness for her father's narrow spite but a sense of self-preservation kept her sitting there. With an unusual, icy coolness, the Reverend Cavanagh rose from the table.

'I have much to do,' he announced. 'I shall be in my study and then I must go to the prison. I am not on any account to be disturbed.' With that he too swept from the room leaving disturbed feelings strewn about like the aftermath of a storm.

Once outside, Gabriel's fury carried him along the route to the prison. On top of everything else, was he now to tell his uncle that his wife could not even have a Christian burial? In the event, he had a wasted journey for the gaoler would not let him in. As he argued, he cursed himself for having spent the shilling the night before. Here was his punishment for drinking in Isaac's house, for with the money he might well have bribed his way in.

'Well, at least tell them that we are thinking of them,' he called out. 'Tell them that we are working towards their release.'

The gaoler smirked at the words and Gabriel, worn down by exhaustion, accepted defeat.

He took another route back leading towards Ephraim's shop. The memory of the vicar's bile, the implacable insensitivity of the gaoler, fuelled his anger. It was going to take a lot of will power not to be drawn into doing something foolhardy. The journey seemed twice as far as before. He kept hoping that someone would come along and give him a ride, but the road was empty.

When he reached the shop, both Ephraim and Betsy were there.

'You look exhausted,' said Betsy. 'Did — how did the night go?'

He resisted the urge to say that no one had disturbed him, for such a remark, even in jest, would only cause her pain.

'All was well,' he answered instead.

'When will be the funeral?'

He kept his voice gentle.

'If the vicar has his way there will be no funeral — not at the church,' he said. 'The minister says they are not part of his flock.'

At Gabriel's words Ephraim, who had been working at his bench stitching a pair of brogues, flung them aside.

'That's enough! I'm going to see some of the others. Aunt Sarah is entitled to be buried in the churchyard and buried she will be.'

For once Gabriel was in agreement with his cousin. The vicar was a stranger to the village. The Lawlesses had lived there all of their lives as had their ancestors before them. It was time they took charge of their own affairs.

Gabriel realized that he was feeling hungry. Betsy had baked a barley-loaf which he could smell, mouth-wateringly nearby. He was glad when Ephraim suggested that they should eat. There was a little cheese too, enough for the four of them to share, for young Matthew was of course there, playing listlessly with a box of buckles near to the fire.

Gabriel looked at the young boy, at his sad, drawn little face, bereaved of both parents. There and then he decided two things — that his father should be brought home safe and well, and that his mother should have a decent burial.

★ ★ ★

That night, under cover of darkness, Gabriel and Ephraim, along with two local men, Tobias Barnes and Jonas Mercer carried Sarah's coffin to the churchyard. Tobias and Jonas were members of Isaac's congregation. Had events turned out otherwise, they would by now have been sworn in as members of the Friendly Society. Instead, circumstances had kept them away on the fateful evening.

Burials at night were not unusual but there was no one around to witness Sarah's interment. The churchyard felt different at night. The peace of the day seemed transformed into menace by the darkness. The tombstones, mementoes of past lives, became hunters, threatening to ambush the men as they struggled along the path between the graves. The sound of an owl caused them all to jump.

It was a relief to put the coffin down for even though it was made of thin wood Sarah and the babe were surprisingly heavy. Between them, Ephraim and Gabriel began to dig a plot, not in the main part of the cemetery where all the current graves were, but across the pathway where the growth was undisturbed. Gabriel had already decided upon the spot, for in the spring this area was alive with cowslips and cow-parsley. Overhead the hawthorn blossomed white in Maytime and would drench Sarah's resting place with petals. By summer the nearby hedge would be pink with dog roses while the ragged robin and cornflowers would cover her like a quilt. In autumn, michaelmas daisies and golden rod would surround her with a canopy of purple and gold. This was a good place for her to be.

It was hard work. The soil had been undisturbed for generations. Underneath, the recent rain had made the clay heavy as lead but on the surface it was frosty. He had no idea that six feet was such a long way down.

When it was done, they lowered Sarah into the ground. Neither Gabriel nor Ephraim had the words or the belief to conduct a ceremony and it was Tobias who led them in prayer, which seemed right somehow, for this was what Isaac would have wanted. Afterwards they each dropped a handful of soil into the hole and said their goodbyes. Tobias had fashioned a crucifix to mark the place, with Sarah's name on it, and also that of the baby, and the date. When they had done they filled in the hole and went home.

First thing the next morning Gabriel's sleep was disturbed by the sound of insistent knocking on Isaac's door. He scrambled from his bed, his heart resisting this sudden intrusion into its gentle slumber. As he pushed the door open he saw the Reverend Cavanagh, his face almost purple with rage.

'You! I am going to have you arrested for trespass and criminal damage. How dare you! How *dare* you interfere with the burial ground.' He was so angry as to be almost incoherent and his fury gave the younger man a perverse sense of pleasure.

Gabriel waited until he stopped to draw breath then he spoke.

'Vicar, if you want my aunt removed from her rightful place in the churchyard, then you dig her up,' he said. With that he shut the door in the vicar's face. It was a good feeling, although one he feared he might come to regret.

Later that afternoon Gabriel was patching up a leak in the thatch of the roof when he heard noises in the lane below him. He looked down to see the village constable at the gate.

He clambered down and nodded a greeting to the man, thinking that he had come to tell him what had been decided about the prisoners. Already he was wondering how, if the men were charged, he would find the money to pay for their fines. He was therefore not prepared for what the officer said.

'Gabriel Lawless, I am arresting you, on the charge that on the eleventh day of November you did help your uncle, Isaac Lawless to administer an illegal oath to . . . ' He began to list the names of the men who had been at the cottage on that fateful evening.

He should have been prepared but the accusation took him so much by surprise that he couldn't think fast enough. What were the advantages in denying the charge? Should he name Ephraim as the other man? His reasons for doing so would have little to do with the truth and more to do with his feelings about his cousin. Besides, what would Betsy think if she knew he was the one who had betrayed her husband? He remained silent.

'I'll have to ask you to come along of me, lad.' The constable's voice was not unkind. He was an ordinary man doing a difficult job. Gabriel bit back the desire to say 'It wasn't me,' and fetched his jerkin.

'You aren't going to give me any trouble, are you?' the constable asked.

Gabriel shook his head. 'I won't run away.'

When the constable mounted the horse he fell into step beside him.

'Can we let Ephraim Carter, my cousin know?' he asked. It wasn't far out of their way and he thought that when Ephraim heard, it would be up to him to decide whether or not to tell the truth.

The constable nodded. He pushed the horse forward and Gabriel walked at its shoulder. In some way, the presence of the animal, its strength, its shape and smell, brought some small comfort.

'What did you hope to gain by such behaviour?' the constable asked.

Gabriel had no answer, except to say:

'You of all people must know how bad things are for the labouring men.'

'Aye, they are bad indeed, but you won't make them any better by breaking the law.'

'We didn't know we were breaking the law.'

The officer shrugged. 'You had better save that for the jury.'

When they reached the shop, the constable dismounted and they both went inside. Ephraim was alone, supping tea, seated close to his fireplace. From habit Gabriel looked through into the living-room to see if Betsy was there but in the circumstances he was glad that she was not.

'Cousin?' Ephraim frowned at him, standing up as they came in. Gabriel had no chance to speak to him alone so he shook his head to warn him that there was trouble.

'I am being arrested,' he said. 'For being the other man at the cottage.'

Ephraim blanched. His eyelids flickered.

Gabriel thought of what he had warned about being the only one who could continue to keep Betsy and Matthew fed and sheltered. When they had talked before, his warning had included Sarah and her baby but they no longer needed protection. Nevertheless, the prospects for Gabriel's employment were uncertain. In any case, even with three mouths rather than five to feed, the wages that Daniel Bridle paid him would not be enough. Another thought occurred to him. If Ephraim was in prison the shop might have to be sold to pay for his fine. Worse, with Isaac arrested, Sir Jenison might well decide to take back the cottage and then, on top of everything else, they would all be homeless.

'Don't say anything,' he whispered.

Ephraim nodded to show that he understood. Behind him, the constable stamped impatiently and already Gabriel could hear the bars of the gaol ringing shut behind him.

★   ★   ★

On the long walk to the prison Gabriel took comfort from the thought that at least he would be locked away with his kin. The conditions in the cells might be bad but it would be good to be once more with Uncle Isaac. In spite of all Isaac had suffered, he knew that his uncle's strong belief in his own innocence and his sense of justice would see them all through. He consoled himself with the thought that when the grief of Aunt Sarah's death tormented him he in turn could tell Isaac about the funeral. Isaac would like the thought of her there, in that leafy sanctuary. For once, Gabriel could be the one to offer support and comfort.

On their arrival however, he found himself subject to the most ungentle treatment. His clothes were taken from him and his head was shorn, the blunt blade of the razor tearing the skin. He protested but it was in vain. Thereafter, worse was to come for a set of shackles and manacles was produced. The memory of that last time in prison, the chafing of the iron against his skin, the hated rattle of the chains, threatened to unman him. His breath came in ever greater bursts as if he had to fill his lungs to overflowing to hold back the darkness.

'Why are you treating me as a criminal? I have been found guilty of no crime.'

The gaoler looked at him with a slow, cynical smile.

'They have already decided that you are guilty, lad.'

The last act was the worst, for once the restraints were in place he was led away to a single cell and locked away from his kin. The realization that he was to be kept apart shook the last remnants of his courage.

'Where's my uncle?' he shouted, but the gaoler did not reply, instead closing the door with a menacing clunk.

The space was so small that even if he sat on the floor there was no room to stretch out his legs. Already the shackles were doing their worst. He could do little more than crouch down, resting his head against the cold slime of the wall. The only small comfort was a narrow window at head height that let in a modicum of light and air.

He stayed awake all night, the combination of anxiety and the cramped conditions giving little respite. Trying to take some small control over his future he resolved to tell the truth as far as possible. As long as the magistrates thought that he was the missing man, he would not disappoint them.

The next morning he was taken to the recorder's house for questioning. He realized then why he had been kept apart from his kin for this way they could not have agreed upon a story.

He found himself facing a bench of three men. He immediately recognized Squire Wetherby seated on an ornate chair in the centre of a raised dais. A young man whom he did not know sat to his right and a minister whom he took to be the vicar for the parish of Lower Rising was on his left. It was Squire Wetherby who was the spokesman.

'Where were you on the night of November the eleventh?' he started.

'At home.'

'At home *sir*. And where is that?'

Gabriel told him.

'Who was with you?'

'Some friends.'

'What friends?' There was irritation in his voice.

Gabriel thought of the men who had been there that evening and who were now in the gaol. He did not reply.

'What were you doing?' This time it was the young man who spoke. As Gabriel turned to face him he sensed that here indeed was trouble. He was certainly younger than Gabriel, perhaps eighteen years of age. There was a plumpness about him, a softness of body that sat at odds with the cruel, downward turn of his mouth. The sound of his light, lisping voice made him shiver. He wanted to ask his name but thought better of it.

'We had met together to discuss forming a friendly society,' Gabriel said.

'To what purpose?'

'To protect ourselves in the event that any of us found ourselves without work.'

'To hold your masters to ransom, don't you mean — is that not it?' The youth looked down at him with contempt and Gabriel found his anger rising.

'No. We wanted to set up a fund so that we would not find ourselves destitute if trouble struck us. It was a way of ensuring that no matter what happened we should not starve.'

He glanced at the minister, who took up the questioning.

'If that was so, why did you feel the need to administer an illegal oath?'

Gabriel shook his head. 'We did not know that it was illegal. We merely thought that if we made the occasion solemn, the men would feel more obliged to abide by their commitment.'

'Whose idea was it, to set up this society?' The minister spoke the last word as if it was something dirty.

'It was something that we all agreed upon.'

'But someone must have organized it.'

Gabriel shook his head again. 'I don't know.'

'You must know, man. You were one of the men administering the oath. Was it you who planned it?'

He did not answer.

'Another thing.' The questioning came again from the young man. 'How many men were there present on that evening?'

Gabriel hesitated. 'Nine or ten.'

'Can you name them?'

'I forget.'

The questioner snorted impatiently. 'And where were you on the evening that Sir Jenison's property was destroyed?'

'What evening might that have been?'

'You know well enough.' The young man sat up straight and stared down at Gabriel. 'Where were you?'

Gabriel shrugged. He took a deep breath. 'I was at home with my family,' he said.

'Prove it.'

Again he shrugged. 'How can I do so? They will tell you but I doubt that they will be believed.'

The questioning continued, bouncing from one to another of the three men. Sometimes two of them would question him at once, leaving him no time to fashion an answer. As far as possible he stuck to the truth.

At the end of a very long time they seemed to sense defeat. Whatever it was that they wanted him to say, he had not satisfied them.

'Right,' said Squire Wetherby, sitting back. 'You will be charged along with the other felons. We have already referred the case to the next assizes.' He nodded to the gaoler who had been standing at the back of the room to take him away.

It was only when he was back in the cubby-hole of a cell that he realized he had not even asked what the charge was to be.

*   *   *

Jonathon Gordon came to see him that same afternoon. As he was led to the conversation room the sound of the chains, the incessant clanking, the weight like a millstone, filled him with a black sense of shame and outrage. Already he was humiliated, charged and found guilty without even the pretence of waiting for the trial.

The room contained a table and two chairs. Gabriel sat facing the solicitor, the silence punctuated only with the rattling of the fetters. Jonathon's face was tense and from his expression it was clear that they were in serious trouble.

'Let me get one thing straight,' he started.

'Were you or were you not at Isaac Lawless's cottage on the night of the swearing in?'

'I was.' He reasoned that he had been there later in the evening so in this he was telling the truth.

Jonathon shook his head. 'That is not what I hear. At the time that the other men were engaged in swearing an oath to form a friendly society not one of the accused has mentioned your name.' He leaned forward. 'You need to be careful. If you were not present then questions might be asked about whether you make a habit of being out and about. They might ask for example where you were on the night of the machine-breaking.' He sat back and sighed. 'Mr Lawless, they are determined to punish you all for something, for anything. If they can pin both charges on to you or your friends then they will be doubly pleased. If you lie to me, I cannot help you or your comrades. What will you gain by lying about such a thing?'

Gabriel shrugged, having no way of explaining to him the complex feelings that bound him to his family.

'What do you think will happen to us?' he asked.

Jonathon held out his hands in a 'who knows' gesture.

'You must know that the charge of

machine-breaking would mean a death sentence. The charge of taking an oath should carry only a fine. The charge of administering it however will be viewed more seriously.'

Gabriel was immediately haunted by the spectre of imprisonment. He sought for some inner courage. A month, perhaps three, even six months he would endure. Besides, it was likely that Isaac and he, as the guilty parties would be together. It might not be as bad as he feared.

He looked up at Jonathon and the lawyer's face was troubled. In response to Gabriel's raised eyebrows he made a visible effort to throw off whatever bothered him.

'No matter,' Jonathon said, then in an attempt to be jocular: 'the masters might not like you but they can't hang you for that. Take courage, my friend. I will see you in court.'

19

Martha learned of Gabriel's arrest later that day.

Her father brought the news on his return from the gaol. He could not hide his pleasure.

'I knew it. I knew that those Lawlesses were involved in all the troubles.' He sat back with a big, self-satisfied sigh. 'Well, they'll get what's coming to them now.'

'What will happen to them?' The words were out before she could stop them.

'What will happen, young lady, is that they will be tried and found guilty and imprisoned.' With malicious pleasure he added, 'I shouldn't be surprised if they are found guilty of the riots and burnings and are all hanged.'

He watched her for her reaction. She tried to outstare him. She alone knew the truth about where Gabriel had been on the night of the machine-breaking and she alone had the power to save him. The knowledge reassured yet terrified her.

From somewhere she found some inner strength.

'I need to go out,' she said.

'And where to?'

'To the haberdasher's. I have a little project in mind for the church. I am going to make a tapestry listing all the ministers who have served this parish, ending up with you, Papa.'

Her father's eyes narrowed. 'You can go another time.'

'But I need to get some materials so that I can start now.'

Her father hesitated. Martha held his gaze, keeping her own steady.

'I shall not be long,' she added.

'Then do not be.'

As she fetched her cape, her confidence was undermined by darker thoughts. Perhaps Gabriel *was* the one who had destroyed the threshing-machine. Perhaps he had set fire to the barn. He had been in the woods, less than a mile away from where it happened. If he was guilty, however, she reasoned that he was very calm when he found her and he had been prepared to take her right to her door. Surely a guilty man would have tried to hide away? There was only one thing to do, to go and see Jonathon and tell him everything. He was the only one whom she could trust.

When she arrived at the offices of Perkiss & Rowhampton, Jonathon was transparently pleased to see her, ordering a hot drink to be brought, for the weather was cold.

'Well, Miss Cavanagh, and how can I help you?' His manner was immediately professional and he sat behind his desk. In the face of the openness, the candour of his expression, all her composure seemed to desert her.

'Have you heard the news?' she blurted out. 'Mr Gabriel Lawless has been arrested.'

He nodded. 'I have heard. I will be the one to defend him, along with the rest of the accused.'

She took a deep breath. 'I need to see him. Can you arrange it for me?'

He continued to look at her with a strange, questioning expression on his face.

'Why would that be, Miss Cavanagh?'

She tried to summon some dignity from somewhere.

'I know that Mr Lawless was not at the cottage when he claims to be,' she said.

'And how do you know that?'

She blushed painfully. 'Because he was with me.'

Jonathon's face still wore that same expression but his jaw tightened. Too late she remembered her thoughts that he might indeed nurse some feeling towards her. For the moment she pushed them aside.

'If I could see him,' she said, 'I could . . . ' She wasn't really sure what she could do. She could ask him outright what he had been doing, whether he was the man who had set light to the barn. She was sure that she would know whether he was telling the truth. If he was not guilty she would give him an alibi, stand up in court and risk derision and condemnation. She did not care. She would think of some good reason why they should have been together. That way he could not be charged with anything.

Jonathon sighed. 'I really would not advise you to take this course of action. For a start, if you do so you may be called upon to give evidence before the court.'

'Then if necessary I shall do so. The truth is more important than anything, would you not agree?'

'Is it?' He sat back and sighed. 'The men will be charged tomorrow. Your father will be one of the men on the grand jury. That has already been decided. It would put you in a very difficult position to be giving evidence against the charge that your father has been instrumental in bringing.'

'But I must! Don't you see?' She began to grow angry. 'I thought you cared about the poor people. I thought you would want to defend them against untrue charges.'

He began to look impatient.

'I do and I will. I am already giving of my

time — and risking my reputation, to see that justice is done. After all, if I earn notoriety as a champion of the poor, then the rich are hardly likely to employ me.'

He stood up and came round the desk. With a sigh he sat down on the edge of it, close to her. She could see the muscles of his thighs moving against his breeches as he crossed his legs. She had not noticed before that although his legs were long, they were also very muscular.

'I hoped you would trust me, Miss Cavanagh,' he said. 'If we are lucky, the men will suffer no more than a fine. Should that happen you will be able to help them to pay the cost. Besides, I think you should respect the fact that Gabriel Lawless might have his own reasons for saying that he was somewhere when he was not.'

'I think it might be to protect me,' she started and Jonathon smiled his disbelief.

'That would be a very noble gesture. Very noble indeed.'

Tears of frustration began to gather in her eyes. Perhaps he was right. She wanted to believe that Gabriel would go to such lengths to protect her, but would he? She remembered how he had shouted at her, the anger he felt with her father. Why should he risk his own welfare to protect hers?

Jonathon reached out a well-manicured hand and patted her on the shoulder.

'You must not worry so much about him — about them. If the case goes badly we can review your evidence again. In the meantime, as you are here, I have some ideas about alternative investments for you. Perhaps you would like to look at them now.'

'No. I don't care. You do what you think.'

He stood up. 'Certainly not. This is your money we are talking about, your future. You must never blindly trust anyone else with something so important.'

She nodded, chastened by his advice. He went to his desk and retrieved a pile of documents, spreading them out before her. Carefully he explained what it all entailed, all the advantages and the risks. She kept nodding to show that she understood but she was not really listening. It struck her that when he was talking about something he felt passionate about, or when he was addressing her in a professional capacity his stutter totally disappeared.

As if to illustrate the point, he ended by saying:

'By investing some of your money in this way you will be helping some of the more vulnerable members of our society. I myself have money in the same scheme.' At this moment he caught her eye and his speech faltered.

'You — you must of c-course think about your own w-welfare.'

His face was quite close to her and she looked at the dark shadow that marked the extent of his beard. He had a long irregular face. Both his jaw and his nose twisted very slightly towards the left. It made him look as if he was permanently smiling at some secret thought. He ran his hand through his perpetually dishevelled hair in a way that she now recognized as being from habit.

Thoughts of Gabriel, of the troubles ahead were still foremost in her mind. She thought how comforting it would be to turn to Jonathon Gordon and have him hug her. It was such a long time since anyone had put their arms about her in a gesture of affection. She realized that he was the sort of big brother she had dreamed about when she was young.

'D-do you want time to think about it?' he asked, indicating the documents.

She shook her head.

'Please go ahead,' she said.

At the door he held out his hand to shake hers. His expression was kindly as he spoke,

'Rest assured that I will do everything in my power to see that justice is done. And I

272

will keep you informed of all developments.'

'You are very kind.'

She didn't know what possessed her, but as she went to pass him to take her leave, she leaned up and kissed him on the cheek!

★ ★ ★

The following morning the prisoners were removed from the gaol to the county court. As a concession the shackles were taken off but instead they were chained together in one line, a guard before and aft. Gabriel felt like a peep-show, as people, ordinary people, many of whom he knew, came to gawp at them.

'Brothers and sisters,' Isaac called out to the bystanders. 'Do not believe all that you see. We may be chained like criminals but we have been convicted of no crime. Indeed, we have committed no crime, as God is our witness.'

There was a murmur of discontent among the crowd and Gabriel sensed that the guards grew uneasy. Isaac's voice was persuasive and to silence him, he received a blow across the shoulders for his pains. The men were urged to walk faster.

It was a miserable journey. Already the men were cold and hungry. Chivvied along by their escort they felt like cattle being driven to

— to their slaughter. The image was not a good one to choose. When they arrived, more disappointment awaited them.

If the cells at Chantry were bad, at the courthouse they were worse, being below ground-level and with little light and less air. For Gabriel the one comfort was in being back with his kin, for on this occasion they were all crowded in together, although there was insufficient room for more than half of them to lie down at any one time.

Within the hour they were bustled up the narrow stairs and into the courtroom. The room was empty except for the jury members and the officers. It was with sinking heart that Gabriel recognized some of their number. Sir Jenison Bowler, Squire Wetherby, the Reverend Cavanagh, the young man who had earlier questioned him and who turned out to be Sir Jenison's son.

As in all such situations, Gabriel found respite by distancing himself from what was happening. He viewed the proceedings as some sort of interesting performance, as if the outcome was of little importance. Looking at Sir Jenison, it struck him as curious that the man rumoured to be his half-brother, and the son who would therefore be his nephew, should be carrying out this interrogation. If he did not like the father, the look of the son was infinitely worse. With a chilling realization he thought that he should not wish to be at the boy's mercy — and yet he was.

They elected Isaac to be their spokesman.

To the first question: What were you doing on the evening of November the eleventh? Isaac told them clearly and simply that, in order to protect themselves from any disaster that might befall them the agricultural labourers had been in the process of setting up a friendly society. He explained about the constitution with a secretary and treasurer and how the money collected would be used to support the members in case of sickness or lack of work.

'On that evening of November the eleventh we were all at my cottage for this purpose,' he concluded.

Next they asked about the damage to Sir Jenison's threshing-machine.

'We have discussed this honestly together,' said Isaac. 'Every one of us is prepared to swear on the Bible that he took no part in such an attack. I am therefore certain that this is the truth.'

One by one the same question was put to each man and without fail each confirmed the story.

Next, Michael Cooper was brought into the court for cross-examination. He looked terrified. As the questions were put to him he could barely answer. What emerged was a simple statement. That he had been at Isaac's cottage on that evening, although he did not know what for. That he had been blindfolded and forced to swear on oath that he would tell no one about what had taken place.

'What did take place?' Sir Jenison asked him.

'I had a hood put over my head sir. I — was made to place my hand on what felt like a book.'

'Then what happened?'

'Some words was said. I don't know what they was but I was made to swear on my children's lives that I wouldn't tell no one what had happened.'

'And did you swear?'

'I had to, sir. I was that scared.'

'Can you name all the men who were there?' asked Sir Jenison.

'I . . . ' Michael looked frightened. He glanced across to see if the men were listening, to gauge whether they were likely to attack him.

'Come along man,' Sir Jenison added impatiently. 'These were local people. You must know who they were.'

'I — uh.'

Sir Jenison said, 'Was Isaac Lawless present?'

Michael nodded.

'Was . . . ' Sir Jenison began to call out names. When he got to Joseph and James, Michael nodded again.

'You are certain that they were there?'

'I — I think I am, sir.'

Sir Jenison sighed in frustration. 'Was Gabriel Lawless present?' he added as an afterthought. 'Was he one of the men who administered the oath to you?'

Like a rabbit cornered by a weasel, Michael hunched his shoulders in a paroxysm of panic.

'I . . . ' His eyes found Gabriel out. Gabriel gave a single nod of his head, encouraging him to answer. Again Michael nodded and Sir Jenison sat down, flinging his list aside.

The questioning over, Michael was led away, the jury members retired from the court and the men were left to wait. The restless pacing of the accused, the clinking of the shackles, the whispered excitement of those members of the public who crowded the gallery, told of the tension that awaited the outcome.

'What do you think is going to happen?' whispered Gabriel to his uncle.

'Who can tell, son. If the government has

anything to do with it, we'll certainly be tried.'

Surely the government could not be interested in the happenings in Midwillow? Gabriel remained silent.

After an eternity, the jury returned and when asked if they found a true bill, their foreman declared that they had. In due course, an indictment would be drawn up and a grand jury summoned to hear the case.

'It's as I feared,' said Isaac. 'They intend to make an example of us.'

Rattling their way back to the cells Gabriel thought: let's look on the bright side, they can't hang us for it.

The next day Isaac and Gabriel were fetched to the conversation room where Jonathon Gordon was waiting to see them. By his expression they knew that the news was bad.

'The charges have been decided,' Jonathon started. 'You two men will be charged with administering an illegal oath. The rest will be charged with taking it.'

'And the machine-breaking?'

'That has been dropped. For the moment they are saying that it was carried out by *persons unknown*.'

Gabriel felt the tension drain away. Jonathon had said that the administering of an oath would be regarded as a misdemeanour. He waited for him to confirm that they would probably receive a fine, not even a prison sentence, but his expression remained grave.

'In the normal course of events,' he said, 'you would be charged under the 1799 Act, whereby you would be accused of belonging to an 'unlawful confederacy'. That indeed would bring a maximum fine of twenty pounds and three months in gaol. As it is however, it has been decided that you will be charged under the 1797 Act and this is much more serious indeed.'

'How?'

Jonathon sat back and his voice was neutral. 'This act was introduced a few years back, at the time of the naval mutinies. It was intended to give the courts maximum power to crush such an uprising.' He paused and looked from one man to the other. 'The charge under this act is sedition and treason.'

Gabriel's brow creased in disbelief. Jonathon would not be joking about such a thing, but the idea that they, Uncle Isaac and his cousins, would be planning the overthrow of the government was laughable. Only Jonathon wasn't laughing.

'My friends,' he said. 'I fear you must prepare yourself for the worst.' As if pronouncing sentence he added: 'it is abundantly clear that the powers that be intend to make an example of you.'

For two days they were left to languish in the filth of the cells. For the first time it seemed that even Isaac was defeated.

'What's going to happen Gabriel? What's going to happen to young Matthew, to all the families?'

Gabriel did not know. 'Try not to worry, Uncle. Ephraim will look after them.'

After a long silence Isaac spoke,

'My poor girl is with child,' he said. 'What will become of her?'

'She has her husband.' It hurt to say it. From Isaac's silence Gabriel guessed that his uncle drew small comfort from the knowledge.

Every time Gabriel closed his eyes the enormity of his situation hit him anew. Should he tell the truth? What would be best for Betsy? For all his shortcomings, was not Ephraim the best hope the others had of being fed and housed and clothed? Betsy's face came back to him. She was so beautiful, so precious beyond words, that only her welfare mattered. Slowly the seconds, the hours ticked by and he was no nearer to resolving his torment.

He was still undecided when they were

once more taken to the court. Perhaps some external force would make the decision for him.

After the gloom of the cells, the light and the hubbub assaulted his eyes and ears. As they were led into the dock he felt a grinding sense of shame. Here they were, dressed in prison garb, their heads shorn like common felons, bound hands and feet. The injustice of the situation made his head swim.

Unlike their previous visit, the court was packed full. Gabriel did not raise his eyes to see who might be there. Once again he tried to pretend to himself that they were not present at all and that the whispered voices were all inside his head.

As the grand jury was sworn in, however, he looked at Isaac in dismay. To a man those chosen were unlikely to have any sympathy for their cause. Daniel Bridle was one of those nominated but he was turned down on the grounds that he was a dissenter. It did not bode well.

In his opening speech, the judge under-lined that the crimes of which the men were accused were to be treated with great seriousness. He laid emphasis on the fact that people who threatened the social order could expect little mercy. Surely it was not the judge's job to express his own views?

The charges were read out. Much of it Gabriel couldn't understand but, watching Jonathon's unfolding expressions of disbelief, dismay and disapproval, he knew that they could expect little sympathy. Next to Jonathon, the prosecuting council, a man of middle years, looked solid, confident, a veritable part of the social order that they were accused of trying to overturn.

As the case got under way the questioning and statements seemed like a repetition of their earlier appearance. Michael Cooper was again paraded before the jury. Today he seemed more confused than ever. He could not remember the date of the meeting. He could not remember who was there or what was said. In the end, the prosecuting lawyer read out a statement that he had made earlier, naming all the men and saying how he had been forced into taking an oath.

'Is this a true account of what took place?'

'I think so, your lordship.' Michael, poor simple Michael, was relieved not to have to think about what had happened any longer. No matter what was read out, he would agree.

'So you confirm that you did swear an oath to keep the society's nefarious activities a secret?'

Michael looked puzzled. It seemed unlikely

that he knew what the word 'nefarious' meant. Indeed, Gabriel did not know himself.

'Well, man? Did you swear or didn't you?'

Michael nodded. 'I — I think I did, sir.'

The prosecuting council slapped the document from which he had been reading on the table with a flurry of triumph.

'Proof enough, I think,' he said. The statement was put forward as evidence of their wrongdoing.

When it was Jonathon's turn, he stood up and began to stroll around the court, his head raised as if he was deep in thought.

After a while he spoke.

'I wonder what secrets the newly formed friendly society wanted to keep so badly that they were prepared to go to such lengths?' he said. 'Did they perhaps intend to kidnap someone — the squire perhaps? Or might they have been planning to take over the government?' He stopped and surveyed the accused as if looking for proof of their dangerous intentions.

'I think, at the last count, there were ten of them.' He went through the motion of counting them, nodding to confirm that they were indeed ten. 'You see them here before you, gentlemen. They must certainly be dangerous characters if they could undertake such a feat as a revolution without help at least from an army.'

He paused and looked around the room to gather everyone's attention.

'Allow me to read to you from the constitution that was drawn up for the society on the night of November eleventh, all quite legally.' He picked up a paper from the table in front of him and held it out theatrically. He read:

'*The object of this society can never be promoted by any act of violence or by breaking the law*. Does that sound like the work of a group of desperadoes who are looking to carry out acts of terror — or is such a charge too absurd to contemplate?'

He continued to point out that the act under which they were being charged was never intended to apply to this situation.

'This is a political charge, gentlemen, and one that should never have been brought. If you believe in justice and in the fairness of our legal system, you will not find the prisoners guilty of any crime other than over-enthusiasm. In seeking to keep their union safe they asked the members to take an oath. The fact that such an oath-taking is not permitted by law is something that they would not have known and is really only a minor offence.'

Listening to him, Gabriel thought that the

sense of what he said was so self-evident that even those who feared them could not in all honesty take the charges seriously.

Isaac had prepared a statement and when Jonathon finished his deliberations, he asked if the accused wished to add anything.

'I do, sir.' Isaac's statement was passed to the judge.

'You wish this to be read out?' his worship asked, glancing at it as if it was something distasteful.

'I do, sir,' Isaac repeated.

The judge turned to the jury and began to gabble what Isaac had written. He raced though it and Gabriel could not hear what he said, even though he already knew the content of the paper.

As the men mumbled their disquiet they were ordered to be silent and moments later the jury were leaving their benches to consider their verdict.

The men were taken back to the cells but they were not there long. Within what seemed like minutes they were returned to the dock. In that same moment, the jury members returned.

Once more, the charge was read out to them and the question asked; 'Have you reached a verdict upon which you are all agreed?'

'We have, my lord.' The foreman stood up.

'And your verdict is?'

'Guilty.'

Amid the clamour, in the emptiness that surrounded them Gabriel was aware of only one thing. Somewhere in his mind a woman's voice let out a long, scream of distress. His eyes settled upon his cousin Betsy, standing alone, her face a picture of anguish.

Everything else faded away. All he could see was her agony, her beautiful brown eyes burning into him as she cried again and again:

'Gabriel, for God's sake, tell them the truth!'

★   ★   ★

They had to wait for two days for sentence to be passed. During that time they were confined once more in the dingy dungeon of the courthouse cells. In any circumstances such a wait would seem like a lifetime. With the prospect of their sentence hanging over them, it was like an eternity.

Something strange seemed to happen to them. To a man they appeared to have forgotten that they could be facing the ultimate penalty of the law. Instead the conversation continued around how long they

286

might get and where they would be sent to serve their time.

Some of them came near to striking wagers as to what would be decided. In respect for Uncle Isaac, though, they desisted from gambling any assets they might have left in the outside world.

'I think three months maximum.'

'No. They mean to punish us. I say six.'

'I think they'll send us away from here so that our kin cannot stir up trouble in the neighbourhood.'

Winchester was the favourite choice of destination.

Jonathon came to see them but he wasn't saying much. Gabriel thought that he too was trying to convince himself that the unimaginable could not happen.

When at last they were called, the court was again full to capacity, for the trial had aroused great interest. The opening words of the judge sank what little hope of mercy that they had until now hung on to.

'In considering this case, there has been very little need to weigh up the circumstances surrounding the crimes committed by the accused. Those circumstances are self-evident. The men brought before this court are dangerous. They are a part of the rebellion that is even now sweeping the south of England and that in its turn is part of the urban unrest that is plaguing our towns to the north. With such men on the loose, our very way of life, the very traditions of England are under threat. Knowing this, I have no doubts about passing the extreme sentence. It is therefore my decision that the accused: Joseph Lawless, James Lawless, (in total eight names were read out), shall be taken from this court to Portsmouth, there to be incarcerated in one of His Majesty's prison ships until such time as passage can be arranged on a ship to carry them to the territory of Australia. There they shall be held captive for a period of not less than seven years.'

A gasp of disbelief ricocheted around the courtroom.

'No!' The accused men called out from the dock, looking to someone, anyone to tell them that there had been a mistake.

All the while, Isaac and Gabriel stood in silence. Gabriel was aware that he had stopped breathing. Somehow, they had clasped each other's arms as they waited.

The judge took up another paper. Turning once more towards the dock, he began to read aloud. 'In sentencing Isaac Lawless and Gabriel Lawless, who have both been found guilty of administering an evil and seditious oath, I have no doubt as to what is a just sentence. It is my decision that they shall both be taken from here to a place of execution and there, at a time appointed, shall be hanged by the neck until they are dead. Thereafter, their heads shall be displayed outside the prison as a warning to anyone else thinking to threaten the security of our country. May God have mercy upon their souls. Take them down.'

Something happened then. Gabriel felt as if there was no one left in the room except for himself and Isaac. Only a few days before he had tormented Miss Cavanagh with a picture of how a hanged man slowly has the life choked out of him, how he struggles and kicks and gurgles. How his eyes bulge and his bladder lets go and his brain feels as if it will burst.

It couldn't be true. He was four-and-twenty. He had a whole lifetime of dreams to make into reality.

Some increasing crescendo of sound dragged him back into the real world. Everywhere there seemed to be shouting and chaos. The people in the court were screaming their anger, the sound rippling like a tide into the far distance. At this display he felt a moment of wonder that his fate should matter to anybody. He was no one of importance. Then he realized that it was what they represented that mattered — he and Isaac, ordinary men, not criminals.

At that moment they heard that there was further protest taking place outside. The word had already spread.

Joseph, James, the rest were quickly bundled back down the stairs into the bowels of the court. Gabriel and Isaac were left behind. The court usher was trying to clear the people out with help from the constable. For a moment Gabriel wondered whether they should not take their chances and make a break for the door but when he glanced at Isaac he seemed to be in a trance.

'Uncle?' He shook his sleeve but Isaac seemed incapable of taking in the situation.

From somewhere, a group of men armed with cudgels arrived and began to beat the protestors, driving them to the door. As the main door to the court was forced shut and barred, Jonathon came across.

'My friends,' he said. 'I am truly sorry, but do not despair. This is not the end. I have already lodged a formal protest. This has not been a fair trial. We will get a just resolution.'

Neither man answered. The gaolers came to escort them away and Jonathon stood back, waving his hand in a gesture that seemed to imply: *God go with you.*

Suddenly, over his shoulder, Isaac called out.

'Justice — that is all we want.'

Gabriel patted him on the shoulder. 'We will get it, Uncle, never you fear.'

Back underground, they were taken along a different corridor and led into another cell. It was about the same size as the previous one only here there were just the two of them.

'What about my sons?' asked Isaac. 'I want to see them.'

The gaoler, not an unkindly man, shook his head.

'I don't think that will happen. If you wish, I will say goodbye to them for you. By first light they are to be transported to Portsmouth.' He looked away, his shame at being a part of this travesty showing in his eyes. 'The authorities will want them as far away from here as quickly as possible,' he said with a helpless gesture. 'There's trouble brewing.'

As if to confirm his words, the continuing hubbub outside was drowned out by the spitting sound of gunfire, a chorus of shouts and screams and the harsh sound of boots on cobbles.

As the cell door slammed shut Gabriel turned to Isaac.

'We had better start praying,' he said, 'for I fear the trouble is only just beginning.'

20

Martha was writing a letter to her friend Rachael Masters when she heard the sound of a horse outside. She went to the window, from where she saw Jonathon slip from the saddle, loop the reins over a gate post and come towards the front door. She hastened to let him in herself.

'This is a surprise,' she started, then seeing his face she stopped. 'What is wrong?'

'I — I, th-the . . . ' Jonathon began to stutter then angrily shook his head. 'Th-the trial. It was a travesty. The men . . . '

'Gabriel?' Martha spoke without thinking, realizing too late the transparency of her thoughts.

Jonathon again struggled with his words. Eventually they came out in a rush.

'Eight of the men are sentenced to transportation. The others, Gabriel Lawless and his uncle are sentenced to — to be hanged.'

Her reaction was swift and violent. Her vision blurred, her very being seemed to lurch and her stomach rebelled against the news. Helplessly, shamefully she began to retch.

Jonathon took her by the shoulders and eased her into a chair.

'Breathe deeply, focus your mind on what can be done to help them.'

She found her head resting against his shoulder, his hand cradling her face as if to shield it from the horror of his words.

'I must see him. I must tell the truth.' Nothing mattered now except saving him.

'What truth?'

She closed her eyes.

'That it couldn't have been him. He — he was with me, you see.'

'When?'

'On the night of the machine-breakings.'

Jonathon shook his head.

'That is no longer the night in question. It is the night that the oath was taken. He . . . wasn't with you then — was he?'

She saw the fear in his eyes and knew that he was willing her not to have any involvement with Isaac Lawless's nephew. She didn't know what to say. All the time she knew that if it would help Gabriel then she would swear that he had been with her no matter when.

'I have already put in an appeal on behalf of all the men,' said Jonathon. 'We must hope that this will delay the transportation and it should ensure a temporary stay of execution.'

Execution! The very word made it difficult to breathe.

'Please, when can we go?' she asked.

He pulled away from her and stood up. She could sense his disappointment but she did not care.

'If — if you have anything important to tell w-we can go now. I have unrestricted access to the prisoners.' He hesitated before adding: 'You do realize that if Gabriel Lawless was indeed damaging the threshing-machine, or carrying out acts of arson, or even poaching, then the penalty would be much the same?'

She nodded.

'Well,' he said, taking her by the elbow. 'We had better go and find out.'

It was the first time that she had ever been to a prison. Head bowed she sheltered behind Jonathon as he arranged for their access. They were taken to a room to wait while the prisoner was fetched.

'Are you sure you know what you are doing?' Jonathon asked. 'Please, Miss Cavanagh, do not perjure yourself to help — this man. Your motives may be noble but you will be making trouble for yourself.'

'Thank you. I — I will only tell the truth, but please, I should like to see Mr Lawless alone.'

At that moment she heard the rattling of

chains and turning towards the door she watched in disbelief as Gabriel was escorted into the room. He had shackles about his legs and manacles about his wrists. His shaved head, the blood on his scalp where the razor had torn his skin repelled and frightened her.

He looked surprised at the sight of her and sank wearily on to the opposite stool. She glanced up at Jonathon and with obvious reluctance he withdrew.

'I want to help you,' she said, struggling with her words. 'Please tell me what you were doing in the woods on that night.' She risked a glance at him, then added: 'My testimony could set you free.' When he did not answer, she asked: 'Were you poaching?' When he still did not reply, she added; 'Or was it you who broke Sir Jenison's machine?'

That familiar smile of derision creased his mouth, humourless, dismissive. She noticed the paler lines on his face where the prison dirt had not permeated the tiny wrinkles that criss-crossed beneath his eyes.

'And if I said I was guilty?' he asked.

'I . . . ' She couldn't answer him.

'What do you want me to say, Miss Cavanagh?'

From somewhere she found some inner reserve of dignity.

'I want you to tell the truth,' she said. 'If

you are guilty of a crime, any crime, then there is nothing that I can do to help you. But if you are not, then I will say that you were with me on the evening that the barn was burnt — and if it helps, on the evening that the men swore the oath.'

He shrugged. 'It is very noble of you to risk your reputation to give me an alibi, but I do not think that you should do that.'

'But — '

'But nothing.' He seemed to be searching around for the right thing to say. With a mirthless little laugh, he went on: 'As you are so interested in my affairs, as you are so eager to help, then please believe me, you can only do so by keeping quiet. I have my own reasons for not saying where I was.'

'But, I ..'

He sat back and the chains rattled horribly as he moved his limbs. He seemed to make up his mind about something very important.

'I don't suppose it matters any more,' he said. 'I will tell you what you want to know, but if you repeat it, I shall deny it. As it is, it may shock you.'

She swallowed down her fear, dreading what he might be about to confess.

'I have been going out often in the evenings,' he said, 'not to poach or to burn barns, but I had my reasons. On the evening

296

of the meeting at my uncle's house, my cousin Ephraim, along with several others, was going to be there, to swear in the first members of the friendly society. It was my intention to join them but beforehand . . . but beforehand, I took the opportunity to visit Ephraim's shop.'

He raised his eyebrows, waiting for some response. She looked confused. 'You see, Miss Cavanagh,' he went on, 'with Ephraim away, I knew that my cousin Betsy would be alone. I wanted to see her. In fact I have been going on many evenings to stand outside their shop in the hope of catching a glimpse of her.' He looked up briefly and a small, embarrassed smile played about his lips.

'It was wrong of me I know, to visit a married woman while her husband was away but — well, the sad fact is that I love her. Even though she has married someone else, it makes no difference. My feelings are — beyond my control.'

Martha stared at him, willing him to stop. Of all the things he might have said, this was the worst. She did not want to hear any more but he was relentless.

'When I came back to Midwillow earlier this year from prison, Betsy was already betrothed to Ephraim Carter,' Gabriel continued. 'For a while I hoped that she might change her mind but the date for the marriage had already been set. In any case, she led me to believe that she was marrying him for her family's sake. As for me, well, in the circumstances, I had nothing to offer her.'

He leaned forward the better to hold her attention, as if it was important to him to make her understand.

'My uncle's family is poor,' he said. 'So poor that you could never conceive of such a thing. No matter how hard Isaac worked, no matter what pittance Joseph and James brought home, no matter that your father paid Betsy a few, insulting coppers, they were still too poor to put sufficient food on the table.' He fixed her with his desolate eyes, hunching his shoulders as if to ram home the futility of the situation.

'If Betsy married Ephraim it would mean one mouth less to feed. More than that, my cousin Ephraim is shrewd. He has some small success as a shoe-mender. He has a cottage that is his by right. He would be able to help the family in other ways.' He looked away and in his expression she saw the hopelessness that mirrored her own heart.

'I did not know what Betsy felt for me but I realized that it made no difference for I had nothing to offer her. So, I kept silent.'

For an eternity, it seemed, he stopped

speaking, lost in his own thoughts. At last he said; 'I wasn't the man who administered the oath, Miss Cavanagh, it was my cousin Ephraim, but the best thing I can do for Betsy is to leave her the support and security of her husband. In that way I hope that she will survive this disaster that has befallen the rest of our family. If you wish to do something for me you will say nothing. You might also ensure that no matter what the future holds, my cousin Betsy and her young brother are provided for.'

In the face of his confession she was out of her depth. She struggled to sound calm.

'Then it should be Ephraim Carter sitting in this cell instead of you?' she asked.

'That is not your concern.' His voice was sharp and he stood up, grasping at the hateful chains that weighed down his wrists.

'Now please don't think that I am ungrateful, Miss Cavanagh, but there is nothing you can do for me other than take care of what remains of my family. Thank you for coming and please excuse me.'

'I — I could marry you,' she called out. 'If you tell them that you were with me on both occasions I will confirm your story. Then they will have to release you. As — as my husband you would have enough money to help all your family.' Her feelings boiled over, shame and hope and a dozen other foolhardy emotions tumbling in the cauldron that was her heart.

He turned round and stared at her, then shook his head in disbelief.

'You are serious?'

She was too ashamed of her need to meet his eyes. He made a sound that was almost a laugh.

'I can't believe that you would be so foolish . . . ' he said.

When she remained silent, he sighed.

'Thank you, Miss Cavanagh, but no. Your kindness is overwhelming but — well, as I said, if you look after Betsy, that will be enough.'

'Gabriel, please!'

Ignoring her, he turned away and went to the door, banging on it with his manacled fist. In response the guard who had been lurking outside came to lead him away and she was left with the pain and humiliation of his rejection.

Outside, Jonathon waited for her. He stood up as she came into the outer room and she could see the concern on his face.

'Are you . . . ?'

'Thank you. I should like to go home now.'

In silence, in blessed silence, he escorted her back to the vicarage. He did not ask her what had passed between them and as the bitter realization of Gabriel's love for his cousin tore at her, she prayed that nobody would ever find out what she had proposed.

She stopped at the vicarage gate and turned to him.

'Please,' she said. 'I — I would prefer it if my parents do not learn of this afternoon's visit.'

Her cheeks betrayed her shame and Jonathon looked down at her with his sombre, gentle eyes.

'I will not tell them,' he said. 'But what of you? You are upset. I fear that, as with all of us, the heart sometimes rules the head.'

She could not speak so she nodded. He looked away and she saw a mirroring hurt in his eyes. Amid her own pain was room for one more thought — that Jonathon loved her.

* * *

Her father returned later that afternoon. Martha was in her room, too numbed by the disclosures at the gaol to do more than sit and gaze out of the windows on to the lawn. Like her mood, the garden was grey and bedraggled. A recent wind had wrought havoc with the flower-beds, crushing the fading stalks, scattering the few remaining petals to be trampled underfoot. In the winter months they employed no gardener and the grass was long and waterlogged.

Gradually she became aware of the sounds from downstairs, the aggressive sharpness of her father's footsteps, the irate way that doors opened and closed, the razorlike tone of his voice in answer to her mother's timid questions, although she could not hear what was being said. Moments later she heard him mount the stairs and her bedroom door flew open.

She resisted the instinct to leap to her fleet, instead gripping the arms of the chair and bracing herself.

'Papa?'

'So,' he said. 'That is what you have been up to all these weeks, is it? Whoring with the scum of the earth!'

'I . . . '

He was breathing heavily. With something resembling a roar, he strode across and wrenched her from the chair by her right arm. She cried out in pain and protest.

'I knew it! I knew that there was something not right with you,' he said. 'Already it is all around the village. They say that you have been to the prison and offered yourself to that scum, Lawless. How could you? What sort of evil has taken possession of you?'

'I have done nothing wrong,' she started, wondering who had betrayed her, but he continued:

'I have sent for the doctor. He will be here shortly. He will know how best to deal with you. In the meantime you will stay in your room. I don't know how your poor mother and I will ever live this down, but whatever it takes I will find a way to stop your madness.'

So saying, he pushed her back towards the chair and she fell against it. Her head rushed with blood, with emotion. Above all the chaos within, she heard only one thing, the turn of the key in the lock.

Hugging her arms about her, she had one thought — that like Gabriel, she was now a prisoner.

The doctor's carriage arrived within the hour. Martha watched from the window as he clasped his bag and hurried up to the front door. Moments later she heard a murmured conversation, her father's voice and the doctor's exchanging information. She could imagine what sort of a story her father might be telling him, of how her mind, always weak, had suddenly cracked and that she was no longer capable of governing her own affairs. She suddenly felt very afraid indeed.

She had heard stories of other girls, young women of good fortune who had been locked away for their own safety, when in reality it was to enable their grasping families to hang on to their wealth. Was this really the case with her father? Was he acting out of any motive other than concern for her welfare?

Her thoughts were disturbed by the approaching footsteps, the rattle of the key in the lock. Doctor Hughes came into her chamber with a false show of *bonhomie*, her mother, hovering like a phantom, to his rear.

'Ah, Miss Cavanagh. Your father tells me that you have been a little unwell of late. Shall we just see?'

Something about his manner awoke a dormant sense of outrage in her.

'There is nothing wrong with me. It is simply that my family and I have a difference of opinion. That does not make me sick.'

'Of course not. Now.' He laughed jovially, the sound grating on her nerves as he seated himself on the side of the couch. Paternal, indulgent, he tried to take her hand. She resisted the overture of friendship.

For a moment he continued to sit there, studying her. The expression on his face implied that perhaps her father was right and that there was indeed something contrary about her that called for treatment. She remembered that he had three, very demure daughters.

'I understand that lately you have taken to wandering out alone, Miss Cavanagh,' he started.

'What do you mean, *wandering?*' she asked.

He smiled indulgently. 'These are dangerous times, my dear. Someone such as yourself, a young lady of refinement, should not be away from home unescorted.'

She did not answer. Whatever she said would no doubt be twisted to imply some mental aberration.

'How is that ankle of yours?' asked the doctor. 'I seem to remember that you damaged it when you were out of the house. On a snowy night.'

Again she remained silent. Some inner sense of preservation warned her that she was in real danger of losing her freedom and indeed her future if she was not very careful.

'Doctor, I am sure that my father wants only the best for me,' she started. 'But I am equally sure you will appreciate that there are times when parents can become over anxious. I assure you that I am in perfectly good health, both in my mind and body.'

He nodded in agreement, cutting her short. She tried again.

'I am really sorry that you have been called out unnecessarily.'

Doctor Hughes stood up. 'Well, I shall come back tomorrow. In the meantime I am going to leave a phial of medication for you. You must take a draught now, and then three times daily. Your mama will administer it for it should not be treated lightly.' He gave another false little laugh. 'We would not want you to take too much, would we?'

She bit back the desire to say that she would not be taking any. Already she could imagine the conversation that would follow. Doctor Hughes agreeing with Papa that she was indeed unstable, that perhaps in the circumstances a few weeks in a 'retreat' would be beneficial.

He left with a cheery wave and after a few moments Mistress Cavanagh came back with a frightened expression and a tumbler of milk.

'Here, my dear. You just drink this now.'

She took it and sniffed it. It smelt strange, not like milk at all.

Her mother's eyes darkened with worry. 'Please drink it,' she said. 'Papa will be angry and it is for your own good.'

'I will, in a moment. At present I am sucking a lozenge for my throat.' Martha made the appropriate gestures with her mouth.

Her mother stood there uncertainly.

'Is — is it really true that you went to the prison and — and offered to marry that Lawless man? Please tell me that it isn't.'

'Who told you this?'

Her mother shook her head, clearly unable to contemplate her daughter's actions.

Martha sat back on the bed. 'Please do not worry, Mama. I — I am feeling a little tired so if you don't mind, I will go to sleep. I will drink the milk in a moment.' She saw how her mother glanced anxiously at the glass.

Seeing that there was nothing else to be done, Mistress Cavanagh moved towards the door.

'Sleep well then, my dear. And do, please, try not to upset Papa. He only has your welfare at heart.'

'I know.'

When her mother had gone she got up again and sat in the chair by the fireside, watching the flames lick and climb about the logs. Taking the glass she trickled the contents carefully to the back of the grate where it hissed and spluttered but did not douse the flames.

She had already made her plans. Her bedchamber was fortuitously situated over the front porch. She walked across and pulled back the curtain to look out. A strange, frosty light emanated from the hazy gloom. Below, the ground would be hard. However, it should not be too difficult to reach the roof of the porch and slide to the ground, although her ankle was still not fully healed.

Somehow she endured the eternity until she was certain that her parents had retired and were both asleep, then she tiptoed across the room and opened the casement.

Her outdoor clothes were in the closet in the hall. She did however have a thick shawl and her slippers, although not really suitable, would have to do.

With an intake of breath she opened the window wide, scrambled on to the sill and then lowered herself out and on to the apex of the porch, sitting astride it like a horse. When she had gathered sufficient courage she tilted herself forward and slid down the side, grasping at branches as she went until she hit the ground with a thump.

The sound reverberated like thunder to her anxious ears but no one came to investigate. Stiffly she picked herself up, wincing at the resulting pain in her foot, and began to hurry away. Breathing heavily she stood in the shadows. Her mind burned with the question of who had betrayed her. Other than Gabriel, who could have heard the conversation. Had he told his companions about what she had proposed. Had they laughed about it, laughed

308

at her for her stupidity? She ached with misery. Gently she tiptoed her way out of the shrubbery and towards the gate. There was only one place to go — to Jonathon Gordon's.

Happily there was a full moon and no wind so in spite of the slippery conditions underfoot and the strange other-world feeling to the countryside at night, she found her way without mishap.

As she drew near to the outer wall of Jonathon's house, the reality of what she was doing hit home. What would Jonathon's parents think? She remembered with trepidation that his father too was a physician. What if Doctor Hughes's diagnosis was correct and she really was losing her sanity? Would Doctor Gordon insist that she be returned home, to be confined in a sanatorium until such time, if ever, that she made a recovery?

She must have made more noise than she thought, for suddenly, from inside the house, dogs began to bark. Their sound was so insistent that after a while she saw the flicker of a candle. She had to fight the desire to run away reminding herself that she had nowhere to go.

'Who's there?'

It was Doctor Gordon who opened a bedroom window and leaned out, trying to shield the flame of his candle from the cold air.

'Doctor Gordon, it is me, Martha Cavanagh. I am afraid that something untoward has happened. I need to see your son.'

'I'm here.' A little further along, another window had opened.

'Wait there, I will be down straight away,' Jonathon called out.

The relief was such that when he opened the door she well-nigh fell into his arms.

'I'm so sorry,' she kept repeating, realizing too late that her behaviour could only add fuel to the belief that she was sick in the head.

In silence Jonathon led her inside. The hallway was huge, a panelled oblong with several rooms leading from it. He took her into one of these and made her sit in a chair near to the fireplace where the embers still glowed.

'Now then, what has happened?'

She told him. Her story must have sounded implausible, incoherent in places, but he did not interrupt.

'You must stay here,' he said, when she had stumbled to a halt. 'You are a free, independent woman, Miss Cavanagh. Your father has no right to persecute you in this way.'

'I doubt if he would agree with you.' She watched him as he lit several candles, bringing warmth and safety to the room. A moment later his mother entered carrying a tray with tea and brandy.

'I am so sorry,' Martha started, ashamed again at her foolishness. Somewhere in the recent past she seemed to have lost her way and there was no route back.

'There is nothing to be sorry about, my dear.' Mrs Gordon looked across at Jonathon. 'I will have a bed made up for Miss Cavanagh,' she added. Then, turning to her: 'You must stay here as long as you need to.'

'That is very kind of you.'

When she had gone, Martha said; 'Do you think that my father might be right? Do you think that I am behaving like a lunatic?'

He laughed. 'That is not the word I would choose.' His face grew serious again. For a long time he appeared to be thinking, then he came over and took both her hands in his.

'Miss Cavanagh, p-please d-don't be offended. W-what I am about to say is n-not to put pressure on you.'

'You are nervous,' she said. 'You only stutter when you are nervous.'

'Do I?' He looked surprised. Her remark seemed to give him courage for he sank on to the sofa next to her and turned her to face him.

'I fear,' he said, 'that although in principle you are a free agent, the law is sometimes applied for expediency.'

She was not sure what he meant so she waited.

'I suspect that you are right in so far as your father does not want to lose his influence over you,' he continued. 'Neither does he want his inheritance to go out of the immediate family. For this r-reason, he would no doubt want to arrange a marriage suitable to wh-what he sees as his station in life.'

Remembering her father's past attempts at matchmaking, his hostility to his only male nephew who would inherit his property if she did not marry, Martha nodded in agreement. Jonathon cleared his throat, stumbling over the next words.

'S-so, he might call upon those men of influence whom he knows to — to . . . ' He snorted with irritation. 'What I am trying to say is, your father will use any means at his disposal to have you safely back under his roof and married to a man of his choice — unless you are already married, that is.'

She frowned at him. It was late. She was tired. She was distressed by the events of the day.

'What are you trying to say?'

'M-Miss Cavanagh, if you married me, I would give you all the independence you are entitled to.' He shrugged. 'J-just an idea,' he added.

'But why should you do that, Mr Gordon?'

He looked uncomfortable.

'Be-because, Miss Cavanagh, I-I love you. I-I know that I am not the man of your choice. Forgive me for saying so but the man of your choice could never be yours. Apart from anything else, he does not care for you. Anyway, this — this is just a suggestion so that you will not be forced back into the arms of your family if you do not w-wish to go back.'

She wanted to argue with him, to challenge his statement that Gabriel could not love her. Perhaps one day . . . Then the brutal truth refused to be denied. He did not love her. He had already told her so. Nothing that she did could ever change that. In a strange way, acknowledging the truth was a relief.

'I don't know,' she said. 'Everything is so confusing.'

'It is.' He let go of her hand and stood up.

'Anyway, just so that you know, if ever you are d-desperate, there is always somewhere to turn.'

'You should not ask a woman to marry you

313

because she might be desperate. Perhaps you should ask her because she might be — fond of you.'

He looked at her. His face was glowing with embarrassment.

'Well,' he said, 'my parents agree that you must stay here as long as you feel the need.' He hesitated and an embarrassed smile played about his lips. She thought what a nice face it was, not handsome, not in any way aristocratic, not conventionally attractive, but kind, humorous, infinitely trustworthy.

'If ever you decide that you might be f-fond of me, perhaps you will let me know,' he said.

Martha exhaled her breath in a rare feeling of relief.

'If ever I do — I will.'

21

The next morning Martha was awoken by a disturbance outside. Her first thought was that it was her father come to fetch her and having looked out of the window her worst fears were confirmed, for standing in the driveway was the minister. She heard him banging loudly on the door, so hastily she dressed and crept down the stairs, bracing herself for the stormy encounter to come. Before she could make her presence known, however, he had already departed.

The maid showed her into the breakfast room where Jonathon was seated at the table.

'My father was here,' she started.

'So he was.'

'What did you tell him?'

'I told him that you were our guest and that you had no wish to be disturbed.'

'Did — didn't he get angry?'

Jonathon wiped his mouth on a linen napkin and put it aside.

'Oh, he did that all right, so I explained to him that you were an independent woman and that if he came here again I would have him taken up for trespass. Now please, Miss

Cavanagh, do have some breakfast.'

In a daze, Martha took a seat. She was not hungry but she was terribly, terribly grateful.

As the weeks passed she discovered a sense of harmony, a mutual affection emanating from Jonathon to his parents and from them to him, such as she had never before observed. It was a revelation. Sometimes her own thoughts were disturbed by the uncertainty of her future but when she expressed her fears, they were firmly but gently dispelled.

'Do not worry. Do not fret yourself. Take your time. There is no urgency.' Gradually she began to feel as if she might stay for ever.

A few days later however, Jonathon came home with disturbing news.

'There has been an incident in Midwillow — a serious one. Sir Jenison Bowler and his son Bartholomew are both dead.'

'How?' His words did not make sense. How could the most powerful men in the parish, indeed in the county, be dead? She could not believe it. When he did not respond she asked:

'What happened?'

They were found in the coach-house. Someone had locked them inside and set light to it. By the time anyone realized, it was too late.'

316

Martha felt herself grow cold at the barbarity of the crime. She shied away from imagining their terror, their pain.

'Do they know who did it?'

'Nothing is known for certain. There are suspicions.' He looked uncomfortable. 'I don't want you to worry but I think it is best for the time being that you stay inside the house. I have to go to the prison. I will tell you of any developments when I return.'

He must have seen the expression on her face for he added: 'Do not fear, I will pass on your good wishes to Mr Lawless.'

At the prison, Gabriel had plenty to think about. His life was in limbo. Wherever his thoughts wandered he always came back to the same realization, that today, this week, this month he might die. In spite of the life-lines that had been thrown to him he still resolutely refused to save himself. He was not sure why. That Miss Cavanagh, poor, innocent Miss Cavanagh should be willing to sacrifice her reputation, indeed, even her virtue, seemed more confusing than ever. It was not something that he could discuss with his uncle. Indeed he had told no one of the nature of Martha's visit although he learned too late that the guard had eavesdropped on the conversation and rumours of their clandestine affair were everywhere.

He was pondering on these things when he was called away to the conversation room. When Isaac rose to accompany him he was waved aside.

'Just you,' said the gaoler.

When he entered the room, Jonathon was standing by the window. It was small and barred but after the gloom of the cell it offered a symbolic hope that there was still light and normality outside.

'I asked to see you alone because certain things have happened,' Jonathon started.

Gabriel took a seat and heaved the offending chains up on to his lap to ease the weight.

Jonathon in turn took a seat.

'I thought you should know that Sir Jenison and Bartholomew Bowler have both been murdered.'

'How?'

Jonathon told him. Much as Gabriel had disliked, nay, hated his reputed half-brother and his detestable son, the thought of their panic, their screams, shocked him.

'What happened?'

'We don't know yet, but there are suspicions. There is more too. All across the country there have been demonstrations, uprisings, clashes with the authorities. The government is struggling to contain them.'

Gabriel took time to digest the thought that because of his friends' actions, their wish to improve their lot in such a modest way, the whole country was at odds.

'How is my cousin?' he asked.

'Your cousin Betsy Carter has organized a petition to be sent to Parliament demanding your release,' Jonathon replied. 'Similar things have been happening everywhere.'

He thought of Betsy, organizing a campaign to set them free and his heart overflowed with love.

'And my cousin Ephraim?'

Jonathon compressed his lips.

'Your cousin Ephraim Carter is making a lot of noise, stirring things up. There is a suspicion that he was in the vicinity of the coach-house when the fire started.'

Gabriel felt that familiar anger. Had he risked his life, taken Ephraim's place in this hell-hole of a prison merely for him to wreak more mayhem? Who would look after Betsy and Matthew if he in his turn found himself arrested?

'What do you think will be the outcome?' he asked, wondering how he was going to relay all this to Isaac.

Jonathon shrugged. 'In the past such disturbances have been easily crushed, and petitions, no matter how large, ignored. In the present extreme circumstances however, I am not so sure. The government has two choices. Either they clamp down on the demonstrations and risk making things worse, or they recognize that a mistake has been made with regard to your trial and they climb down. That, they will not find easy to do.'

Gabriel thought of his cousins. 'Do you know how the others are faring?'

'I have been to Portsmouth to see them,' answered Jonathon. 'At present they are incarcerated on the old *Serenity*.' He snorted. 'Whoever gave that old hulk its name I do not know.' Realizing that he was adding to Gabriel's worries, he simply added: 'They are well enough but let's just say that their accommodation is not as spacious as yours.'

Gabriel tried to imagine being crammed into a rotting ship, the constant movement from the waves, the ever-present chill of a wind. He had heard tell that these old hulks were never watertight. They leaked. The floors were always awash. Guiltily he reasoned that in this respect at least, Isaac and he were better off.

'There was a suggestion that they should sail on the next convict ship, the *Reliance*,' said Jonathon. 'but in view of my appeal, they are being held back — for the moment.' He looked across at Gabriel and his words had a prophetic quality. 'Everything will depend on what the government decides.'

The next morning Martha had a visitor.

Going to the breakfast room, where the caller had been taken, Martha was shocked and confused to find Betsy Carter.

All of those hot, shameful feelings about Gabriel came back to plague her, made worse by being in the presence of the woman who inspired such emotions in him. Martha's first thought was one of shame, in case Gabriel had told her about the marriage proposal. Perhaps they had laughed about it, derided her for her foolishness. She could not have borne the humiliation had Betsy learned of what had passed at the gaol.

'What is it that you want?' Her voice sounded querulous.

Betsy looked pale and anxious. There were dark smudges under her eyes and she kept fingering the material of her skirts in a fretful manner. She was obviously pregnant.

The jealousy that flared in Martha's bosom gave way to concern.

'Are you unwell?' she asked. Thinking of Gabriel's request she thought that perhaps she should give the girl some money.

'I have here a petition asking for the release of my father, my brothers and their friends,' said Betsy. 'I have come to ask if you will sign it?'

For a moment Martha hesitated. She had been raised to obey the law. Petitions challenged the decisions of the powers-that-be. Her father's voice, condemning the unrest in the country intruded, unwelcome, into her head.

'What is it that you are demanding?'

'That the men be released straight away. That their sentence is unjust, being based on prejudice and not on the law. That they have committed no crime.' Betsy was near to tears.

She was right. They had committed no crime, at least, not one that justified such treatment. Martha knew that it was time that she found the courage to match the younger girl's. She signed her name. Most of those others on the petition were marked with a cross but there were a few local men who could write their signatures. As she looked down the list she saw Jonathon's name boldly scrawled across the page, also that of his father and mother and she felt ashamed that she had hesitated even for a moment. She rose to indicate that the meeting was at an end but Betsy did not respond.

'Your husband is well?' Martha asked, for politeness.

Betsy's expression turned to one of desperation.

'Miss Cavanagh, I fear that Ephraim is heading for certain disaster. I — I have threatened him that I will leave if he persists with his madness.'

Martha frowned. What had he done? What was she asking?

'Where will you go?'

Betsy shrugged. 'Gabriel said that if ever I needed help, to come to you.' she said quietly.

Did he? Martha felt the irony of her situation.

'This is not my home, Mistress Carter,' she answered. 'I am in no position to issue invitations.'

'Why have you left your family?' Her question took Martha completely by surprise.

'I — because . . . ' She had no answer. As Betsy stood there, waiting, she found herself saying: 'I left because I do not see eye to eye with my father. You are lucky, Mistress Carter, your father is a fine man who stands up for what he believes. My father . . . ' She could not say more. Even in these extreme circumstances she did not want to expose her family as being flawed. Instead, she said: 'I went to visit your cousin in prison. He confessed to me that he — that he has certain feelings for you.'

She watched the colour flood the young girl's cheeks.

'He said that?'

'He did. He asked me to help you if the need arose — do you need money?'

Betsy shook her head.

'Well?'

Betsy shrugged helplessly. 'Now that Sir Jenison is dead, your father's influence will be stronger than ever.' She stopped and looked imploringly at Martha. 'Your father knows me, Miss Cavanagh. In spite of everything he must know that my family are not criminals in the way that they are being portrayed. Is there no way that you can approach him and ask him to intercede on our behalf?'

'You don't know my father,' Martha said. 'He has no compassion. He thinks that God put us in our positions for some reason of his own — in your family's case as a punishment, perhaps. I don't know. I cannot share his views. I cannot help you.'

Betsy stood up, her shoulders weighed down by her worries. As she prepared to leave Martha asked:

'What about you, Mistress Carter, do you have feelings for your cousin Gabriel?'

Betsy shook her head, but not in denial.

'Please, Miss Cavanagh.' She reached out and touched Martha's arm. Martha looked down at her small work-worn fingers.

'I am a married woman,' said Betsy. 'As such I can think of no man other than my husband. I do not wish to bring more trouble to my family.'

Martha's jealousy seemed to fade.

'I think you have answered my question,' she said.

In silence Betsy left the room, the petition crushed to her chest.

Martha watched from the window as the girl hurried down the drive. For some reason the visit made her feel stronger. She began to think that it was time to take control of her life. At present she had done little more than run away from one source of oppression and then leave all the decisions to Jonathon and his family. Now she must act for herself.

Jonathon and his parents were all away from home. She thought that she would take a walk and visit the stables. She fetched her outdoor clothes and let herself out into the morning air. Beneath her feet the ground was solid, and for this she was grateful as, for too long, the rain had presented them with nothing but mud.

What happened next was so fast, so unexpected that later she could not recall the exact details. Her mind preoccupied, she was about to turn into the stable yard when she sensed a movement behind her. Before she could turn she was grabbed and a sack of some sort was pulled over her head.

She screamed in fright but two pairs of very strong arms lifted her from the ground and bundled her into a vehicle. Seconds later they were bumping perilously along a track. She struggled but her hands were tied behind her back. She tried to call out to demand who they were and where they were taking her, but the musty, distasteful smell of the sack made breathing difficult and in a fearful moment she thought that perhaps she would suffocate.

They did not seem to have travelled very far before she felt the horse slow down and heard the crunch of its hoofs on stony ground. The carriage or whatever it was came to a halt and she was lifted bodily and carried away. As she struggled to free herself, she heard a knock at a door and sensed rather than saw the darkness as they stepped inside.

'You've got her.'

There was no doubting the voice. She was lowered to the ground and the sack unceremoniously pulled from her head. Shaking, bruised, her eyes blinded by the change of light, Martha came face to face with her father.

She was torn between disbelief and panic.

'Well, miss, I hope you will come to regret the trouble you have put me to.' He spoke with such a cold, impersonal tone that she began to tremble.

'You cannot do this,' she shouted in an attempt to assert herself.

'Do not presume to tell me what I can do, madam! And how dare you embarrass me in the way that you have. You are an ungrateful, wicked creature and you will live to regret it.' He stopped to draw breath. 'Anyway, there will be no more of this nonsense. Doctor Hughes is on his way. He will confirm what is obvious — that you have lost your reason. A place is ready for you at the infirmary. Your affairs will be handed safely back to me — for your own protection.' He seemed to be bubbling over with resentment, then he snorted. 'That fortune seeking, wretched creature Jonathon Gordon will very soon find himself arrested if he so much as tries to see you again.'

'Papa, please! You cannot do this. I am my own mistress. I have done nothing wrong.'

'Silence! Nothing you say will make any difference. You will have a few weeks respite at the infirmary and I plan to negotiate a satisfactory marriage settlement that will be of great advantage to us all.'

Who with? A series of nightmarish shapes

floated into her mind of old, evil-looking men without compassion. Seeing her shock, he added: 'Do not fear, you will be well looked after.'

Something shameful happened to her then. It was as if the years were stripped away and she was a child again. She wanted to shout at him and tell him *I am not, I repeat* not *going to marry anyone*, but the words would not come.

Taking her by the arm, her father started to drag her towards the door when all of a sudden there was an almighty crash in the hallway. They both stopped struggling and stared in the direction of the noise. Seconds later, the front door was heaved open and a man stumbled into the hall. He held a pistol in his right hand. It was Ephraim Carter!

'What the blazes!' Ignatius flung her aside but Ephraim raised the pistol and aimed it at the minister's chest.

'Get back. I have several things to say to you before I use this.'

Martha stood where she was and stared at him. He was hardly recognizable as the man who once mended their shoes. The set of his face was wild, almost animal in its haunted, hunted expression.

'Mr Carter,' she started.

'Get down.' He indicated that she should fall to her knees and she did so for there was something about him that was beyond reason. She glanced around the room, wondering if there was any means of escape. Ephraim was standing in the doorway, breathing heavily. It took her only seconds to realize that the enemy had now changed. Moments before she had been fighting her father, now they had a mutual foe.

Ephraim turned back to the vicar.

'You should have listened. You should have stuck by the agreement.' he said. 'If you had, then my uncle, my cousins would not be facing death and destitution. Now it is your turn to pay.'

Martha screamed as he raised the pistol and he shook his head in irritation.

'Quiet, Miss Cavanagh. I have not finished with your father yet. I am going to give him a chance to ask for forgiveness before he meets his maker. Good of me, do you not think? It is more than he did for the labourers.'

'Please, Mr Carter.'

Papa cut her short. 'Do not plead with him, girl. He is not worth your breath.' Turning to Ephraim, he said: 'Come on. Give me that gun.'

'Papa, he means to shoot you!'

She heard the click of the pistol as it was

cocked, closed her eyes against the dreadful consequences to follow.

Her father hesitated and for the first time he seemed to realize that Ephraim was serious.

'Come along now,' he said in a more conciliatory tone. 'Do not be stupid. Just give me the gun.'

'You sound just like Sir Jenison Bowler when you speak like that, minister,' said Ephraim. 'He used the same words, pretended the same understanding.'

Simultaneously father and daughter realized that it was Ephraim who had killed Sir Jenison and his son.

'What is it you want?' Martha called out. 'Tell us what you want us to do and we will do it.'

Ephraim glanced at her.

'You keep out of this, Miss Cavanagh,' he said. 'My wife says that you are a decent enough woman. Not like him.' He turned his attention back to her father. Slowly, waving the pistol gently up and down in his hand, he said: 'It is too late for you, *Reverend* Cavanagh. You have been judged and found wanting. You had better start praying to that God of yours, although if he has as much compassion as you have — then God help you!'

She knew then for certain that her father was going to die.

Until that moment she had not even wondered where her mother was. Never had she prayed more fervently that she should not walk in. Something strange happened then. Her prayer indeed was answered for her mother did not appear but in that same moment someone else entered the hall and was walking along the passageway towards them. It was Jonathon.

Ephraim felt his presence at the same time and swung round, the pistol aiming crazily at him. Turning back towards the vicar, he looked desperately from one to the other, backing up against the wall so that he could keep them both in his line of vision.

Martha's instinct was to run but she was afraid that any sudden movement might unleash the shot they all feared. Jonathon stood still, his expression reassuringly calm and she thought of how she had first perceived him. Here was no bumbling, inarticulate youth but a confident compassionate man.

'Ephraim?' said Jonathon. 'What are you doing? Come now, this is no way to solve your family's problems.'

'Get back!' Ephraim was close to collapse. Push him one more step and one of them would be dead.

'Why not let Miss Cavanagh go,' said Jonathon. 'None of this is her fault. Then you and I and the minister can talk about ways to resolve this mess.'

Ephraim shook his head. For a second he looked as if he might keel over but then the fire returned to his eyes.

'You,' he said, turning towards the vicar. 'You dismissed my wife from your service. Did you consider for one moment that she might have needed the few pence you gave to her each week?'

The Reverend Cavanagh started to answer but Jonathon forestalled him.

'Perhaps you should let Mr Carter have his say, Minister. Believe it or not, he may have a just complaint.'

'Mr Carter, please think about your wife and her baby,' Martha said.

Ephraim turned his attention to her and she immediately regretted having spoken. He blinked furiously.

'My wife and baby? My wife and that bastard Gabriel's brat, more like.'

'No! No, I am sure that's not true. Your wife — Betsy, would never betray you like that. You must know that.'

His breath was coming fast and shallow. He was like a raging bull, standing proud and pawing the ground before a charge. 'It's too late, Miss Cavanagh,' he said. 'Things have gone too far. People must be punished.'

Thinking of Betsy's anxious face that morning she wondered whether he had harmed her.

As if making up his mind, he turned again to focus on her father.

'Well, Reverend. You have had time to reflect, time to ask for divine forgiveness. Are you prepared to meet your maker?'

'Don't be ridiculous.'

Everything seemed to happen at once then. As Ephraim raised the gun, Jonathon rushed at him with such force that they both fell to the ground. Martha stood transfixed, her eyes following the direction of the weapon that thrashed and flailed along with the assailants.

Jonathon had wrestled Ephraim on to his back and was sitting astride him but the cobbler was far stronger. With a bout of arm-wrestling, they both held on to the pistol.

'Give me that!' Papa strode forward to wrest it from them and in that moment Ephraim gave a huge thrust and pushed Jonathon off him. As he went to swing the pistol in the direction of her father, Jonathon grabbed him again and there was a horrific, deafening report from the gun. An explosion of acrid smoke began to permeate the air and Jonathon flew back with such force that he hit the wall and slid down it.

In that moment, her blood froze in her veins. If Jonathon, good, caring Jonathon died she did not want to live.

Something outside herself must have taken control for she found herself reaching for the pewter tankard that stood on the table in the hallway. With all her might she brought it crashing down on Ephraim's head. The impact reverberated along her arm and he fell like a sack of corn let loose from the miller's pulley and lay still.

'Jonathon!' Martha ran to him. His eyes were open and he blinked as if he could not quite remember what had happened. Across his shoulder and chest, a deepening patch of red spread, gradually enveloping his side.

'Oh Jonathon! Please do not die!'

She fell to her knees beside him, willing him to say that he was not hurt, even though the evidence was before her. Without even knowing that she had done so she reached out and grasped his hand, holding it close to her bosom as if she could will life into him. No matter what else happened she wanted him to live.

'I think,' he said, 'you had better send for my father.'

Jonathon was carried home, the constable was sent for and Ephraim Carter was arrested. Martha remained at the vicarage. Her father's confusion and the paralysing shock of what had just happened seemed to have taken away her ability even to walk. Somehow she groped her way to a chair and sat dawn. It was her mother's return that released her from the torpor that claimed her.

'Oh Martha! You have come to your senses at last.' It took Mistress Cavanagh a few moments to realize that something momentous had happened.

Her father stumbled over some sort of explanation. He sounded stunned, as if he had lost all his certainties. Martha wondered if the brush with death had brought about in him the very change she had so often fantasized about. She turned to her mother. 'Ephraim Carter tried to kill Papa,' she said. 'Jonathon saved his life. He has been wounded.' At the gravity of what she said she rose to her feet.

'I have to go to him. He has asked me to marry him. I am going to accept.'

Her parents were silent and to herself she added: *if he lives. Please God, let him live.*

22

The carriage carrying Jonathon home had already left and as soon as she could escape, Martha set out on foot to pursue it. It began to rain, an angry powerful swell from the north-east that quickly soaked through her clothes. In places the ruts along the lane were so deep that the water came over her shoes, bruising her toes with the cold. The rain beating against her face hid the tears that coursed down her cheeks. *Please God, I will do anything, but anything as long as he survives.*

Several times she stumbled and once she fell, drenching her cloak, but nothing mattered except reaching Willow Halt.

When she arrived, breathless and frozen, the news was not good. The bullet wound was deep. Jonathon had lost a lot of blood and there was a danger of infection. She was not allowed to see him.

His mother descended from the sickroom, her face taut with grief.

'I think,' she said, 'It might be best if you return home.'

'You blame me for what has happened.'

Martha felt the agony of guilt on top of everything else.

'Of course I do not blame you, but there is nothing that you can do here.'

'Please, please let me stay and nurse him.' She wanted to be with him more than anything in the world.

Something of her intensity must have touched the other woman, for she seemed to hesitate.

'It would not be seemly for you to undertake such a role, but — '

'Jonathon has asked me to marry him.'

She saw the surprise on his mother's face.

'If he will still have me then there is nothing more that I want in the world,' she said.

'You had better change out of your wet things.'

When at last she saw him she was shocked by his appearance. His skin was the colour of the linen and a glistening dew covered his face. Martha took his bloodless hand and held it in hers.

'Jonathon, please fight, please don't leave me now.'

His father was in almost constant attendance.

'I am so sorry,' Martha repeated. 'I feel as if it is all on my account that this has happened.'

Doctor Gordon shook his head. 'You are not responsible for the madness of Ephraim Carter.'

'If I had not come here Jonathon would not have followed me to the vicarage and been present at that fateful moment.'

'If he had not done so then both you and your father would be lying dead.'

She nodded. 'I had rather it had been me.'

The doctor inclined his head the better to look into her eyes.

'You sound as if you are fond of my son.'

'I love him, more than anyone else in the world.'

At night she had vivid dreams. Sometimes she was with Jonathon, laughing, picnicking, dancing and they were extremely happy. Once she dreamed that he was betrothed to Betsy Carter and she watched in an agony of jealousy while Jonathon escorted the young girl on his arm. At another time she told him that she wanted to marry him and he laughed. *Please, Miss Cavanagh, the time for such nonsense is over. I no longer love you.* Once, he was dead.

The days crept past, then a week. Jonathon burned with fever, then froze with chill. He vomited, he rambled, he seemed unaware that she was there.

Along with his mother Martha kept up a

constant vigil. Looking at her distraught face Doctor Gordon insisted that she should rest and gave her a draught to induce sleep.

She awoke to the shadow of his mother, bending over her.

'Jonathon?'

'The fever has broken. Praise God he will live!'

When Martha was up and dressed she went along to his chamber. He was dozing and she slipped quietly into the chair beside the bed and waited. After a while he opened his eyes. They widened as he realized that she was there.

'Miss Cavanagh!' Painfully he eased himself up.

She smiled and took his hand. 'I am so glad to hear that you are making a recovery.'

'I am glad that you are glad.' He gave her a quizzical look. 'How is your father?'

'I have not seen him although he has sent messages asking after you.'

'How long have you been here?'

'For an eternity.'

'And you? You were not harmed by what happened, although in truth I remember very little of it.'

'You were very brave. You saved my father's life.'

'Then I am glad to hear that too.'

They were both silent. All the time momentous thoughts circled in her head. 'Mr Gordon, you once asked me that if ever I felt myself to be — fond of you, I should — mention it,' she found herself saying at last.

His eyes widened. 'Are — are you mentioning it now?'

'I — I think that I am.'

'Does that mean . . . ?'

'I think I am asking you to marry me.' This was not how she had intended it to be. She blushed at her shameless words.

He laughed, wincing with pain as his shoulder jerked uncomfortably.

'Well, Miss Cavanagh, what can I say? To refuse would be to insult a lady of quality and I cannot do that.'

She must have looked uncertain for he added, 'Your words have made me the happiest man alive.'

His eyelids looked heavy. 'I think that you should sleep now,' she said.

'Will you be here when I awaken?'

She nodded.

'Then I will.'

Gradually Jonathon gained strength and his mother insisted that Martha should go home.

'You need to be away from here,' she said. 'You should get some rest and give time to your parents. They have suffered a great shock.'

Reluctantly she agreed, but two days later she was back at Willow Halt to visit the patient.

To her joy, Jonathon looked much more like his old self. At the sight of his crooked smile, his thatch of unruly hair, her heart swelled with love.

'All is well?' she asked.

'It is, but something — strange has happened.'

She waited for him to go on but he seemed reticent.

'Well?'

'Well. It concerns the death of Sir Jenison and his son.'

Again he stopped.

'Go on,' she said impatiently.

'Well, they leave several aunts and cousins but — but the terms of the will state that the property must be entailed to a male relative. You will find this difficult to believe — I do — but — it seems that my father is the nearest male relative.' He grinned in embarrassment. 'It seems that he is to be the new lord of the manor.'

'Your father?' She could not take it in.

'My father. I only learned for certain yesterday. It has given us plenty to think about, I can tell you. For a start I — we — will be moving into Bilton Manor. Also, there are many reforms that we can make.' He leaned forward and she saw colour come to his face at the pleasure of considering all that he might do.

'The wages and hours of the men in our employ will certainly have to be amended,' he continued. 'There is a lot to sort out with regard to housing too. I — I still don't quite believe it.'

Martha didn't believe it either. It just wasn't possible and yet she had known, that like her, he had a distant kinship to Sir Jenison.

'When will all this happen?' she asked.

'It will no doubt take a few months to finalize the probate but one day . . . you, Miss Cavanagh will be lady of the manor — unless the news has made you change your mind?'

She shook her head, feeling glad that she had been in ignorance of this when she had agreed to marry him. Never would she wish him to think that she was doing so because of his likely change of status. It also crossed her mind that any reservations her father might have had would be well and truly swept aside at the prospect of his daughter living at Bilton Manor.

Jonathon grasped her hands, that welcome gleam of enthusiasm brightening his face. 'We have so much to do in the parish,' he said. 'You, my dear, will be able to give your thoughts to the welfare of the women and children. I will concentrate on the working conditions for the men.'

It suddenly occurred to her that as the lord of the manor his father would have the right to grant the living at the church to whomever he might choose. Could he and her father ever work together when they saw the world so differently? If not, this could be a very delicate situation.

In the weeks since the shooting, though, her father had been so much quieter. Perhaps indeed he was having a change of heart. Perhaps he and Dr Gordon and Jonathon could come to some sort of working arrangement that would benefit the entire Parish.

For the first time her thoughts turned to Gabriel and the men in gaol.

'Is there any news of the imprisoned men?' she asked.

Jonathon shook his head. 'I fear there is news, but you will not wish to hear it. Ephraim Carter is to be charged at the next assizes. You might be called as a witness although the testimony of your father might be enough.' He shook his head sadly. 'There is too much evidence against him to even hope for a verdict of not guilty.'

A feeling of emptiness opened up inside her at the prospect of his violent death. She thought about Betsy.

'What will happen to his wife?' she asked.

Jonathon smiled. 'My mother has taken her and young Matthew Lawless into the house. Betsy is to work for us and in the fullness of time Matthew will be sent to school.'

Her dream came back to her, of Jonathon escorting Betsy on his arm.

'Betsy is very pretty,' she observed.

'So she is. I — I understand that perhaps she has some sort of affection for her cousin Gabriel.'

He looked at her closely to gauge her reaction. Those recent feelings of longing and jealousy did not erupt.

'Where did you hear that?' she asked.

'Oh, rumours.'

She realized that he had only answered half of her question.

'What of the other men, Isaac Lawless and the rest?'

Jonathon shrugged. 'No news as yet. These things take time. I only know that the response from the country has been such that only a very foolish government would ignore what has been happening. It will be down to them to put pressure on the judiciary to see things in a different light. Patience, my dear, I am sure that all will be well.'

The news came a week later. Martha made her daily visit to find Jonathon downstairs and seated in a chair near to the window.

'Look at that,' he said by way of greeting. 'Daffodils in the garden and almost in bud. Winter is behind us.'

She took a seat and followed the direction of his gaze on to the panorama outside.

'Perhaps it is a good omen.'

'It is. This morning I received word that the Government has taken the unprecedented step of intervening over the trial. The scandal of the charges, the uproar that has followed has persuaded them to quash the case.'

'Then the men . . . ?'

'They are all to be released.'

Such a surge of joy swept through her. At last the nightmare was coming to an end.

'I am going to visit the prison this afternoon to break the news to Isaac and Gabriel,' said Jonathon.

'Are you sure you are well enough?'

He smiled. 'Good news is the best medicine. I feel well.'

As he prepared to leave, he asked: 'You wish me to take any message to the men?'

She smiled and shook her head. 'Only that I am delighted.'

When Isaac and Gabriel were led to the conversation room they were still in chains. Jonathon frowned his disapproval but nevertheless invited them to take a seat.

'You are well?' he asked.

'Well enough. Is — is there any news?'

His face creased into a smile. 'The best, gentlemen. The charges are dropped. I will get those confounded fetters removed immediately.'

Uncle and nephew looked at each other, hardly daring to believe his words.

'What of my sons?' Isaac asked.

'They will be on their way back from Portsmouth within the week.'

'And us?'

'You are free to leave.'

'Now?'

'Now.'

'We — we aren't likely to be re-arrested and charged again?' Isaac asked.

'No. It has been agreed that what you have already gone through has been punishment enough for your misdemeanour in swearing the oath.'

Both men sat still as if they did not quite believe what he had told them.

Now that it came to the point of leaving

Gabriel felt a strange sense of unease. Could the reality ever live up to his dreams of freedom? Besides, where were they to go?

As if picking up on his thoughts, Jonathon spoke.

'There have been one or two developments while you have been here,' he said. 'There is a new heir to Bilton Manor.'

'Who?'

Jonathon looked uncomfortable. 'It is my father.'

'Your father?'

He nodded.

Gabriel felt a strange bitter-sweetness at the news. In truth, as half-brother to Sir Jenison he must be far nearer in terms of blood, but he had no claim, for bastardy was an insurmountable hurdle. Anyway, he did not care. If he owned all that land, what would he do with it?

'Your cottage is waiting for you,' Jonathon said. 'If — if you wish to continue to work as you did before you will be able to do so . . . '
He looked away and his cheeks reddened as he added: 'But I have been thinking. There is nigh on a hundred acres over on the southern boundary of the parish. It was once a part of the old abbey but it has been abandoned for many years. There is an old house on the site together with several outbuildings. It would

please us to see it once more in full production. Perhaps between you all could work it and make it pay?'

Isaac's brow creased. 'You wish to employ us to farm it?'

Jonathon shook his head. 'No. We were thinking more of giving it to you. It will be hard work but you two men together with Joseph and James could probably make a living from it.'

They looked at each other, disbelief mingling with their unexpected joy. As they went to thank him, he said, 'From what I can gather, the Bowlers harmed your family more than once. Now is our chance to tip the balance. I hope you will agree.'

'Where is my daughter?' Isaac asked, his face sombre again.

'At present she and your young son are under my roof. If you move to the farm they may wish to accompany you.'

In a daze the two men parted from their solicitor. The chains were removed and their clothes returned to them. Within half an hour they stood outside the gate.

As they left the gaol Gabriel's one thought was for Betsy. Betsy had lost her husband in a most terrible way. Thanks to Jonathon she had a roof over her head and food in her belly, but he thought: there is another dimension to life that cannot be mended by kindness alone. He ached to see her.

Together they walked to Isaac's cottage. The loss of the chains made them feel feather-light. The warmth of a spring day seemed to herald a new beginning. Neither man spoke for they were both immersed in the possibilities of land of their own, a future they could never have foreseen.

When they reached the cottage, Isaac hesitated on the doorstep. Tears rimmed his eyes and Gabriel recalled that the last time he was here he had had the comfort of his wife. Poor Isaac, he had lost so much. He touched his uncle's arm, indicating that he would stay with him but the older man shook his head.

'I think I would like to be alone, son. Why — why do you not go across and see Betsy? Tell her that her father is well and loves her and that there is a home for her with us — that is, if she wants it.' He smiled. 'Bring young Matthew back with you too — again, that is if he wishes to leave his sister. If not, I will visit them on the morrow. For today I am too weary to go another step.'

As Gabriel went to turn away, Isaac said, 'I have not been blind all this time. I know what my daughter means to you.'

Gabriel could not speak. He patted his uncle on the shoulder and turned his back on the cottage. Walking away felt like a release from that old life. In spite of his recent incarceration he felt vibrant and energetic.

As Jonathon's house came into view he stopped to absorb the moment. He stood very still and listened to the sounds of freedom. Today had already changed his life. Could the next few moments alter it further — and for ever?

He made his way round to the back of the house and knocked at the kitchen door. Mrs Price, one of the Gordons' servants, opened it. She stared at him and he said:

'I wish to speak with Mistress Carter, please. I am her cousin, Gabriel Lawless.'

'I know who you are.' Her expression was neutral and he waited. His hands felt damp with anticipation. A moment later the door swung wide and there she was.

Standing there, in spite of her large belly, Betsy looked smaller somehow, her face thinner, her eyes dark and gentle and sad.

'Gabriel?' Her hands were clasped against her bosom and he could feel the pent-up pain that she must have suffered for too long.

'Your father sends his love to you,' he said. 'We are all free. He has gone back to the cottage but he is too tired to make another journey today. He says that if you wish, you must come home with me — Matthew too.'

She looked at him and teardrops formed silently in the corners of her eyes.

'Betsy, I am so sorry.' He acknowledged the loss of Ephraim. He wanted to touch her but to do so at that moment would have been wrong.

She stood very still, fighting with her hurt, then with an intake of breath, she said:

'Perhaps for the time being it is best that I stay here. I have work and a place. I should not give them up lightly.'

'Mr Gordon has offered to give us a farm.'

Her eyes widened in surprise.

'It is the old Abbey Farm, a hundred acres down by the bourne,' he explained. 'As a family we can run it. Between us we have all the skill, all the labouring power to make it work. It — it would be a good place for young Matthew — and to raise a baby.'

She bit her lower lip to hold back her emotion.

'It — it will need a woman's hand, though.' he said. 'We — your father and your brothers are going to need someone to look after them.'

She looked up and met his eyes.

'And you, Gabriel? What do you need?'

He held her gaze and his heart surged with love.

'Me, Betsy? I want to take this chance. I

want to cast off the slur of prison and to prove myself. I want to be respected for who I am — but most of all, when the time is right, I want to marry the woman I love.'

She looked away. 'And Ephraim?'

'We will do all we can to help Ephraim but I think it would take more than the goodwill of his family to save him from his punishment.'

His certain execution hung in the air, a louring, angry presence almost as if Ephraim himself was there.

'Even before I married him I knew that he was unstable,' Betsy said. 'What with his shop and everything I thought that together we could make a good life, but . . . ' She raised her shoulders, invoking the fates. 'I think he was determined upon his own destruction.'

'There is time now, time for a new beginning,' said Gabriel. 'The bad things in the past were not of our making. The good things though — we can make those happen.'

She looked up and smiled. 'Tell father that Matthew and I will visit on the morrow. For tonight I think I need to prepare him for all the changes. He has had an unhappy time of late.'

She was right. He stood there awkwardly for a moment.

'Did you know that Doctor Gordon is

going to marry Miss Cavanagh?' she asked.

'You are serious?'

'Very.'

He grinned. Dear Miss Cavanagh with her small peaky little face and her good works.

'They will make a perfect couple,' he answered.

Again they were silent for a while.

'Well, I will go back to the cottage,' he said at last. 'I — I will see you tomorrow?'

She nodded. As she moved away, she called out, 'Gabriel?'

He turned back to look at her. She smiled her gentle smile.

'That evening, the one when you came to the cottage — why did you not tell them where you had been?' she asked. 'Was it — to protect my reputation? You might have died.'

He shrugged as if it was of little importance.

'At the time I thought that Ephraim would be better able to look after you than I could,' he said. 'I guess that I was wrong.' He held her gaze, wanting her to know without words the depth of his love. Then he said, 'That's all in the past now though, isn't it?'

She looked at him and her expression softened into one of warm, gentle, precious love.

'Yes,' she said. 'That's all in the past.'

We do hope that you have enjoyed reading this large print book.

Did you know that all of our titles are available for purchase?

We publish a wide range of high quality large print books including:
**Romances, Mysteries, Classics
General Fiction
Non Fiction and Westerns**

Special interest titles available in large print are:
**The Little Oxford Dictionary
Music Book
Song Book
Hymn Book
Service Book**

Also available from us courtesy of Oxford University Press:
**Young Readers' Dictionary
(large print edition)
Young Readers' Thesaurus
(large print edition)**

For further information or a free brochure, please contact us at:
**Ulverscroft Large Print Books Ltd.,
The Green, Bradgate Road, Anstey,
Leicester, LE7 7FU, England.
Tel:** (00 44) **0116 236 4325**
Fax: (00 44) **0116 234 0205**